A Love by the Bay novel

by Stephanie Kay

Unmatched

participate in or encourage the electronic piracy of copyrighted material. Your support of the author's rights is appreciated.

UNMATCHED

A Love by the Bay Novel

Lexi Wells has been searching for her perfect match online. Not that he needs to be perfect. Just someone who she can hold a conversation with, who will give her mind-blowing orgasms, maintain a steady job, and fall in love with her six-year-old daughter. Why is that so damn impossible?

Grant Parker isn't looking for forever, at least not yet. He's moving in a few months for his final four years with the Coast Guard, and then he'll think about settling down. Now is not the right time for happily ever after, much to his family's frustration.

Then he rescues Lexi from a horrible date. Over chocolate lava cake they decide to have some fun before he leaves. Where's the harm in two consenting adults enjoying dessert and each other for the next few months?

They're just scratching an itch until he leaves, so why does it feel like so much more?

~*~

Stephanie loves to hear from her readers. Please sign up for her newsletter, on her website, http://www.stephkaybooks.com, for upcoming releases and exclusive excerpts.

Dedication

To my Dad for always encouraging me to follow my dreams.
I wish you could be here to see mine finally come true.
Miss you every day.

Acknowledgements

There are so many people to thank that I don't know where to start.

To Samantha Wayland and Victoria Morgan, thank you for taking me under your wing and molding me into the writer that I am today. With every line edit and critique, you've made me a better writer. I cannot thank each of you enough for all of your guidance over the last few years.

To Susie Warren, my newest critique partner, thank you for the great feedback. Sometimes you can have too many awful and unneeded dates.

To Chelsea Kuhel, my awesome editor, thank you for polishing up my writing and catching every word I missed. Your feedback was invaluable.

To Iveta Cvrkal, proofreader extraordinaire, thank you for finding every comma I missed...I hate commas!

To the members of Rhode Island Romance Writers, New England chapter of RWA, New Hampshire chapter of RWA, and all the writers I've met in the last eight years, thank you for your workshops, conferences, and critiques. I've learned so much since I joined RWA. I shudder to think of how horrible that first historical romance is in comparison to my writing now.

To Penny Watson, Bobbi Ruggiero, Samantha Wayland and Victoria Morgan, thank you for our brainstorm sessions over ginger chicken and mango martinis. Your knowledge base is extensive and truly valued.

To Christine Depetrillo for listening to me every time I doubted myself and for encouraging my love of Damon Salvatore.

To Aviation Survival Technician First Class Chad A. Smolar, thank you for answering all of my questions, no matter how random. The fact that you willingly jump out of helicopters into freezing water to rescue people amazes me. Thank you so much for your service.

To my mom. You and Dad showed me how to have a successful 40+ year marriage through laughter and affection. You've also shown me that even in grief, you can become the strongest woman I know. So glad you are finally able to travel the world and have a social life I envy!

To my amazing in-laws...yes, I actually like mine. Thank you for letting me watch your hysterical Italian family for the last 10+ years. And to my mother-in-law for reading my first book and loving it. I'm not sure if I can give you this one...there's lots more sex in it!

To my family for always encouraging me to go after my dreams and for your unwavering support, even if most of you don't read romance novels...I'll forgive you for that last indiscretion.

And of course, to my husband, John, for more reasons than I can count. You were the one who encouraged me to get back to writing when I was laid off from my day job in 2008. Probably so I would leave you to your books and guitars. Chicken has dried out on the grill and sweet potatoes have been burned because I was working on a scene instead of focusing on dinner, but you never complained...well, not that loudly. And you agreed to let me live out my romance dreams and get married over the anvil in Gretna Green, Scotland, even if you did refuse to wear a kilt. Thank you for loving my craziness and putting up with discussions about the characters in my head not doing what I want them to.

And to my readers, thank you for taking the chance on a new author. I hope I make you laugh out loud and fall in love.

Chapter 1

Lexi Wells took a fortifying gulp of wine. Okay, it was more like she shotgunned half the glass, but who was keeping track anyway? Buzzy warmth spread through her body, and she instantly regretted skipping lunch. The granola bar she'd inhaled a few hours ago did nothing to soak up the booze. She swore she'd sip her next glass.

Lexi glanced around the trendy wine bar. *Desperately Seeking Desperate* should've been the tag line for tonight's event. She'd attended a few of these local cocktail parties that eMatch had set up, and while it wasn't as bad as speed dating, it was still awkward. Some people were mingling, but there were also large clusters of same-sex groups, like a junior high dance. Online dating was torturous, and interacting with real live people, when you stepped away from the computer screen, was daunting. At least she knew the wine would be stellar, unlike the last event where the booze had been cheap and the mechanical bull in the corner of the bar had taunted her to relive her college days. She shuddered. No thanks.

So, here she was—looking pretty hot, if she did say so herself—in a deep purple wrap dress and mile-high strappy heels that always gave her a boost of confidence, ready to meet other singles. Her cousin had found love online, so how hard could it be?

But that was over two years ago…

Well, it was fucking hard, and not in a good way. She needed to get good and laid—repeatedly—according to her friend, Amanda. She sighed. The last time she'd had sex had been with her ex-husband, and they'd been divorced for almost four years. Wow. Maybe she should listen to Amanda. Was it possible for her virginity to grow back? She looked down, expecting to see a sign saying, "Closed due to lack of interest."

Not that she hadn't had some offers, but she wasn't going to sleep with just anyone. When they said trolling the Internet, they meant it, and there were a lot of trolls she stumbled across in her search for the perfect man.

Not that he had to be perfect. Just someone she was attracted to, who she could hold a conversation with, who could give her mind-blowing orgasms, hold a steady job, and fall in love with her six-year-old daughter. Was that impossible?

She'd been tempted to make that her bio, but her friend Penny had warned her that if she put the word "orgasm" in her dating profile, she'd probably attract the wrong kind of guy. Who was she kidding, even without that word she didn't seem to be attracting the right kind.

She set her empty glass down and glanced around the bar. She would allow herself one more drink, hopefully purchased by her imaginary dream man while he told her about his steady eight-to-five job, healthy performing 401K, and desire to settle down with a few kids and a white picket fence. And maybe a dog. She'd always wanted a pet.

Good luck with that.

"Can I get you anything?" the hunky bartender asked her with a suggestive smile.

She'd caught him looking her way a few times tonight, but he was so young, probably early twenties. She'd like to ask him about his healthy performing…

No. Absolutely not. Way too young for her. Not that she was expecting her AARP card in the mail anytime soon at the ripe old age of thirty, but he was still too young for her.

She never thought she'd be here at this point in her life. She was supposed to be settled and happy with at least two kids and a loving husband. She had one child—Abby was amazing—but the loving husband thing hadn't really worked out. More like Captain Douchebag had done a number on her, and she was still trying to recover.

No, she wasn't going to get all maudlin thinking about Joe. Tonight was about her. She'd ruined enough years of her life on him. It was time to move on to bigger and better.

She smiled at the bartender. "Can you refill my wine glass with ginger ale? I'm not ready for another drink yet."

"Of course."

Twenty-one. He couldn't be more than twenty-one. *Step away from the child.*

"Thanks," she said as she grabbed her mocktail and moved away from him.

The bar had filled up in the hour since she'd arrived. She hated these events. And if you were alone—forget it—it felt like high school all over again. She was tempted to join the small group of women at the other end of the bar, but she knew that men tended to avoid packs...fear of rejection or the inability to draw out the weakest in the herd.

She internally snorted. Clearly, she needed to lay off the *Animal Planet* marathons, although it was a pretty accurate representation of the dating world. She would stay right here, sipping her soda, nibbling on the appetizers they'd just set out, and hopefully sending out pheromone-enriched vibes to all the sexy and successful men in attendance.

* * *

A couple hours later, Lexi was ready to throw in the towel. Apparently, her pheromones were on the fritz, since she'd been sucked into one mind-numbing conversation after another with guys she had no interest in. At least she'd gotten a glass of wine out of the last one, who was currently talking her ear off about computer code.

She darted her gaze around the room hoping to recognize anyone in order to politely excuse herself, but the crowd had started to diminish, people leaving in pairs. At least some of them were successful tonight.

She paused on a guy at the other end of the bar. It wasn't the first time she'd seen him tonight. Not that her eyes were following him around the room or anything, but he was just so nice to look at. And his smile…

He had one of those panty-melting smiles where his eyes crinkled, and she wanted to bury herself in his arms and feel that dark scruff against her cheek. A slate gray button down stretched across the breadth of his chest as he leaned against the bar, drinking a beer. He was about a foot taller than her and could probably pick her up while she wrapped her legs around his waist and nibbled on his lower lip.

12

Whoa. Where had that very detailed thought come from?

She pushed that image away and tried to focus on the guy in front of her. He was talking about operating systems and what his company preferred to use. She nodded, taking a sip of her wine. Hopefully she hadn't just agreed to another date. This was why she needed a wingwoman. Amanda would've made up an excuse and had her out of this conversation in one minute flat.

Fiddling with the stem of her glass, she glanced down the end of the bar again. Shit. He was looking at her, smile still in place. She turned her attention back to the guy in front of her, took a final sip of her wine, and set it down on the bar.

"I hate to do this—" What was his name? Steve, maybe. God, she sucked at remembering names, and she always felt like an ass asking for it at the end of a conversation.

A hand settled at the small of her back. A warm, large hand that obviously hadn't come from Steve, unless he was super flexible.

"Sorry that took so long. Are you ready?" A deep voice rolled over her in waves, sending shivers down to her toes.

She half-turned to face the voice, her gaze traveling up, over well-defined, broad shoulders to a scruffy jaw accentuating a plump lower lip—the one she'd fantasized nibbling on—before stopping at his eyes. They looked like melted chocolate. The corner of his mouth tilted up in a cocky smile, and she held back the desire to lick her lips.

"What?" That totally sounded like a breathy squeak. Apparently, she'd lost her vocal abilities.

"Dinner? I was able to get a table at that Italian place a few doors down." He glanced over her shoulder at Steve before smiling at her with a small nod.

"If you already have plans…"

Steve stuttered beside her, but she was still caught in her mystery man's gaze. "Oh, right, dinner," she said, but it sounded more like a question.

"I guess I'll go then. Maybe we could see each other again?" Steve asked, pure hope in his voice.

Lexi turned back to Steve. "I'm sorry, but we did make plans," she said, trying to sound polite, but not encouraging. "It was nice chatting with you, Steve." When he brightened at her comment, she wished she'd kept her mouth shut.

"If you ever want to grab dinner," he said, handing his card to her, "give me a call."

"Thanks," she said, pocketing the card as he walked away.

"Poor sap, and you're welcome," her rescuer said, leaning back against the bar, his grin widening, cockiness brimming from his voice.

She bristled at his arrogant tone. Sure, he was nice to look at, but she knew his type and had no desire to have dinner with another controlling, arrogant man. She'd had enough of that type to last a lifetime.

Yes, he'd saved her, but she wished he'd stayed at the other end of the bar, looking hot, mysterious, and mute.

The woman Grant had been trying not to stare at all night caught his gaze again. He'd spotted her across the room an hour ago and had watched her eyes dart to the door and down the hall to the bathrooms a few times, before she scanned the bar. Their eyes had met twice, this time her smile had been pained before she'd turned back to the most recent guy in front of her. She'd had "rescue me" written all over her, so he'd pushed away from his end of the bar to step in, unable to stop himself.

And now her hazel eyes, that only moments before had held clear interest, held only clear irritation. She flipped a loose wave of auburn hair over her shoulder, drawing his attention to the deep V of her dress. The dress that wrapped around her body, accentuating her lush curves. She was stunning, and he wanted to whisk her out of this stupid meet-up and have her look at him with clear interest again.

She shifted away from him, his hand falling to his side, but that brief touch still tingled in his fingers, and he wanted more.

"Thanks, but I could've handled that myself."

The words sounded forced, drawing him out of his thoughts. "Yeah. Looked like it."

She huffed. "You do realize how cocky you sound, right? Does that work on most?"

Her cheeks were pink in annoyance, but he was undeterred. He grinned. "Usually."

"Seriously? I didn't need your help. Now if you'd excuse me," she bit out, grabbing her bag and stepping away from the bar.

"Leaving so soon? Can I get you another drink?" he asked, ignoring her snippy tone, not ready to let her leave. Damn. He was usually better at this, and he was sure he hadn't hallucinated her interest earlier.

"No thanks," she replied, pulling her purse strap tighter on her shoulder, glaring at him.

"Just one drink. You wouldn't want Steve to think you'd used me to blow him off, right? That wouldn't be very nice of you," he said with mock seriousness.

"But if we stayed for a drink, then he'd definitely think you made up those dinner reservations," she shot back before glancing over her shoulder.

He followed her gaze to see Steve a couple spots down the bar, already talking to another woman.

"Looks like he's fine," she said, turning back to Grant, amusement in her tone.

Wow. Go Stevie boy. Grant hadn't thought the guy would move on so quickly. He'd looked crestfallen when Grant had stepped in. "Right. So dinner it is."

"You can't be serious?"

"Completely. Come on. The event is almost over and, for the last hour, you kept looking at the door." Her eyes widened, and he wanted to kick himself for being obvious. "Not that I was watching you or anything." Now he just sounded creepy.

"Right. Well, I'm going to go now," she said, moving slowly away from him.

He usually had better game than this. "And what? Just chock the night up as a loss? You should get at least one good conversation out of the evening. I'll even pay for

16

dinner." He was glad his friend, Matt, couldn't hear his pathetic attempt to convince her.

"How generous of you. Good conversation *and* dinner? How could I pass that up?"

She was laughing at him. He shook his head. Jesus. He was floundering. *Get it together, man.*

"Great. So how's Italian sound?" he asked. "I'm Grant, by the way."

"And, I'm going to pass," she said.

"Maybe I should walk out with you?"

She stared at him. "Why?"

"You know, so that Steve doesn't think you just blew him off."

God. He sounded like a moron. *Stop talking, you idiot.* But he caught the hint of a smile before she masked it with annoyance again.

"I think I'll be alright, but thanks again."

She turned and walked away before he could say anything else, her dress swishing around her curves. He almost called out for her number, but he refused to be that pathetic. He took a long pull on his beer before rolling his shoulders back. The drills at work today had been brutal, but not as painful as that brush off had been.

He shook his head and made his way back over to Matt, hoping for a quick goodbye so he could escape. Why he'd agreed to this shit, he didn't know. He wasn't even on eMatch, but he had tagged along since his friend hated going to these things alone.

"I'm going to head out," Grant said once he stopped next to Matt.

"Dude, who was that? And why didn't you introduce us?" Matt asked.

"Just a woman who looked like she needed rescuing."

Matt grinned. "Always trying to rescue someone. And how did it go?"

"Saved her from a guy that was boring her to tears, but she claimed she didn't need my services."

"Her loss. There's plenty of women to pick from," Matt said.

"Whatever. This online dating is your thing, not mine," Grant said, placing his empty bottle on the bar.

"Don't knock it until you've tried it. You're going home alone, and I'm taking Lisa," Matt nodded at the svelte blonde who was walking toward them, "out for a late dinner."

"Glad to see your night was a success," Grant replied, rolling his eyes. "But I'm not looking for anything long term right now."

"It's dinner and drinks, not a marriage proposal."

Grant chuckled. "Yeah. I know. Next time, get one of the other guys to be your wingman."

"You definitely had some options tonight, except the one you wanted. Maybe if you'd had better game, she wouldn't have shot you down," Matt quipped.

"Whatever, man. I'm heading out since you clearly don't need my assistance anymore," Grant said, just as Lisa stopped next to Matt, who made quick introductions.

"Enjoy your night, and I'll see you on base tomorrow," Grant said to Matt. "Nice meeting you, Lisa."

Grant walked out into the brisk night, pulling his collar up as he jogged to his car. He tried to push aside thoughts of his mystery woman. He wished he'd gotten her name. He shook his head. No. It didn't matter. She'd probably been there to find an actual relationship. He didn't have time for that. He had four years left of moving around, then he could retire. When the time was right, he'd settle down, and it would work. He always succeeded when he set a goal for himself.

Chapter 2

"I'm becoming bridezilla," Lexi's friend, Penny, announced a few days later. Lexi had noticed the frazzled look in her friend's eyes and had gently shoved her out of the office for an early lunch. Drinks received and sandwich orders placed, Lexi sipped her iced tea as Penny pulled her ever-present tablet out of her bag, swiped it on, and began scrolling through a multitude of lists that Lexi had only glimpsed at.

Lexi laughed, putting her hand over the tablet. "I promise you are not a bridezilla. I haven't been asked to do anything crazy yet, and it's still a few months away, so I think we are safe. It's just stress, and it's totally normal."

"It's just nonstop, and Michael isn't helping. Although, aside from cake tasting and listening to possible bands, I'm not sure how else he could help. We were supposed to go see a band tonight but he just texted me that he has to work late. Again," Penny grumbled, tapping at the screen.

Lexi kept her mouth shut. Michael worked late a lot, but he was aiming for partner at Penny's father's law firm, so Lexi guessed it was to be expected. She didn't want to push her own issues onto Penny, especially during wedding crunch mode, but after Joe, Lexi didn't trust men who claimed to work late constantly.

"You know I'd go with you, but I'm pretty sure bringing a six-year-old to a bar is frowned upon. What about

Amanda?" Lexi asked, pushing Joe from her mind. He had no business being there anymore.

"She said she'd go, but I wanted to pick the band with Michael. It's his wedding, too. We never see each other anymore. With the planning, and my hours at work, and his hours at work," Penny said.

"I get it. I know you want everything to be perfect, but just think of it as a big party, and try not to stress."

Penny's eyes narrowed. "A party?"

Lexi pulled back and chuckled. "Okay, bridezilla, retract those fangs. I promise not to call it *just* a party again."

"Sorry. See, I told you I was getting crazy." Penny laughed.

"It's totally normal. And it's going to be perfect, don't worry about it. With all those lists you have, what could possibly go wrong?"

Penny's eyes narrowed. "Very funny."

"Just trying to be helpful." Lexi held her hands up in surrender.

"I know. Or maybe you're trying to avoid talking about your meet-up the other night. How did it go?" Penny shoved her tablet back in her purse.

Shit. That meant she was really going to pay attention now.

"Nothing special. I don't know why I bother with these events." She focused on the sandwich the waiter had just placed in front of her. She didn't want to talk about her dating horror stories or the fact that, after two years, she was still looking. It was so damn frustrating.

"Is it all the same people? You didn't talk to anyone new?"

"Honestly, it was so boring that I couldn't wait to go home. I talked to a few guys, but I wasn't interested in any of them."

She was such a liar. She hadn't wanted to be attracted to Grant, especially after his cockiness had cancelled out his hotness, but she did, and it'd pissed her off for the last three days. She'd finally caved and tried to find him on the eMatch website, without any luck. There'd been a few Grants in the San Francisco area, but the pictures didn't match. It was for the best. He'd been irritating, and she had no interest in him. Except his smile and how adorably awkward he'd been once the cockiness had faded away.

Nope. Not interested.

"What are you muttering?" Penny asked.

Lexi focused on her friend again. "Nothing." She shifted in her seat, willing back the heat in her cheeks.

Penny grinned. "You know you're a terrible liar, so fess up. Did you meet someone?"

"No, of course not." The words rushed out of her mouth, and Penny's grin widened.

"I totally don't believe you. So what's he like?"

"It's not important," she muttered.

"You sure about that? Your blush says otherwise."

"Fine," she huffed. "So, I was talking to this guy about computer code."

"You don't know anything about computer code," Penny interjected.

22

Lexi laughed. "No shit. I told you I was bored. Anyway, I was just about to sneak off to the bathroom and this guy comes up and pretends that we had to leave for our dinner reservations, just to get Mr. Boring to leave me alone."

"Oh. He rescued you. How romantic. I like where this is going," Penny said, nodding along.

"Yeah, so did I, until he said 'you're welcome' all cocky. I even called him out on it." She was impressed with herself for actually saying something.

"Seriously? So then what happened?"

"He said we should grab dinner to keep the ruse going, but I said no. He was very persistent, but the cockiness was a complete turn-off. I mean, he just waltzed over and took control of everything. I don't get why guys think being an alpha-hole is a good idea."

"Okay. Okay. So we don't like him. Got it."

Penny focused on her drink, but Lexi saw her smirk. Dammit. Lexi hadn't meant to get so heated over Grant.

"Anyway, it doesn't matter. I'll probably never see him again." She fiddled with her straw, pushing away the unwanted thoughts. Yes, he'd been cocky and used to getting his own way, but she couldn't forget his adorable awkwardness when she refused to go out with him. He was definitely her type, but that type had screwed her over too many times.

"But you want to. It's okay to admit it," Penny teased.

Lexi glared at her friend. "You're not helping. How about we talk about that party again."

"Don't start with me. I'll find the ugliest bridesmaids dress possible, just try me."

Lexi grinned. "I already bought my dress, and I'm not changing it for your bridezilla freak-out."

"Whatever. I think we need to do another girls night and go through that dating app. A few bottles of wine and Amanda's expert advice, we'll find you a winner," Penny teased.

Lexi snorted. "Yes, because that worked so well the last time. Drunk messaging on a dating site just screams morning after regrets."

"Maybe we can find this guy from the other night. What was his name?"

"Grant. But I couldn't find him on the site." *Dammit.* She hadn't meant to let that slip.

"Oh really?" Penny perked up. "Did a thorough search? Didn't think you were interested?"

"I'm not. I was just browsing the site." She really was a horrible liar.

Penny grinned, looking totally unconvinced. "Maybe you'll see him again."

"I doubt it. And it doesn't matter, since I'm not interested."

"Of course not." She ignored Penny's silent laughter.

Lexi focused on her sandwich and steered the conversation back to Penny's wedding. She was not interested in Grant and that stupid smile. Or the heat that his brief touch on the small of her back had shot through her body.

Nope. Not interested.

Lexi drained the rest of her afternoon coffee, hoping to stay awake after spending the last hour reading over the changes to the employee handbook. It was one of her least favorite things to do as office manager, but she'd promised the company's owner the completed update by next week. An hour left and then she could head home to wine, yoga pants, and dinner with her daughter.

Her phone chimed.

Pick up Abby.

She glanced at the clock. Crap. It was just after five. She'd totally forgotten that her mother wasn't getting Abby from daycare today. Lexi zipped through the rest of her emails. Payroll was done and everything else could wait until tomorrow. Even with rushing to shut everything down, it still took another ten minutes to finish. She was definitely going to be late. Mother of the year.

Grant walked through the halls of his old elementary school. He was dog-tired and frustrated after coming off a twenty-four hour shift that afternoon. He'd been the ready swimmer and had completed two rescues yesterday, but this morning's call hadn't ended well. Two kids were still missing out there. He'd been called back and relieved, his shift over, but he wanted to go back and help. He hated that part of the job. Especially when it was kids. The more time that passed after that initial search, the bleaker the likely outcome became.

As much as he wanted to just go home and crash, getting his sister Lily's call to pick up the kids was exactly what he'd needed. He'd take all the extra time with them that he could get. He'd miss the little monsters when he moved in a few months. In the meantime, he'd do anything he could to help Lily out, especially since her scumbag, soon-to-be ex-husband had bailed on her.

If he'd known what Billy had really been like, Grant would've kept his sister away from him, but Billy had seemed like a stand-up guy. Lily had only recently confided to Grant about Billy's drinking and lashing out at her and the kids. Grant could kick himself for not noticing the changes in his sister. His boisterous sister had become silent, her ready smile disappearing. She was better now. Almost completely back to her annoying, little sister self.

He couldn't even blame it on not being around because he'd been home for the last four years. Luckily for her ex, Billy had transferred to Los Angeles a few months ago, so he was out of Grant's reach—for now. But if he ever came back….

Grant shook his head. He knew violence was never the answer, but a few well-placed punches wouldn't hurt. He curled his hands into fists at his side.

Grant reached the auditorium and poked his head in. Kids were clustered around in groups since it was too cold to play outside. He spotted Nathan in the corner, bouncing around with his friends. Grant chuckled. That kid had way too much energy. Grant had promised Lily he'd do his best to tire both kids out in the hopes that bedtime would be painless, but it was easier said than done with Nathan. As

26

tempted as Grant was to bring Nathan to the base with him to run drills, part of him was afraid that his almost seven-year-old nephew would outlast him, and then he'd never hear the end of it with the guys.

Keira was, of course, center stage, singing along while one of the after-school workers played the piano. Keira's brown curls bounced as she sang her heart out. After she finished the song, and the teacher praised her, Keira's brilliant smile reached out to him at the back of the room. That little girl had no fear, and her confidence amazed him. They'd practiced that song so many times that he heard it in his sleep, and, he'd found himself humming it when he'd been working on some rigging the other day. Matt had ribbed him, but Grant shrugged him off, insisting that Matt needed to get his ears checked.

Grant paused to greet some of the parents he'd met at other events as he made his way down the center aisle. Two small bodies crashed into him. He ruffled Nathan's hair and crouched down for a hug. At least they hadn't grown out of that yet, as two sets of skinny arms wrapped around him. Man, he needed those hugs today.

"Keira, you sounded great up there," he said, pulling back to smile at his niece.

Keira grinned, puffing out her chest. "Told you I could do it."

"Never doubted you for a second," Grant replied, before turning to Nathan. "Having fun? Maybe a little tired?" he asked, trying to mask the hope in his voice.

"Nope. Can we go home? I got a new video game," Nathan said. He started rambling about building new worlds and slaying monsters. The kid loved his video games.

"Only after you finish your homework, buddy. You know the rules," Grant said.

"I don't have that much," Nathan said, staring down at the floor and scuffing his shoe, before looking back up at Grant with pleading eyes.

Grant chuckled. Yeah, he was a big softie when it came to these kids, and they knew it. "We'll see when we get home."

"I'm hungry. Let's go," Keira said.

"Any requests for dinner?"

They started rambling off food options as they gathered their backpacks.

"I'm so sorry I'm late," a harried voice spoke from behind him. It sounded familiar, so he turned around and came face-to-face with the woman who'd shot him down the other night at that stupid meet-up. Not that he'd thought about her since then. Or her fiery hazel eyes and curves he wanted to trail his fingers down. He shook his head, clearing that image, and caught her shocked expression as her gaze locked with his.

"What are you doing here?" she blurted out.

"Picking up kids. Probably the same thing you're doing here," he replied, with a smile. A variety of emotions rolled over her face, stopping on a mixture of shock and confusion. What was her problem?

"You have kids?" she asked, her brow furrowed.

Before he could answer, a little girl walked over to her. "Hi, Mom."

Grant's mystery woman gave him one last questioning look before she crouched down to her daughter's level. "Hi, honey. Sorry I'm late."

His attention was drawn to the way her suit skirt stretched along her curves. He shook his head.

Nathan tugged on Grant's sleeve, trying to get his attention. Great. Ignoring the kids to check a woman out. His sister would kill him.

"I know. We're going." He reached over to straighten the straps of Nathan's backpack.

"I'm starving," Nathan said. "And I thought Mom was picking us up today?"

"She had to work late, buddy. She'll be home in a couple hours."

"Mom?"

Grant heard the barely audible squeak next to him. He turned to see the look of horror on his mystery woman's face.

⌒‿⌒

It never changed. Men never freaking changed.

"You're married?" she gasped.

"No, it's not—" he started.

"I can't believe you're married," she sputtered.

"How about we take this out of earshot," he gritted out, taking her elbow and guiding her away from the kids.

"Of course you're married. And you flirted with me and asked me to dinner. Unbelievable," Lexi spit out. She should've grabbed Abby and ran, but she was determined to put him in his place, to give him a piece of her mind. Why

29

did this keep happening to her? One nice guy who didn't lie. That's all she wanted. Did they not exist? Were they like unicorns? Mythical creatures that might've lived at some point but hadn't been seen in so long that they only existed in fantasy stories and movies?

Oh God, and she knew their mother, Lily. Not well, but enough to know that Lily was married, so the man that Lexi had contemplated climbing like a tree was apparently Lily's husband. If the floor could open up right about now, that would be awesome.

"I'm unbelievable? You know what they say about assuming?" he replied, his mouth tight.

"Seriously? You flirted with me, and you're married," she snapped.

"Again, assuming."

He had the audacity to glare at her. Cheating bastard.

He crossed his arms across his broad chest, his blue, short-sleeved t-shirt stretching at the shoulders, black ink peeking out from the edge of his right sleeve.

"You're here to pick up your kids. I've met their mother, Lily, a few times, and I know that she's married," she said, trying to regain her composure.

"Yes, she's married." Lexi caught his brief glare of anger before he continued. "But not to me, since I'm pretty sure it's illegal to marry your brother."

"What?" She blinked.

"I'm not married. Lily is my sister," he said, with strained patience.

"But you made it sound like you all lived together," she sputtered, looking around to see how loud her outburst had been. Luckily, most of the parents had picked up their kids and cleared out of the auditorium. There were only a few people left, and none within hearing distance, as long as she didn't yell at him again.

"Again, you assumed who I was."

"Why isn't their father here?"

"Not that it's any of your business, but he's out of town," he said.

His anger was clear, and the hole she'd just dug only expanded. She needed to stop talking. "Umm…"

"Exactly," he bit out.

She was well aware she was responsible for the current awkwardness, but she still stiffened at his tone, even if it was justified. "I'm sorry for the accusation, but it was an understandable mistake."

He barked out a laugh. "What a nice, backhanded apology." He raked a hand through his short, dark hair.

"There's no need to be rude. I'm trying to apologize," she shot back.

"Fine. But most apologies go down better with a glass of wine. You should take me out for dinner," he said, offering her a deadly smile, his quick shift in attitude almost giving her whiplash.

Hell. He had a dimple in his left cheek right above the edge of his scruff. She tried not to return the smile. Damn him.

"It was an innocent mistake. I hardly think it's worth dinner," she replied, biting down her smile. *She would not cave. She would not cave.*

31

"Uncle Grant, I'm hungry. Can't we go?" His nephew tugged at Grant's hand, and Grant looked down at him, flashing another dimpled smile.

"Sorry, buddy. Yes. We should get going." He glanced back up at Lexi. "It was *interesting* seeing you again," he trailed off.

"Oh, it's Lexi, by the way. And, again, I'm sorry. Have a nice night," she said.

"You too, Lexi. Think about dinner," he said, his voice low.

Her name rolled off his tongue like a warm caress. She refused to acknowledge the sparks in her belly, as he led his niece and nephew up the aisle. She remembered her daughter and tightened her grip on Abby's backpack. "Ready to go?"

Abby nodded. "Yep. How do you know Mr. Parker?"

"What?"

"Keira and Nathan's uncle?"

"How do you know him?" Lexi asked.

"He picks them up sometimes, and he came to talk to our class last month."

"Really? What did he talk about?"

"His job. He's a swimmer," Abby said, tucking a blond strand behind her ear while walking up the aisle to the door.

"A swimmer?"

"Yes. He rescues people for the Coast Guard. He must be a really good swimmer." Abby babbled on about what Grant had talked about in her class, but Lexi only half heard her.

He actually rescued people for his job, was obviously great with kids, probably had a healthy performing everything, *and* had dimples. He was a cocky unicorn.

Hell, no one was perfect.

Chapter 3

"Umph." Lexi reached down, rubbing her freshly kicked shin, and hoping her favorite knee-high boots didn't have a huge scuff mark on them. Dammit. She loved these boots.

"Sorry about that," Sean, her most recent eMatch find, mumbled around a rather large bite of steak. "Leg day today. Had to stretch out."

"What?"

"Leg day at the gym. Don't want to stiffen up," he said, his mouth free of food before he spoke, for once.

She focused on her wine, hiding her grimace behind her glass. This was Amanda's fault. Amanda and Penny invaded her house last weekend, and after one too many glasses of wine, Lexi had stupidly allowed them to go through the eMatch site. Clearly a recipe for disaster, but Lexi had struck out so many times that she'd mentioned mixing it up a bit, and Amanda had dared her to go out with five guys who weren't her type.

Before they'd left for the night, Sean had winked at her online. His profile had been decently intelligent, aside from the gym bathroom ab selfies, and she'd been at least three glasses deep at that point, so she'd agreed to dinner. Amanda said she couldn't weasel her way into making each date a coffee date. It had to involve dinner and drinks.

And here she was, listening to him talk about his daily workouts, for the last freaking hour. Wine should come with a warning label. Don't drink and online date.

34

"So what's your exercise routine? You're in decent shape. Could use some toning, but not that bad. I'm also a personal trainer on the side. I could tighten you up in no time," he said, with complete sincerity.

Seriously! Who says that on a first date? Someone who isn't looking for a second. She stared at him, and he tilted his head to the side, like a puppy waiting for a treat or a command. She was going to kill Amanda.

"Ah, thanks, but I'm happy with my routine," she replied, twirling the stem of her wine glass and debating if she should toss it in his face. Nope. She refused to waste good wine. Gulping down the rest, she wished it would magically refill itself. She glanced around the restaurant, plotting her escape. How much longer did she have to sit here? Thank God she'd taken her own car.

"Just a suggestion," he replied, shoveling in more food as he continued to discuss the great merits of mixing up chest days and arm days and leg days. She pictured him walking through the gym, dropping large weights to the ground as he grunted like a damn caveman. At least she could cross this type off her list. One and done with gym rats.

"I'd like to think I have a healthy mix of activities. Yoga, cardio, some weights," she said, not sure why she bothered to continue this strained conversation.

"Yoga, huh? Bet you're really flexible."

He leered at her. He *freaking* leered.

She eyed her water glass, not nearly as attached to her water as she had been to her wine, she was sorely tempted to upend it over his disproportionately small head. Luckily, the waiter stopped at their table asking if they needed anything else, and Lexi requested the check. She'd wanted dessert, but had no desire to listen to his potential comments about her need for toning, while she inhaled the chocolate lava cake listed on the menu.

"You can just split that check right down the middle, man," Sean said.

Lexi hid her irritation. Not that she minded paying her own way on a first date, but his meal had been significantly larger and more expensive than hers. She wasn't going to quibble over the check if it got her out of here faster, though. She'd enjoy her dessert at home, from the comfort of her couch, in the comfort of her yoga pants.

"I had fun tonight. We should do this again," Sean said, shoving cash into the bill folder the waiter had just dropped off.

He'd had fun? Maybe listening to himself talk. Aside from a few cursory questions about her life at the start of the meal, he'd done most of the talking. He'd seemed so charming in his profile. This was why she kept her first dates to coffee. Fifteen minutes tops and she could've escaped.

"Mmhmm," she muttered, refusing to agree to another date.

"Not that the night needs to end now," he continued.

She was adding delusional to his list of finer qualities. "I really should get home."

"We could grab another drink at the bar. Or if you want to get out of here, there's an awesome club across the street. I've got moves like you've never seen," he said.

"Let's keep it that way," she mumbled behind her glass of water.

"What?" He did that head tilt thing again.

"Thanks for the offer, but I really need to get home," she said, rising from her chair, and hopefully ending the conversation.

"Next time, I'm getting you out on a dance floor," he said, standing up. He reached out to help her straighten her coat. It would've been a nice show of manners if he hadn't followed it up by palming her ass. She shifted away from him, biting down the desire to grab something of his and twist, but he crowded against her, his arm snaking around her waist.

"Are you sure I can't interest you in extending the night?" he asked, his breath against her hair.

"Thank you, but no thanks." The time for pleasantries was over, and she squirmed to break free.

"Lexi. I'm so glad I found you," a tight and familiar voice said from behind her. She peeked over her shoulder and found Grant glaring at her date.

"Grant? What are you doing here?" And why did he look pissed?

⌒⌒⌒

"We have to hurry. Mom fell. Dad took her to the hospital, but we have to meet them," he rushed out, eyeing her date, who still had his hand on her ass.

Lexi stared at Grant like he had two heads. Not that he blamed her. He hadn't noticed her at first when he'd stopped by for a quick dinner and a few beers with two of his coworkers, who, he'd bet anything, were watching him with rapt attention and amusement. They would rib the shit out of him, but he was too focused on Lexi to care.

He'd planned to leave Lexi and her date alone, until he'd caught the guy grabbing her ass. She clearly hadn't been interested in the grab, her evading techniques obvious to everyone except to her date. Apparently the guy was blind on top of being an idiot. Grant had instantly wanted to rip the guy's arm off and beat him with it. His reaction had been palpable, and he'd slid out of the booth without a word to his friends.

He elbowed the idiot in the ribs, effectively separating Lexi from her date.

"Hey man," the idiot yelped.

"Oh, sorry about that. Lexi wasn't answering her phone, and I had no other choice but to come find her. Mom's not doing well," Grant said, further driving home his ridiculous story.

"That sucks. We were just about to head to the club across the street," the idiot continued. Jesus. How dense was this guy?

Grant turned to Lexi, giving her a look that hopefully translated to *is he for real*? He caught her faint smile before she plastered on a look of pure concern.

"Oh no. I told Mom to be careful on the stairs. Why does she never listen to anyone? I knew this would happen. She already has one bad hip," she tutted before turning back to the idiot. She was laying it on thick. Grant wanted to laugh at the guy who looked confused and concerned at the same time.

"Of course. Give me a call later. We can set up another date."

Clueless moron for the win.

"We have to go," Grant said, tugging her toward the door.

"I just hope Mom is going to be okay. She's too young to need a new hip, but I think it's come to that." Her voice sounded watery, as if she was about to burst into tears.

"Uh. Yeah. Sorry about that. I'm going to go," the idiot said, moving toward the door. Apparently the guy didn't handle tears well.

"Good night, idiot," Grant chuckled as the door shut behind the guy. "And I know I shouldn't say it, but you're welcome."

Lexi stiffened and turned to face him. "Always have to end with that line, don't you?" He could hear the smile in her voice as she tried to sound annoyed. "And how did you even find me? Are you following me?"

"What? No. I was finishing up dinner with friends," he gestured toward the booth in the bar section of the restaurant. He could see Matt's smirk from here. Damn bastard. "I was going to leave you alone, until that moron grabbed your ass, and you tried to evade him."

Her cheeks heated. "Saw that, did you?"

"Yes. What the hell is wrong with that guy? First date?"

She nodded.

"Who goes in for an ass grab on the first date? That's at least a third date move." He shook his head. "Another eMatch winner?"

"Yep. It was awful. I'm having the worst luck on that site, and my friend convinced me to go out on dates with five guys who aren't my type. Sean was bachelor number one. I still can't believe he grabbed my ass. Maybe he was testing its plumpness. He'd asked about my workout routine, after spending an hour discussing the merits of chest days versus leg days. And then suggested how he could help me tone. Why am I telling you this?" She grimaced and pulled her purse strap tight to her body. She did that a lot.

Grant chuckled. "That guy is an idiot and needs to get his eyes checked. You look perfect to me."

Her eyes widened. "Umm, thanks. I wasn't fishing—"

"Just stating a fact. He's not worth your time. I would've jumped in at the first bicep flex, but I didn't want to get yelled at for a preemptive rescue if you were actually enjoying your date."

"Oh God. You saw that, too?" She ducked her head, shoulders shaking with laughter. "Again, I am sorry for yelling at you the other day. And in front of the kids. I'm normally not like that, I swear. I know rescuing is your thing."

"Checking up on me, are you?" He tried to ignore the small thrill that rocketed through him.

"Of course not," she scoffed, fiddling with her purse again.

"Of course not," Grant echoed. Her denial was adorable, as was the deep pink color in her cheeks.

"My daughter, Abby, mentioned that you spoke to her class." She brushed an auburn curl from her cheek, tucking it behind her pink tinged ear. He wondered how far her blush spread. She was pale, so probably everywhere. Heat pooled low in his belly, and he mentally shook his head, clearing the image of her spread out before him, with only her blush covering her.

"Umm, well thanks for the rescue, but I should let you get back to your friends." she said, her tongue darting out and licking her plump lower lip. *Not helping.*

"Do you want to join us?" Not that he wanted to share her with anyone. Where the hell had that thought come from?

She glanced at the booth he gestured to. "I don't want to intrude, and I really should get home."

He heard the hesitation in her voice. "Come on," he said, lacing his fingers with hers and pulling her along. Heat shot through his arm as their palms met, and he itched to tug her closer.

Matt eyed him as Grant and Lexi stopped in front of the table. "Beers?" he asked.

"What?" Grant asked.

"Wasn't that why you jumped up from the table? To grab another round?" Matt's grin and nod toward Lexi were not subtle.

"Hi, I'm Matt." He stuck his hand out to Lexi.

"I'm Tyler," the young swimmer popped out of his seat, giving her a big smile.

"Hi. Do you guys work with Grant?" she asked.

"Yes, we do. You know, you look really familiar." Matt looked over Lexi's shoulder, smirking at Grant. Man, he was such a pain in the ass sometimes.

"Oh. I don't think we've met before. Maybe I have one of those faces," she replied.

"And what a great face to have," Tyler piped in, and Matt groaned.

41

"Kid, we need to work on your lines," Matt said.

"What? It's true," Tyler sputtered, his cheeks as pink as Lexi's had been. "Should I grab the beers?"

"I don't want to intrude. I should probably go home," Lexi said, pulling away from Grant's side, but he kept her close, not ready to let her escape.

"Nah. Ty and I were just leaving anyway. We are both in early tomorrow," Matt said.

"Oh, do you have to go, too?" Lexi asked Grant. He swore he heard faint disappointment in her tone, but he couldn't be sure. Maybe he just wished he'd heard it.

"I'm off tomorrow, and they have this chocolate lava cake here that I'm dying to have. Could I interest you in sharing one with me?" he asked.

"I'd hate to leave you to eat dessert alone."

He heard the smile in her voice. He didn't like to share dessert, but he would just this once.

"Great." Grant ignored Matt's grin and quickly dispatched his friends before gesturing for Lexi to slide into one side of the booth.

"You decided to stay." The waitress popped up next to the table, staring intently at him, and giving him an over-the-top smile.

"Yes. Lexi, what do you want to drink?" he asked, focusing on Lexi and not the waitress with the cloying perfume that he feared he'd smell for days.

They placed their order, and the waitress left.

"So no date number two with the eMatch winner, right?"

42

"Ugh. Definitely not. I must be doing something wrong on that site. It's one bad date after the next. At least I'm getting lava cake out of it," she grumbled.

He grinned. "You're lucky I'm sharing. I typically like my own dessert."

"We can order a second one if need be."

She was completely serious. "I knew I liked you."

Lexi laughed as the waitress set down their dessert and drinks. Her laugh rolled over him, warming him more than the lava in the cake.

They both broke into the dessert, the fudge flooding the plate. He clinked his fork against hers in a toast. "Dessert will always fix a bad date," he said.

"No kidding," she replied before taking a bite, and making a soft moan.

He shifted in his seat, sipping his beer to distract himself. He was jealous of a fork. That was new.

"So good. I would learn how to make this at home, but then I'd eat it every night."

"I see nothing wrong with that idea," Grant replied, taking a bite. "So who's next on your non-type date list?"

"Not sure yet. You know, I never asked why you were at that meet-up since you aren't on the website," she said in between sips of wine.

"Wait. How do you know that?" he asked, watching the flush creep up her throat again. "Did you search for me? I'm flattered." He'd thought she hated him after their first run-in, but she'd looked him up. That had to count for something.

"Ah. I just wanted to find out about the overbearing guy who thought he was rescuing a damsel in distress," she said, her cheeks still pink.

"I wasn't overbearing. I was trying to be helpful," he replied, pretending to be offended.

"Sure you were. So why were you there if not to find your soulmate?" she asked.

"My soulmate?" he scoffed. "Not sure I'm going to find her at a meet-up in a bar."

"Why not? They say one in three marriages starts with online dating. That's a pretty good percentage," she said.

"Are you sure about that? Seems a little high."

"That's what the eMatch site says," she replied.

"But are they happy couples? Soulmates? Isn't the divorce rate still hovering around fifty percent? So what's the difference between finding love online or randomly in a bar?" he asked.

Her lashes dropped as she focused on the dessert in front of her.

He was an ass. "Sorry. I'm ruining our dessert."

"No. You're right. I'm just trying to be optimistic in my search, but it's becoming one comedic punchline after the next with these dates." She shook her head.

"You can't leave it there. Give me a few dating horror stories," he said, trying to bring humor back into a conversation that had turned darker than he'd wanted.

"I'd rather not relive them, thank you very much," she said, eyeing him over her glass.

"So, worse than the ass-grabber tonight?" He needed to know more.

"Oh my God, so much worse. Profiles can be very deceiving. They seem so normal online, and then we meet." She shuddered and he couldn't stop his laugh.

"Stop hedging and give me some examples."

"Okay. There was the guy who seemed totally normal, until he started showing me pictures of his cats. Like fifteen of them. He even had a picture of a hairball one of them had thrown up just before he'd left to meet me. Do you know what you don't want to see when you're eating dinner? A freaking hairball. So gross."

He laughed. "Okay. Crazy cat man. Give me another one."

She was adorable. The freckles on her nose danced as she scrunched her face with each terrible story. He sat back and nursed his beer, not wanting the night to end. He couldn't remember the last time he wanted to just listen to a woman. It freaked him out, but he did not intend to stop her.

An hour later, they were halfway through their second lava cake, and Lexi was still waiting for the conversation to wane. They'd shared horrible dating stories, then he asked her about her job and Abby. And he'd listened. His eyes hadn't glazed over when she went into mom mode, talking about her daughter, and she'd just about melted when he talked about his niece and nephew. He clearly loved them as if they were his own.

Why was he still single? Gainfully employed, attractive, great conversationalist, awesome with kids. Why

45

hadn't a woman snatched him up already? Not that they'd discussed their pasts. For all she knew, he could have three ex-wives and a half dozen kids, but she doubted it.

She set her empty glass on the table. He really was too attractive for his own good. His dark gray shirt stretched across his broad shoulders. A lock of brown hair fell across his brow, and she itched to brush it aside just to see how soft it really was. He had a spot of chocolate at the edge of his smile, and she wanted to lean across the table and swipe it away with her finger.

Hell. Who was she kidding? She wanted to swipe it away with her tongue, but even she wasn't that bold. She could feel a miniature Amanda hopping up and down on her shoulder, egging her on, but she resisted. She hadn't felt this strong of a pull to a man in ages.

"You still haven't told me why you were at the meet-up."

"What? Oh, right. I was there as Matt's wingman. He hates going to those things alone, so I agreed to go," he said, with a shrug.

"Yeah, me too, but my wingwoman bailed on me."

"Then I'm glad I was there to step in and save you from Steve. Wait, Steve, Sean? You should stay away from those S's." His eyes twinkled under the low light as he grinned at her.

She couldn't fight returning the smile. "I'll keep that in mind."

"You should let me know when you have your next date, in case I need to swoop in and save the day."

She snickered. "Very funny. I can't wait to see what family member falls down the stairs next."

His laugh sent a spark through her body, not that she wasn't warm enough already with the three glasses of wine and just being around him. His lips pulled up in a full smile when he laughed, like he was putting his entire body into it.

She shook her head. "I still can't believe you spouted that story out of nowhere."

"Just wanted to be helpful. But you. You really went with it, you know. All I said was she fell, and now Mom has a bad hip and never listens to you. Oscar-worthy performance," he said, tipping his beer bottle toward her, and leaning back against the bench seat.

"I try. Maybe no injured family members next time," she teased.

"I'll keep that in mind."

"So is that why you became a rescue swimmer? To fulfill your need to be chivalrous?"

"I don't have a need to rescue people, I'm just good at it," he replied with a wink.

She rolled her eyes and laughed.

"To be honest, I love my job. I have good days and bad days, just like anyone else, but it feels good to help people. And I've been able to travel and live in different places that I wouldn't have had the chance to if I worked a normal desk job."

"Where was your favorite place to live? Actually, where have you been stationed?"

"Started in San Diego, then Detroit, Washington, Alaska, and here. So far, Alaska was my favorite. Only two years there. Have you ever been? It's beautiful," he said.

"Wow. No. I haven't done a lot of travelling, but I've always wanted to take an Alaskan cruise. The pictures are always stunning." One day she'd take that vacation, and every other amazing trip she'd dreamed about, but there never seemed to be enough time.

"So much better in person. I'm excited for my next assignment. Final four years in Florida. Finally some warmth, and the base also serves the Bahamas." He grinned. "Detroit, Alaska, Washington, San Francisco. I'm always ending up in cold, windy places."

"Do you get to choose where you're stationed?" She could never just pick up her life and move every four years. Moving sucked every time she'd done it, and she'd never ended up in places she'd actually wanted to move to.

"We choose a few spots and then they try to give us our top choice. Just depends on where we're needed. It's been great being home for the last three years, but I'm ready for something new."

"Do you know when you're leaving?" she asked, already dreading the direction of this conversation. She actually liked this guy, and he was most likely going to pick up and move in the near future.

"Yeah. Early June. It'll be hot as hell there in the summer, but that's when we move."

Four months. She kept her smile in place, although it wasn't as genuine as it'd been moments before. "That's great. Florida sounds awesome. Warm. So, then you would go somewhere after Florida?"

"No. I can retire after Florida, or continue my service at another station," he said.

In four months he'd be gone for at least four years.

"No wonder you're still single," she muttered.

"What?" he asked.

Shit. That had been out loud.

"I was just thinking how difficult it would be to start a relationship when you know you are leaving town every few years," she said.

"It is. That's why I'm not looking for anything serious until I'm out. Another four years and then maybe I'll end up with a profile on eMatch." He set down his empty beer bottle. "Another drink?" he asked.

"No, I should probably get home soon," she replied.

"So what about you. I know you've had some horrible dates, but still nothing?"

"Honestly, I'm tired of the game. I agreed to finding five guys who aren't my type so that when it doesn't work out, I can say I gave online dating a try, and it didn't work. I mean, seriously, it's been four years since the ex. Since I've had sex." Her hand shot up, covering her mouth. "Hell. I can't believe I just told you that."

"Really? How is that possible?" he asked, with complete sincerity. Some of her embarrassment faded when he didn't immediately laugh at her.

"I've been so focused on finding the right guy that I've missed out on just having fun." Why was she being so honest with him? He was practically a stranger, and yet, she felt completely comfortable with him.

"Well, if you ever want to scratch an itch, I volunteer as tribute," he said matter-of-factly, not a leer in sight.

"Ahh. Good to know," she sputtered, willing away the heat rolling through her body at the image of them together.

"Sorry. Just a suggestion. Normally I don't offer my services like that, but…" he trailed off. It was adorably awkward.

"No. No. I get it. And thanks. It's just been so long, and…and why am I having this conversation with you?" Her shoulders shook with nervous laughter.

"I don't typically proposition people, but I'm not looking for long term, and you're looking for some fun. And, that came out weird," he rambled.

"Who knows if we're even compatible. You could be a terrible kisser," she said. Again, filter. Where was her damn filter?

"I've been told I'm an excellent kisser," he said. His eyes darkened as they drifted to stare at her lips. She was out of her side of the booth and next to him before she'd realized she'd moved.

"Oh really?" she asked, taunting him. Her heart sped up as he leaned closer. She was never this bold.

"Really," he whispered before his lips met hers. It started soft, just a brushing of lips, then his arm snaked around her waist, pulling her closer. Her eyes fluttered closed, and he pressed against her. She bit back a moan at the contact. How long had it been since she'd been held this close? Or for that matter, just held?

Her head tilted to the side, getting a better angle as he deepened the kiss. She melted from the top of her head to the tips of her toes, and would've slid off the bench if his hold weren't so tight.

He nibbled her lower lip before tracing the seam of her mouth with his tongue. She allowed him entry, tangling her tongue with his. He devoured her, absorbing every moan as he kissed her. Her nipples tightened with need, and she barely stopped herself from climbing into his lap.

Her hands released the grip they had on his shirt and traveled over his broad shoulders before tangling in the hairs at his nape. She sighed against his mouth. His hair was as soft as it looked, her fingers sinking into the short strands.

When he finally pulled away, she felt like she'd run a mile. They definitely needed to do that again. And soon.

"Did I pass?" he asked, touching his forehead to hers. His rough voice skated over every nerve in her body. She feared she'd spontaneously combust.

"Uh huh," she said, not looking up, mesmerized by his fingers tangled with hers. His thumb traced over her palm and a shudder rolled through her.

"Want to get out of here?"

"Uh huh," she repeated, words failing her.

"Your place or mine? I'm only five minutes from here," he said. It was completely unfair that he was still in possession of all his faculties when she couldn't string more than two words together.

"Yours," she said. Was she really going to do this? Yes. She would not talk herself out of it. She wanted this, and it was high time she took control of her life and had a little fun.

He paid the check, refusing to let her split it with him. Another point for Grant.

"Ready?" he asked. He linked their fingers again, pulling her from the booth and up against his chest. He was solid and warm. She couldn't wait to strip him of every layer he had on, like a belated Christmas present she was dying to unwrap.

"Ready," she echoed.

He brushed a kiss across her lips, then shot her one of his smiles that stopped her breath before linking her arm through his and escorting her out of the restaurant.

"Holy crap it's cold," she mumbled into her scarf when they stepped outside. The slight buzz she had from the wine evaporated into the night air.

"I'll keep you warm," he said, dipping his head down to run his nose along her cheek before nibbling on her jaw.

Heat burst through her, warming her from the inside out. She tilted her head back to expose as much skin as possible above her scarf for him to nibble on. His scruff against her skin felt amazing, and she couldn't wait to feel it against other parts of her body.

He kissed back up her jaw and fused his lips to hers. His hands cupped her face, cradling her gingerly in his palms while his mouth attacked hers. Holy hell, that was hot. She traced the seam of his lips with her tongue before delving into the warm recesses of his mouth and sucking on his tongue. He tasted like chocolate, and she wanted to inhale him.

She didn't want to stop, but the heat of their shared desire wasn't enough to ward off the brisk winter night. She broke the kiss, pressing her forehead against his as their breath intermingled and puffs of frozen air floated between them.

"Is your car here?" he asked.

"Yes," she said.

"Follow me."

She almost whispered *anywhere*, but resisted, and nodded instead.

"You aren't going to ditch me, right?" he asked.

She heard the smile in his voice. "No," she said, stopping next to her car. "This is me."

He pressed a hard kiss to her lips, stealing her breath again. "To hold you over for the short drive," he said when he pulled away, his dimple peeking out at her. She was definitely going to trace that with her tongue tonight. As she watched him walk to his car, she couldn't stop the voice in her head questioning her decision. But she told it to shut the hell up and she followed Grant home. Thank God she'd shaved her legs that morning.

Chapter 4

Lexi parked her car outside Grant's townhouse but didn't get out. In the five minutes it'd taken to drive here, her brain had turned into a freaking tennis match. Back and forth, weighing the pros and cons of what was about to happen. It'd been four years since she'd last had sex. What if she did it wrong? Maybe things had changed in the last four years.

She snorted. *Stop being ridiculous and get out of the damn car.*

Tonight was about scratching an itch. About letting loose and having some fun. And if his kisses were any indicator, she was about to have *a lot* of fun.

A sharp knock sounded on her window, and she jumped a mile.

"Are you coming?" she heard through the glass. She almost responded with, *hopefully*, but her filter had finally shown up.

She opened the door and Grant reached in, pulling her to stand in front of him.

"No second thoughts?" he asked, heat in his eyes.

She'd had second, third, and fifteenth thoughts, but she'd pushed them all aside. "None." The confidence in her voice belied the swirling emotions coursing through her, but she wanted this. Wanted him.

"Great," he said, guiding her toward the steps and into his home. "Do you want a tour?" he asked.

"Not really," she said, peeking up at him through lowered lashes, watching his darkened eyes take in every inch of her. Hell. If she had to pick the perfect guy to reinstate her into the world of mutual itch scratching, he was definitely it.

He chuckled, helping her out of her coat and shedding his own outerwear. "Want a glass of wine?"

"Nope," she said. "But I would like you to kiss me again." Seriously, she'd never been this demanding before. She liked it, but kept her need to fist pump to herself.

"I always do what the lady asks," he mumbled, lowering his head, and brushing light kisses over her cheeks, nose, and chin.

His tongue darted out and licked at the corners of her mouth, but he didn't press his lips to hers. She growled in frustration, gripped his chin in her hands, the scruff rasping against her palms, and fused her lips with his, swallowing his chuckle.

She released his face and curled her hands into his shirt as he deepened the kiss. He had one arm wrapped around her while his other hand glided leisurely up and down her spine, sending sparks of desire rushing through her body. She pressed closer to him, moaning against his mouth, trying to burrow into him.

She trailed her hands down his chest, cruising over every bump and ripple of muscle that she fully intended on tracing with her tongue in the very near future. Her fingers skirted along his waist, slipping under his shirt to the warm flesh beneath.

"You have too many clothes on," she whispered against his lips.

"I'm sure we can fix that," he said, unbuttoning the first two buttons of his shirt before yanking it off with one hand.

She tried not to gape. A dusting of hair covered his chest, barely concealing his flat nipples before narrowing into a line and disappearing into his jeans. She reached out, trailing her fingertip along his warm skin, tracing the line of hair to his waistband. His abs were amazing—like, able to do laundry on amazing.

Ink swirled over his right shoulder, the upper part of his arm covered in a mix of blues and blacks. She stepped into his body, getting a closer look at an anchor resting in the waves, a few names in tiny script wrapped around each point.

"It's like you're photoshopped," she blurted out, unable to stop herself or the giggle that followed her statement.

"What?"

She grinned. "Sorry. From the movie *Crazy, Stupid Love*. Great movie, I just never imagined being around a guy I could actually use that line on. Couldn't resist." Heat flooded her already warm cheeks.

He chuckled. "I'm not sure how to respond to that without sounding conceited."

"Mute is always good," she said, smiling. His eyes darkened, and she no longer missed her filter.

He pulled her closer. "Or I could just kiss you."

"That works, too," she murmured before he sealed his lips to hers in a hard kiss. Her arms snaked around his neck, her fingers sinking into his soft hair.

He broke the kiss and fiddled with the tie that held her wrap dress together. "Now you're overdressed."

She felt a brief moment of panic at being seen naked by a man for the first time in so long, but she took a deep breath, pushed her insecurities aside, and pulled on the bow. Her dress gaped open, and she shrugged it off her shoulders, standing tall as it pooled at her feet.

His heated gaze traveled down her body, his pupils fully dilated so that only the faintest ring of chocolate remained. All her doubts vanished at his perusal and blatant interest. She rolled her shoulders back, pushing her breasts out.

"Gorgeous," he said, a hint of reverence in his tone.

"You're not so bad yourself," she said, trying not to lick her lips. She reached down to unzip her knee high boots.

"Leave them on," he growled, snaking an arm around her waist so they pressed together from chest to thigh. The heels helped with the height difference but he still had more than a few inches on her, even in her three-inch heeled boots.

His hands trailed down her back to her satin covered ass, cupping her, pulling her closer still. His arousal nudged against her stomach and she needed him naked now.

His grip tightened, and he lifted her clear off the ground, a quick kiss muffling her squeak of surprise. She instinctually wrapped her legs around his waist. God, that was sexy as hell.

Wrapping her arms around his neck, her fingers sank into his hair as their lips met. Their heads tilting, lips fitting together like perfect puzzle pieces. She swallowed his groan and tightened her fingers on his skull, holding him close as

57

they ravaged each other's mouths. Her nipples pebbled to hard peaks, rasping against the lace and satin of her bra.

She broke the kiss. "Bedroom," she gasped.

His eyes darkened, and he fused his lips back with hers before walking down the hall at a good clip, his palms gripping her ass. The friction from her wet panties rubbing against his belly was driving her insane. She hadn't been this turned on in a long time. If ever. God, she'd missed this.

He walked her into his bedroom, ended the kiss, and sent her flying. And not just figuratively. She swallowed her startled squeak, a noise she wasn't used to making, but he'd caused it to emerge twice tonight as she bounced on the bed.

She heard him move around the bed before the room flooded with the soft light from his bedside lamp. Sitting up, she scooted to the edge and grasped his belt loops, pulling him toward her.

"Anxious?" he asked, his voice rough with desire, as he slipped a condom under the pillow.

She nodded, and ran her finger down the length of his fly. He hissed in a sharp breath as she pressed a soft kiss to his rock hard stomach, just below his belly button.

"You're overdressed for this party," she said, dragging the zipper down and reaching inside his jeans to cup his hot arousal. He pulsed in her hand, and she wanted him inside of her more than her next breath. She pushed his jeans down his trim hips and over his ass. The tight pair of dark green boxer briefs left nothing to the imagination.

She almost swallowed her tongue when he toed off his shoes and socks, and then turned around and kicked his jeans away. His ass. Sweet God, it was a perfect tight bubble.

The man should never wear pants. She touched her mouth to see if she was drooling before he turned back to face her again.

"So beautiful," he whispered, trailing a rough fingertip down her cheek, over her throat, and along the lace edging of her bra.

She gulped. "Thanks." Not the sexiest reply, but that's all she had right now.

His smile deepened, his dimple winking at her. She was sure she should be doing something other than memorizing every inch of his body and clutching the comforter in her fists, but she couldn't stop staring at him.

"We don't have to do this if you don't want to," he said, leaning down to brush a kiss across her forehead.

"Oh, I definitely want to," she said matter-of-factly, taking a deep breath and releasing the comforter. Her hands gripped his shoulders, the muscles bunching under her palms. She scooted back on the bed, pulling him on top of her. "I want you," she said against his mouth, her tongue running against the seam of his lips before surging into his mouth, tangling with his.

His hips settled between her spread thighs, his hard cock pressing against her heated core. He groaned when she rolled her hips against him, and she swallowed the sound, sucking on his tongue.

He nipped along her jaw, his tongue soothing every small bite before kissing the spot behind her ear, her entire body shuddering at the light touch, and she moaned.

She ran her fingers through his hair, pulling on the short strands as he pressed kisses along her collarbone. She tilted her head back, giving him complete access to her body, her heart racing at the touch of his tongue.

He kissed down her chest, licking along the edge of her bra, his hands reaching behind her, popping the clasp. The straps fell down her arms and he pulled the fabric away, tossing it over his shoulder. He held himself over her, one hand stabilized on the bed while he cupped her right breast with his other hand, his thumb brushing over the pebbled peak. The roughness of his fingers shot bolts of pleasure through her entire body.

"Oh, yes," she moaned when he tweaked her nipple between his fingers, pulling on her. She writhed on the bed, pushing her breast into his hand.

His eyes gleamed in the soft light as he stared at her. "Oh Lexi," he whispered before dropping his head down, pressing a kiss along the top of her breasts. His tongue darted out, licking a small circle around her nipple before engulfing her right breast in the heat of his mouth, sucking.

Her back arched off the bed, her hands anchored in his hair, holding him to her when he moved to torment her other breast. She felt every pull of his mouth deep in her core, and her legs shifted against his belly, squirming for some relief, fearing she would combust beneath him as he continued his assault on her body and her senses.

He released her breast with a pop and leaned back. His fingers trailed down her belly and hooked into her panties, pulling the scrap of satin down her thighs and over her boots. He pressed a kiss to the inside of her knee before standing up and locking his eyes with hers.

He shucked his boxers, and her gaze travelled down his body. She sat up and grasped his hard cock in her hand, stroking him from root to tip.

"Yes," he groaned, his head thrown back, his hard flesh pulsing her in hand, a drop of moisture at the tip.

She ran her thumb over the head, pumping him in her hand, loving the complete power she had over him.

"If you keep that up, I won't last," he muttered, pulling free of her grasp, pushing her back onto the bed, and settling on top of her.

His hands cupped her face and he kissed her, his tongue sweeping between her parted lips and twisting with hers.

She moaned against his mouth, raking her hands over his shoulders and down his chest, scraping her nails over his flat nipples.

"Don't stop," he groaned against her mouth.

His fingers ran down her body, brushing over her trimmed curls, and she tensed. It'd only been her hands down there for the longest time, and she wanted him so much that the anticipation was killing her. She needed him inside her, to feel him pulsing in her core.

His thumb brushed over her clit in small circles, pressure building with each pass. His calloused fingers had felt good against her breasts, but holy hell, pressing against her clit, she tried not to instantly explode. Her stomach clenched as he continued to torment her, his finger delving between her slick folds, curling up to that magical spot.

"Yes. Oh, God, yes," she moaned, her head rolling from side to side as he continued to drive her insane.

He leaned down, capturing her lips with his, a second finger joined the first, his thumb still rubbing her clit. He swallowed her gasp. The pressure built until she thought she would disintegrate under his touch.

With a final moan, she shattered around him, her core clenching his fingers. She broke free of the kiss, taking in a deep breath, a full body shudder rolling through her. She opened her eyes to see him staring at her, his breathing labored, his fingers moving slowly through her folds as she came down from her high.

"God, you're beautiful when you come," he whispered. If her body wasn't sporting a total flush already, it would have at his comment.

"I want you inside me now," she growled against his lips, her hands moving down his body, grasping his ass. Holy shit, his rock hard ass.

He grinned, pressing a kiss to her throat and reaching for the condom. She yanked it from his hands and tore open the package. She grasped his cock and rolled the condom down his hard length, giving him a few quick pumps.

He gritted his teeth, and she nipped at his scruff-covered jaw. He rocked his cock against her folds, slipping through the moisture, his eyes held extreme concentration as he slowly pushed inside of her.

She gasped, her body stretching to accommodate him.

"Are you okay?" he asked between short pants.

She reached up, cupping his face, amazed at the concern in his gaze as he tried to hold back. "Yes," she said, lifting her hips off the bed in an attempt to draw him deeper into her body.

He slipped in, inch by glorious inch, until he was seated to the hilt. They both took in a shuddering breath, and he dipped his head, capturing her lips with his, his tongue moving in and out of her mouth in perfect rhythm with his cock in her body.

She wrapped her legs around his waist, her heels pressed into his ass.

"Oh Lexi," he groaned against her mouth. His body pumped in and out of hers. His cock hit the spot guaranteed to make her explode around him.

His mouth found her breast again. His teeth lightly bit her pebbled nipple. She arched her back, and he rocked against her. "Oh, yes. Yes," she moaned, her hands skating down his back and over his shoulders, the muscles bunched beneath her hands as he took her in slow, measured strokes.

"Don't stop. Don't stop," she moaned.

He drew his hand down her body, finding her clit again, applying just enough pressure. He rested his forehead against hers, their heated breaths intermingling with each thrust.

"Oh God. I'm close," she panted.

"Me too," he said, lifting his head and gazing at her.

She moaned as he moved inside her, his thumb still tormenting her clit, his cock filling her. Desire coursed through her, centering at her core before she burst and shouted out her pleasure.

He pumped into her a few more times before groaning his release. He dropped his head, collapsing on top of her.

"That was amazing," he groaned into her neck.

Lethargic warmth rushed through her from her head to the tips of her toes. She ran her fingertips along his upper back, unable to fight her grin. She'd never gotten off that hard from a man. He'd been incredible. Was this what she'd been missing all these years?

She wanted to go again. Was that possible? She'd already come twice. Lowering her legs, her boots rubbing against his thighs, she let out a soft laugh.

"It's not nice to laugh when I'm still inside you," he grumbled, his labored breathing evening out.

She giggled. "Sorry. I just realized I'm still wearing my boots. That's a first."

He lifted his head, his deep brown eyes twinkling under the soft lamp light. "Looks like you died with your boots on. That's frowned upon, you know."

"What?"

"An orgasm is sometimes called a mini-death, so technically you died with your boots on."

Her shoulders shook with laughter. "Well, that's a new one."

"I watched a lot of westerns with my step-dad when I was a kid. No one ever wanted to die with their boots on. And, I'm realizing how ridiculous this conversation is," he said, pressing a kiss to her lips before pulling out of her body and lying next to her on the bed. He removed the condom and tied it off, rising from the bed. "Don't move."

"Wasn't planning on it," she muttered, watching him walk into the bathroom. God, his ass was a piece of art. She could stare at it for hours. He shut the door on her view, and she flopped back down on the bed, stifling her giggle.

She'd had sex tonight. *Finally*. She inwardly cheered at her four-year drought ending. And it had been amazing and wonderful and she wanted to do it again. She felt desired and well-loved, two qualities that she hadn't felt in some time.

Grant finished up in the bathroom and walked back into the bedroom. Lexi was spread out on his comforter, her flushed skin glowing in the low light. She was stunning, and he wanted her more than he'd wanted anyone else in as long as he could remember. He shook his head. How could she have gone so long without having sex? Were the men in this city blind and stupid?

Not that he was complaining about having her to himself, even if their time was short. She claimed she wanted to have a little fun, and who was he to discourage that?

He climbed back onto the bed and pulled her close.

"That was quick," she said.

"Two things you shouldn't do or say to a guy you just slept with. Laughing and saying that was quick."

She chuckled. "You know that wasn't directed at your performance."

He wrapped his arm around her shoulders. "Good to know."

She snuggled into him, her legs tangled with his. Her hand trailed down his chest and belly, his stomach muscles vibrating under her touch.

He gripped her hand, stopping its descent. "If you keep that up, I can't be held accountable for my reaction," he groaned.

"Maybe I don't want you to be." She nipped his shoulder before bathing the spot with her tongue. Pure heat shot through him again.

His hand moved down her back, squeezing her ass, and he rolled her on top of him.

She rocked against his stomach, and his cock twitched against her ass. He wanted to shift her over him and slide back into heaven.

She ran her fingers down his chest, playing with the crisp hair, her head thrown back, her dusky, pink-tipped nipples begging for his mouth. He sat up, ready to take one pebbled tip into his mouth.

"Shit," she said.

He paused, dropping back down to his elbows. "Ah. Not the response I was going for."

"I have to go," she said, climbing off of him, her suede boots rubbing against his hip.

"What?" He shook his head, trying to clear the desire-induced fog.

She rushed around the room, gathering her clothes. "I only have my babysitter for another thirty minutes."

Nude except for her boots was an image he'd file away for the future, and he almost swallowed his tongue when she bent over and slid her panties up her legs, covering her delectable ass.

He barely heard her mumble, "Mother of the year," before she snatched up her bra and slipped it on.

"It's fine," he said, slipping on his boxer briefs and following her out of the room.

She was in her dress and coat in no time, and he pulled her hair free of her coat collar, brushing his fingers along the soft skin of her nape before leaning in to press a soft kiss to her neck. A shudder rolled through her, and he wrapped his arms around her waist, nibbling at the spot where her neck and shoulder met.

"You have to stop," she said, her voice breathless.

He was an ass for trying to keep her, but he didn't want to let her go just yet. "I know," he said, pulling back.

She spun in his arms. "Thank you for the rescue and the..." she trailed off, waving her hand instead of speaking.

He chuckled. "You're welcome. And, any time."

She pressed a hard kiss to his lips and pulled away. "Have a good night."

"You too," he said.

She gave him one last peck and was driving away before he realized he still didn't have her number, nor did she have his. He grabbed a glass of water and flopped down on the couch, the list of things he wanted to do to her flipped like a slideshow in his head. Of course, that might be a little difficult if he couldn't actually ask her out. She'd said she just wanted to have some fun, but he wanted more than just one and done. Not forever. Just four months of great sex before he left. She had a lot of lost time to make up for, and he was selfless enough to let her have her way with him for as long as he was in town.

He contemplated volunteering to pick up Keira and Nathan at school until he ran into her, but stalking and using his niece and nephew as bait wasn't something he'd be proud of. And if Lily thought he was using her kids to pick up women, she'd hand him his ass.

Chapter 5

"Did you get the cakes?" Grant's sister asked as soon as he walked into her house the following Sunday.

He lifted up the large white box currently resting on the flat of his palm. Years of waiting tables at his step-father's restaurant, and he still had it. "Nope. Just picked up a cake-sized box filled with beer," he said, pretending to wobble the box. He chuckled at her irritation.

"If you drop that I will kill you," Lily snapped.

"You can't kill me. I'm your favorite brother," he said, lowering the box to the kitchen island.

Lily laughed. "You're my only brother, smartass."

"Be nice to your brother," their mother, Rose, said upon entering the kitchen.

"Hey Mom," he said, pulling his petite mother in for a hug. He rested his chin on her head and mouthed *I'm the favorite* to his glaring sister.

Lily huffed and turned her attention back to the stove.

"You'd think you two were still kids," his mother scolded, stepping away from him to give Lily a hug. "How long did you let this simmer?"

"Three hours," Lily said, rolling her eyes as their mother tasted the sauce and added a dash of salt.

Grant grinned, snagging a calzone from the tray on the island. Both women turned to glare at him. "I'm hungry."

"You're always hungry. When are you going to find a nice girl to settle down with? Who will feed you? You're not getting any younger, you know," his mother said.

He checked the clock on the stove. Two minutes had passed since she'd walked into the kitchen. She was slipping.

"Mom, don't you understand how difficult it is to find someone as amazing as you? It's impossible."

"Suck up," Lily mumbled.

He walked around the island, snagging a tiny meatball on his way to the fridge. The spoon came out of nowhere, and he yanked his hand back. "Jesus, Mom." He swore she kept them in her pocket.

"Help your sister and stop eating all the food."

"Fine," he said, ignoring his stinging hand as he eyed another meatball. "And you know I'm not looking for anyone. Four more years and I'll have my full pension, and then I'll find her."

"Ridiculous. Life is going to pass you by while you wait for the perfect moment. And I want more grandbabies," his mother said.

"I'm thirty-four, not eighty. There's plenty of time to give you more grandchildren and you already have two, but I'll keep that in mind," he promised. She was fucking relentless.

She eyed him, and he couldn't help his squirm. She always had that look. "Make sure that you do."

"So, let's see this cake," he said, shuffling around the island and attempting to push the topic away from his love life. He lifted the lid. "I hope one of them is chocolate."

"Of course. Nathan wanted chocolate and Keira wanted white with sugary buttercream. Do you know what a pain it is to find white cake? Not yellow?" Lily grumbled.

"It's not the same?" Grant asked, debating if he could swipe some frosting without anyone noticing. He peeked at his mother, wondering if she had another spoon nearby.

Lily laughed. "No. Just ask Keira."

"Grandpa, that's the wrong button. You're going to die." Nathan's voice carried in from the family room.

"You said push this button to beat the monster," Grant's step-father, John, grunted and Nathan giggled. Grant loved that giggle. He was grateful about how happy the kids were after everything that had happened with his sister and Billy, but he was hesitant to assume Nathan and Keira were fine. He sure hadn't been when his parents had split when he was ten. Nathan was only three years younger than Grant had been, and he hoped the anger he'd felt as a kid wouldn't consume Nathan's sweet nature.

"So, I died," John said, walking into the kitchen, making a beeline for Grant's mother.

"You just need more practice," Nathan shouted from the living room, and Grant heard that giggle again. He bet Nathan hadn't told his grandfather the correct buttons to push.

"No yelling," his sister yelled back at her son.

John snagged a meatball and popped it in his mouth. "Lily, these are fantastic. Just as good as your mother's," he said.

Lily beamed at him. "Thanks, Papa," she said before turning back to the stove.

Grant watched John lean down and buss Rose's cheek and whisper, "Yours are still better."

His mother whispered something back, the love clear on her face as she smiled up at her husband.

That's what Grant wanted. Sure, his mother hadn't found it on the first try, but she'd found it, and Grant would be forever grateful for the Lanzi's coming into his life. He'd pushed them away as a surly teen, but he'd learned a lot from his step-father in the twenty-two years since his mother had started dating John. Grant's teenage years might've been filled with loud voices, but behind that yelling was love and affection, not the pure anger that had filled the walls of the house when his father had been around.

Grant hadn't spoken to his father in years, and he preferred it that way. He loved seeing his mother blissfully happy. She deserved nothing but the best.

"So, how many people are coming to this party? Looks like you could feed the whole town," Grant said.

"Oh, hush. We wouldn't want to run out," his mother replied, swatting his arm.

Grant chuckled. "I think we're safe." He eyed the platters covering the kitchen island, the rather large kitchen island. "At least I can take leftovers home," he said, snagging another calzone slice.

"Hey," his sister and mother yelled simultaneously.

He shot his mother a pleading smile. "I'm a growing boy, and I'm hungry."

"Keep that up, and you'll be growing sideways," Lily quipped.

"Not possible. Punch me. My abs are rock hard," he said, patting his flat stomach. One of the perks of his job and the extensive hours of training was that he could pretty much eat whatever he wanted.

"Don't tempt me," Lily muttered.

John chuckled. "Give it time, son. Eventually those abs of steel will become abs of meatballs."

"I'll take your meatballs any day," Rose said, wrapping her arms around John's no longer svelte waist, gazing up at her husband.

Grant choked on a large bite of calzone, and Lily snickered. "*Mom.*"

"What?" his mother asked, looking at the two of them. Grant detected a faint blush under her olive skin when she realized what she'd said. "Grant William Parker, really? What are you? Thirteen? You know that's not what I meant."

John guffawed before squeezing Rose tighter and pressing a kiss to her curls.

"What did I miss?" Maddie, Grant's half-sister asked as she walked into the room.

"Just Grant acting like a thirteen-year-old," Lily said, still stirring the sauce on the stove.

"What else is new," Maddie said, snagging a meatball as she walked by.

"Hey. Not until everyone gets here," Lily shouted.

"Oh, calm down. There's plenty. Did you invite the entire school?" Maddie asked.

"Shut up," Lily said and glared at Grant.

"Hey, she said it," he said, holding up his hands in surrender.

* * *

An hour later, after twenty kids and a handful of parents arrived, Grant escaped to the den, a pilfered plate of food and a beer in hand. The guests were scattered between playing games in the living room and decorating cupcakes in the kitchen. The high-pitched squeals of that many kids were deafening, and he'd needed to hide.

He settled into the overstuffed sofa, propping his feet up on the coffee table. On coasters, of course. Lily was a freak about feet on the coffee table. He polished off his plate. Man, he was going to miss this food. Lily's calzones and meatballs were almost as good as his mom's.

He crossed his arms across his chest and wiggled deeper into the cushions, hoping to squeeze in a nap before anyone came looking for him. He had a long week of training and test flights ahead and was scheduled for another twenty-four hour shift later that afternoon. He had to catch up on his beauty sleep anytime he could.

"Oh, sorry. I was looking for the bathroom," a voice said from behind him. A voice he'd been waiting to hear all week.

He sat up, looking over the top of the couch. "Hi Lexi," he said, hoping his tone wasn't too overeager.

"Grant," she gasped. "What are you doing here?"

A faint blush darkened her cheeks, reminding him of their night together and how her blush spread across her entire body.

"My niece and nephew are the birthday kids," he stated, trying not to chuckle.

"Right. Of course," she rushed out, backing out of the doorway and into the hall. She pushed a wavy auburn strand behind her ear, and his fingers itched to tangle in her hair.

"I wondered if you'd be here." He stalked closer to her, hungry for something other than his sister's calzones. He hadn't seen her since that night, but he'd thought about her— a lot. He still kicked himself for not getting her number, but he wasn't going to let her escape so easily this time.

"Really?"

He caught her faint smile, her hazel eyes bright.

"Well, we were running late and just got here. Abby's decorating cupcakes, and I was just looking for the bathroom. That's what I get for sucking down a large coffee in under twenty minutes, but I slept awful last night and..." she paused. "And, why am I telling you this?"

"I could've helped you with the sleeping part. I know the perfect activity to wear you out."

"You don't say," she deadpanned, but he caught the hint of a smile.

"And that sounded way creepier than I intended," he said.

She laughed. "Maybe a little."

"How are the dates going? Any rescue worthy ones this week?" he asked, willing himself not to reach out for her hand and pull her into his body.

"Nope. No dates this week. Umm, I'll be right back," she said, slipping down the hall before he could say anything else.

He smiled. Lexi flustered was adorable. Today was starting to look up.

God dammit. Verbal diarrhea at its finest. Why couldn't she function like a human around him? It'd been so long since she'd had sex that she clearly had no idea how to act around a hookup, aside from looking like an idiot.

And she'd wanted it to just be fun. One and done and drought snapped, but she liked him. She liked how he made her feel. Cherished and sexy and...

Stop. Nothing could come of this. He'd be gone in four months and she was determined to find a man who would stay put. Why else would she subject herself to one awful date after another? She didn't want to feel something for a guy who wouldn't be sticking around. It's not like he'd change his job for her.

What the hell. She was seriously getting ahead of herself. She'd shared a total of three conversations and two orgasms with him. Ugh. Why did he have to be here?

She bit back her laugh. Of course he was here. It was his freaking niece and nephew's birthday party. She'd thought about seeing him again as soon as she'd looked at her calendar and remembered the party. Now she just had to figure out if she should meet him back in the den or hide from him in the kitchen with everyone else.

She finished up in the bathroom, straightened her shoulders, and walked into the kitchen where she could be a coward and snag a cupcake. She always excelled at multitasking.

"Hi, Lexi," Lily said as Lexi entered the room.

"Hi, Lily. Thanks for having us," she said, scanning the room for Grant. Luckily, he was still missing.

Introductions were made and Lexi grabbed some food, finding an empty chair and overseeing the cupcake decorating. Abby already had frosting smeared on her cheek, with a few sprinkles mixed in, which reminded her of the chocolate sauce on Grant's face the other night and her overwhelming desire to lick him clean. She ducked her head down, focusing on the calzone in front of her and willing away the heat in her cheeks.

"You finally emerged. Did you enjoy your nap?" Lily asked.

"Very funny." Grant's voice sent a shudder through Lexi. Her escape hadn't lasted long.

"Grant, have you met Lexi? She and her daughter, Abby, just got here," Lily said, forcing Lexi to look up and catch Grant's smirk.

"Hello, Grant, is it?" Lexi asked, unsure if she wanted the entire room to know that he'd rocked her world last week, and she was still trying to recover.

"Hi. Nice to meet you," he replied, engulfing her hand in his.

Was her palm sweaty? She should've brushed it on her jeans first. Nothing worse than clammy hands. His, of course, was warm and inviting. How the hell was a hand inviting?

"You've met before," a small voice piped up beside them.

Lexi looked down to see Nathan looking back and forth between them and his mother.

"Oh, maybe at school? Grant picks up the kids sometimes," Lily said.

"No. She was yelling at Uncle Grant. He must've done something wrong."

Flames. Lexi had flames shooting up her cheeks and Grant just stood there, fighting his smile. She'd kick him if she could manage without getting caught.

"Yelling? Really?" Lily asked her son.

"Yep," Nathan said.

"What did she yell at him about?" Lily asked Nathan, eyeing both Lexi and Grant. Lexi tried not to squirm.

"I think he lied to her about something," Nathan said.

Lexi hid her groan. She could use a black hole right about now. She really shouldn't have yelled at him in front of the kids. She knew better than that. Kids picked up on everything.

"It was nothing. Just a case of mistaken identity," Grant piped in, saving her again. He really was good at that.

"Yes, I thought he was someone else," Lexi echoed.

"Why do I feel that there's more to this story?" Lily asked.

"Because you're a pain in the ass and always looking for trouble," Grant replied.

Lexi couldn't stop her awkward bark of laughter.

Lily huffed, glaring at her brother. "I resent that."

"Truth hurts, sis," Grant said, his arms crossed over his broad chest.

His shirt stretched across the breadth of his shoulders, and she remembered nestling between those shoulders. Lexi bit the inside of her cheek, willing away the heat in her belly. So not the time for these thoughts, with inquisitive family members and children milling around. She really could go for that cupcake.

"Still don't believe you," Lily said, her gaze drifting back and forth between Lexi and Grant, as if trying to figure out if there was more to the story. Thankfully, Grant wasn't spilling any other details. Lily turned to look at Lexi, nodding her head toward Grant. "He can be a total pain, so yelling at him is par for the course."

"I'm hurt, and you're always making assumptions," he said to his sister, holding his hand to his chest as if truly maligned.

"Just calling it like it is," Lily replied, bumping his shoulder.

Lexi watched the interplay between siblings. As an only child, she'd always been jealous of sibling relationships. To have someone who understood your family. To share annoying parent stories with, and childhood memories. Her parents had tried for more kids, but it hadn't been in the cards, and Lexi had never wanted to have just one child. She wanted Abby to have the siblings Lexi hadn't had.

"I still think there's more," Lily said, pulling Lexi from her thoughts.

"Of course you do," he grumbled, before looking back at Lexi, and gave her a small grin. "Nice to see you again."

"You too," she said, trying to will away her blush, painfully aware that Lily was still watching them.

"What's going on over here?" their mother asked.

Lexi smiled at Rose as Grant mumbled, "Nothing, Mom."

"Lexi, dear. Did you get something to eat?" Rose asked.

"Yes. Thank you," Lexi replied. There was something infinitely warm about Rose. Lexi had met her a few times at various school functions, and she'd gravitated toward the woman.

"What'd I miss?" Rose asked, looking back and forth between her two children.

"Grant and Lexi pretending not to know each other, and I was fishing for dirt," Lily replied, a mischievous twinkle in her eye.

"Oh, really?" Rose asked.

"It was nothing, Mom. We've just run into each other a few times recently," Grant piped in.

"Yes, we were picking up the kids at the same time and ran into each other at school," Lexi said.

"And there was yelling," Lily said.

And just when Lexi was starting to like Lily.

"Really?" Rose asked.

"Total misunderstanding and I would appreciate it if you would stop bringing it up," Grant said, glaring at Lily again.

"I still say there's more to the story," Lily grumbled.

"Don't torment your brother," Rose admonished.

Lexi caught Grant mouthing *favorite* at his sister, before Lily walked away, and Lexi couldn't fight her smile. Lexi turned her attention to Rose, who was staring at her, her head tilted to the side, as if trying to figure out exactly what was going on.

"Abby is such a good girl, Lexi. You should be proud," Rose said, nodding toward the dining room where Abby and her friends were finishing up their cupcakes.

Lexi smiled. "Thank you."

"And she and Keira get along great," Rose continued.

Where was she going with this? "Yes, they do."

"You're single, right?" Rose asked.

Lexi looked at Grant to see his eyes widening. Clearly, he knew where his mother was going.

"Yes."

"I've been trying to find a good girl for my Grant," Rose said.

"Umm." Wow. Straight in for the kill.

"Really, Mom," Grant groaned.

"What? Just stating a fact." Rose nudged Lexi, "And he's great with kids."

Lexi bit back her chuckle as Grant shook his head.

"Oh, looks like the kids need more snacks." And with that, Rose departed for the living room.

"Well that wasn't awkward at all," Grant said, looking uncomfortable.

Lexi laughed. "No. Not at all."

"Sorry about that."

"She means well."

"She knows I'm leaving soon. It's like she wants me to find someone and knock her up just so she can have more grandkids now, instead of later, when I'm ready. She's relentless," he groused.

"It's because she cares," Lexi said, understanding his frustration. "My mom harps on me all the time to provide more grandkids. I swear if I hadn't signed up on eMatch, she would've created a profile for me."

"Honestly, I fear there's an account out there for me that she's made. She's probably had in-depth conversations with multiple women, and she's going to spring them on me any day now."

Lexi grinned. "That's quite the overactive imagination you have."

"I want to kiss you right now, but I fear my mother would start planning our wedding before I even slipped you some tongue," he said, dropping his voice.

She snorted, trying to ignore the heat that rolled through her. "You're ridiculous."

"Admit it. You want me, too."

"Nope." Yes she did. But she wasn't going to admit that to him now. Surrounded by his family. In front of her daughter. His dimple peeked out from his scruff, reminding her that she'd forgotten to trace it with her tongue the other night. Damn it. She willed the flush from her cheeks. Stupid pale skin.

"What are you thinking about?" he asked.

"How much I want a cupcake," she stated, looking over his shoulder at her daughter. "If you'll excuse me," she said, trying to step around him.

His smiled deepened. Stupid panty-melting smile. "You're such a liar."

"You know I love dessert," she said.

His eyes darkened, most likely remembering what had happened after dessert.

"Before you escape, hand me your phone."

"What? Why?" she asked, even as she pulled her phone from her pocket and handed it to him. His fingers brushed against hers, pooling heat in her belly as he took it.

"I never gave you my number, you know, just in case you need another rescue from your dates." He plugged his number into her phone before handing it back to her. "Now you can text me whenever you're in the mood for dessert. Enjoy your cupcake."

She should've been irritated at his suggestion, but she couldn't stop the thrill of pleasure that rocked through her as she made her way over to her daughter. He was going to drive her to distraction, and she wasn't sure if she was actually upset about that.

Chapter 6

"Thanks for coming, man," Matt said.

"You should bring Ty to these things," Grant said, nursing a beer. They were at another meet-up. Why did he agree to this shit? Right, he'd agreed because he hadn't heard from Lexi in over two weeks and thought she might show up tonight. He scanned the room again, still no sign of her.

Matt laughed. "Ty wouldn't know what to do with himself. You saw how badly he blundered with what's her name."

"Who?" Grant knew exactly who Matt was talking about.

"You know. Your damsel. Lexi, right?"

"Yeah, Lexi." Why hadn't she called him?

"How's it going with her?"

"What are you talking about? We aren't together."

"Of course not."

Matt clearly didn't believe him and Grant had no desire to talk about Lexi with him. "So, what happened with Lisa?" Grant asked.

"Lisa?"

"The blonde you took home after the last meet-up?"

"Didn't work out. We went back to her place, and she had these dolls in her room. Freaking creepy. They were staring at me, and I couldn't function. She gave me a pitying look, and I zipped up and got out of there as fast as I could."

Grant doubled over with laughter. "Oh, man. That is awesome."

"I instantly regret telling you that," Matt grumbled.

Grant smirked. "Storing that for future blackmail."

"Whatever, man."

"I thought you go to these meet-ups to find the one, not the one for the night."

"Hey, I liked Lisa. It was the dolls. Seriously, she had like twenty of them in one room. Her bedroom." Matt shuddered. "It's like she never wants to have sex again!"

"Maybe other men aren't insecure around dolls."

"Not these ones. They stare at you, with dead eyes, like they're going to suck out your soul."

Grant let out a bark of laughter. "Suck out your soul? You need to lay off the horror movies. You sleeping with a nightlight to keep the scary dolls away?"

Matt glared at him. "Again, instant regret at sharing that with you."

"I know what I'm getting you for Christmas," he said between chuckles.

"You won't even be here at Christmas."

"I'll ship them."

"You're an asshole." There was no malice behind that statement since Matt's shoulders were shaking with laughter. "Seriously. Fucking dolls. That's not normal."

"You should mingle. Maybe find someone who understands your fears," Grant said, putting his empty beer bottle on the bar and grabbing another round.

"Very funny," Matt said. "What are you going to do? Just stand around?"

"Aren't these women looking for long term? I've no interest in that."

"They're not all looking for forever. Have some fun before you leave," Matt said before walking into the crowd.

Grant's phone dinged in his pocket.

Lexi: Another winner.

He grinned.

Grant: Feel the burn. How's your workout routine?

Lexi: The waitress just called my date my father. Seriously.

He laughed.

Grant: Does he look that old?

Lexi: A lot more salt than pepper. I think his profile pic is fifteen years old.

Grant: Those pics should be timestamped.

Lexi: I know, right?

Grant: Aside from that, how's it going?

Lexi: Not good.

Grant: You sure can pick them. Where are you?

She texted him the address.

Grant: I'll be there in ten.

Lexi: No stories about busted hips please, he might be able to commiserate.

He shot her back a grinning emoticon and hunted down Matt.

"I've got to go, man," he said.

Matt pulled away from his latest conquest. Another blonde. "Everything okay?"

"Yeah. Got to go rescue someone," he said.

Matt smirked. "Tell Lexi I said hello."

"Hope your night is doll free," Grant shot back, biting back his chuckle at the curious expression on the face of the woman Matt was interested in.

"Why did I invite you to this?" Matt said.

Mission accomplished.

"Enjoy your night," he said before making his way out of the bar. The excitement of seeing Lexi again rolled through him, and he couldn't wait to see what current train wreck she'd gotten herself into.

Grant made it to the steakhouse in under ten minutes and spotted Lexi's auburn hair glinting under the soft light. She looked bored out of her mind as grandpa continued to blather on. Man, the guy looked old. The waitress had been kind calling him Lexi's father.

He ducked into the corner, out of sight, but still able to see her, and dialed her number. She picked up on the first ring.

"Unless you want me to make a crack about grandpa's hip, pretend I'm the babysitter," he said.

"Mya? Is everything okay?"

"Did you already have dessert?" he asked.

"No. What happened?" she continued.

He chuckled. "You picked another dud, that's what happened."

"She fell?"

"What is it with you and people falling?"

"Oh no. She might've broken her arm." She should've been an actress.

"I know this great place one block over. They have a flourless chocolate cake that will knock your socks off."

"Oh, yes. I'll be right there," she said.

He didn't miss the excitement in her voice. She should probably tone that down.

"I'll be right outside the front door. I say we start with two desserts this time. I'm not sharing." He was having way too much fun with this.

"Can't wait. Umm, yes, I'm leaving now."

He chuckled at her slip and watched her make apologies to her date before pulling on her coat and heading right toward him.

He slipped outside into the cold night air and waited.

She rushed out the front door and looked around.

"Well played, but I think we need to work on your search settings on that site."

"Oh, shut up," she said, grinning up at him.

He grabbed her arm, pulling her close. "I believe the words you are looking for are thank you."

"Thanks."

"Anytime," he said, squeezing her hand.

"Now where's that cake?"

He chuckled, her one-track mind clearly different from his, but he could wait. "One block over. I'll meet you there," he said, giving her the address and leading her to her car.

Within ten minutes, they were seated at a small corner table, extensive dessert menus in hand.

"How am I going to pick? And you're damn right, I'm not sharing," she said.

"So how awful was this one? Did you have to pay because his Social Security check is mere peanuts compared to what he used to make?" he asked.

She glared at him. "Not funny. And he wasn't that old. Definitely older than what his profile said, but not of actual retirement age. But the age wasn't the worst part."

The waitress came over before she could continue and they placed their orders.

"So, what was the worst part?"

"After the waitress made the comment about him being my father, he laughed and said that's what people said about his last wife. Not his first wife, or his only wife, his *last* wife. His profile didn't say anything about him being married before. I asked him how many times he'd been married, and he said five. Five freaking times."

"Wow," Grant said.

"Yep. And the last one left him because he was into, as he put it, really kinky shit." She shuddered.

"How many dates have you gone on with this one?" he asked.

"This was the first date. Shouldn't you feel a person out, and I don't mean literally, before you start confessing your sexual preferences?"

Grant choked on his drink. "Seriously. What are your settings on that site? Looking for a breathing male?"

"Very funny," she said as the waitress set down their desserts. "Too bad they don't serve wine. I need a drink."

"Next time, I promise to take you to a dessert place with booze," he said.

"So what were you doing tonight? Did I interrupt a hot date?" she asked, before taking a big bite of cake. "Holy shit, that's good," she moaned.

His heart sped up as he watched her lick the chocolate from her fork. And he was jealous of a fork again, but this time he knew exactly what it felt like to have her tongue against his. He shifted in his seat, taking a bite of his own dessert, trying not to hone in on the little sounds of pleasure she was making.

"Grant?" she asked.

"Yep?" He'd been staring at her. What had she asked him?

"Tonight?"

"I was Matt's wingman again."

"You went to another meet-up? You're not even on eMatch. You didn't go to find some other woman to rescue, did you?"

"Nope. I'm saving all my rescuing for you," he replied.

Her eyes widened, and a blush stole over her cheeks.

Where the hell had that statement come from?

She swallowed her bite of cake, trying not to read too much into that statement. "Ahh. Good to know. So, how did the rest of the party go? Lily grill you after Abby and I left?" Lexi had escaped as soon as the presents were opened and the cupcakes consumed.

"Lily's a pain in the ass. She tried to get more out of me, but I didn't say anything, which of course makes her think I'm hiding something. Sisters are the worst," he grumbled, but she could hear the clear love he had for his family, regardless of how annoying he found them.

"I always wanted a sister or brother, but I'm an only child. One day I hope I can give Abby a sibling, it just hasn't been in the cards yet." Why was she telling him this?

"Sometimes siblings aren't worth it. Especially pesky little sisters."

"But you'll miss them when you move."

"Mostly the kids, but it's just four years."

He shrugged it off, but she caught his gaze, her heart warming at the obvious love he had for his family.

"And then what?"

"I don't know. Haven't thought that far ahead. Probably try to find a position that will keep me here, but you never know. I love my job, and I'm not sure if I'll be ready to give it up in four years."

Her stomach clenched at his words. Not that she was expecting anything long term with him, he was leaving in four months, but a part of her wondered what would happen if he stayed. Would he settle down in San Francisco, or keep moving around? No. She needed to stop thinking about "what if" with him.

"So I take it this guy was experiment number two? What non-type bullet points did this one hit?" he asked, oblivious to the melancholy direction her overactive thoughts had taken.

She laughed, focusing on his face. He had a spot of chocolate on the corner of his mouth. She reached out, swiping it away and then sucking it off her finger.

"You taste good," she murmured, keeping her eyes locked on his. Focusing on the pure physicality of their relationship.

His eyes darkened. Mission accomplished. He shifted his chair closer to hers and swiped his finger through the whipped cream on his plate, dotting the corner of her mouth with it.

"I bet you taste better," he said, leaning in and licking the whipped cream from her lips, then sealed his mouth with hers.

His tongue darted into her mouth when she gasped, tangling and twisting with hers. He swallowed her small moan and turned his body to face hers.

Her head tilted, giving him better access. Her hands fell to her lap. She wanted to grab him, twist her hands in his shirt, but a part of her, a small part, remembered that they were in public.

After an eternity that still seemed too short, he broke the kiss.

"We should get out of here," he panted against her mouth.

She nodded. "Uh huh."

"Do you have to be home soon?" he asked, desire in his eyes.

"My parents took Abby for the weekend. I made up the babysitter in case I needed to escape the date," she said.

"Perfect," he said, dropping a few bills on the table to cover their bill and more, and pulled her to standing. "Let's go."

She followed him home, without any question. Any thoughts of him moving and where this was going were pushed aside as soon as he'd kissed her at the table. She wasn't even sure she'd finished her dessert, and that was saying something.

"I've been thinking about this all week," he said, dragging her into his house and pushing her up against the wall, the front door shutting beside them.

"Me too," she gasped between kisses. She shrugged out of her coat before pushing his from his shoulders. Her hands deftly unbuttoned the top three buttons of his shirt, and he yanked it over his head, ruffling his hair in the process. She sank her fingers into the short strands and rocked against his body, his heat seeping through her blouse. His cock pressed against her, and she relished in the friction.

"You need to strip now," he ordered, pulling back from the kiss and reaching for his belt. He shucked his pants and boxers in one fell swoop, his cock straining toward her.

She reached out, wrapping her hand around the hard length, giving him a few tugs. He groaned, grabbing her shirt and pulling it up.

She lifted her arms, forgetting about the button at the back, getting stuck with her shirt half over her head, her arms in the air.

"What the hell," he said.

"There's a button," she said, trying to lower her arms and pull her shirt back down. Way to kill the moment.

"Not that I'm not enjoying this view," he said, reaching behind her and finding the button. He flicked it open and had her shirt off before she could say anything else.

93

She rid herself of her pants, kicking off her boots and socks, until she stood in front of him in her matching bra and panty set. She wanted to tell herself that she'd randomly picked the matching set tonight, but she knew that part of her had worn it in the hope that he would see it. That was horrible. It wasn't as if she'd planned for her date to go terribly wrong. She just liked to be prepared.

"Gorgeous," he murmured, dipping his head and tracing along the edge of her bra with his tongue.

She sucked in a shuddering breath, and undid the clasp on her bra. He groaned his encouragement before taking one of her nipples into his hot mouth. She anchored her hands at the base of his skull, holding him in place as he ravaged her body. She would never get enough of the sensations that rolled through her at his touch, at his fervent need to consume her.

* * *

They'd spent the weekend christening almost every surface of his home, and now it was Monday, and she was walking funny. Was it possible to strain your vagina? The second day, after strenuous exercise, was always the worst. Maybe sex wasn't like riding a bicycle, you couldn't just hop back on and pick up where you'd left off.

"You feeling all right?" Penny asked, walking into Lexi's office and plopping down in the chair on the other side of Lexi's desk.

"Is it possible to strain your vagina?" she asked, then covered her mouth. "I can't believe I just asked you that."

Penny had just taken a sip of her coffee and sputtered. "What? You should warn a girl before you say something like that," she said, wiping the liquid from her suit jacket.

"Sorry," Lexi grimaced. "At least you aren't wearing a light color today."

"Oh, don't worry about that. I have a stain remover stick in my office."

Of course she did.

"Now can we go back to talking about your vagina? Wow, that's a sentence I never thought I'd utter."

Penny looked both horrified and intrigued, and Lexi fought back a giggle. "Never mind. Forget I said anything."

"Yeah, that's not happening." Penny stood up and shut Lexi's office door before sitting back down, her full attention on Lexi. "Now spill. Because the last I heard, you hadn't had sex in ages, so how exactly did you potentially injure yourself down there?"

She felt a twinge of regret for not confiding in her friends, but she'd wanted to keep Grant to herself. If she didn't talk about it, they couldn't question her decisions.

"Umm. So, remember that guy I told you about? The rescuer," she said, shifting in her chair.

Penny's eyes lit up. "That was weeks ago. Grant, right? I knew you didn't hate him."

Heat flooded Lexi's cheeks, and she looked down at her hands twisted in her lap. "Yeah, guess not."

"So you found him online and asked him out?"

"Not exactly—"

"I'm so proud. Wait, you've been having sex for weeks and didn't tell me? We're supposed to be friends.

95

You've never held anything back before. And I thought you'd had a few more horrible dates." Lexi hated the hurt look in Penny's eyes.

"I should've told you and Amanda, but it's nothing. Just sex."

"Spill."

Lexi glossed over the last few weeks, mentioning Grant's multiple rescues, to which Penny sighed.

"He's just in it for the dessert and sex," Lexi said.

Penny scoffed. "For some reason I doubt that. What guy is always available to swoop in and rescue you?"

"It doesn't matter. We are scratching a mutual itch, and he's leaving in three months, for at least four years. I'm not getting involved with him," she stated, hating how her chest clenched at her words.

"So you went four years, including dating for the last two years, and no sex, but this guy comes along, and you're banging him left and right, and not looking for more? That itch is taking a hell of a long time to scratch. How many times have you seen this guy?" Penny asked, her eyebrow raised.

"Umm. Maybe five. But we didn't start having sex until the third time."

Penny laughed. "It's like you had a three date rule, but without the actual dates."

Lexi shook her head. She hadn't thought about that. "You know I never sleep with someone on the first date. I'm a lady."

"Ha. Says the woman who's sleeping with a guy she hasn't actually dated."

Lexi grinned. "Semantics."

"Wait. How have you gone on five dates in the last few weeks?" Penny asked.

"Oh, he hasn't just interrupted dates. His niece is in the same class as Abby, and we ran into each other at school when I was picking Abby up."

Penny scooted to the edge of her seat, her smile wide. "Seriously? What are the odds?"

"Yep. And then we were at his sister's house for a birthday party. But that was after we'd had sex, so it was super awkward." She grimaced, remembering Nathan trying to out them.

"This is awesome. Amanda is going to have a field day with this. What are you and Abby up to tonight?"

"Nothing," Lexi said, and instantly regretted it when Penny pulled out her phone, her fingers flying over the keys.

"Great. Amanda will be at your house at six with pizza."

She groaned. "What did you tell her?"

"Just that you had a surprise to tell her and Abby misses her Auntie Manda."

"That's low. You taunted her with a secret and with my daughter," Lexi grumbled.

"Yep. That'll teach you to keep things from us."

Maybe Abby wouldn't want to go to bed tonight. Lexi was a terrible mother, hiding behind her daughter to keep her friends from grilling her. "Don't you have some work to do?" Lexi asked, ignoring Penny's grin.

"I was going to ask if you wanted to grab lunch, but I can get you take-out if you aren't up to moving around. Maybe put some ice on it to cool you down."

Lexi glared at her friend. "Go away. You're not funny."

Penny laughed. "I can't wait for the rest of this story tonight," she said before exiting Lexi's office.

Lexi dropped her head to her desk with a groan. She needed new friends.

Chapter 7

Grant walked into the school office. He had the day off after his twenty-four hour shift ended yesterday afternoon. He should be packing but he'd agreed to chaperone the kids' field trip. Agreed was a nice way of saying that Keira and Nathan had guilted him into it. Claiming that since he was moving so far away, he would never be able to chaperone again. It was also his first field trip, so it's not like his attendance at these things was something they were used to.

Keira was becoming quite the actress with her sad eyes as she'd pleaded with him, so he'd caved. He could never say no to them. Those two kids had him wrapped around their little fingers, and they knew it. It didn't help that Lily never sided against them. Although, they were her kids so what did he expect?

Well here he was, wishing he were still in bed sleeping and not about to join dozens of first graders on a trip to a kid's museum.

"Hello. Can I help you?" the receptionist asked when he entered the office.

"Hello. I'm Grant Parker. I'm chaperoning the first grade field trip today," he said, handing her his license.

She glanced at the ID and then at him. "Yes. Glad you could join us. The kids aren't ready just yet, so if you want to have a seat over there, I'll let you know when you can head out to the bus."

"Thanks," he replied, taking a seat and flipping through his phone to kill time. He hated sitting in a school office. It reminded him of his many trips to the principal's office as a kid. The years leading up to his father leaving had been rough, and his focus had definitely not been on school. He remembered the strain in his mother's eyes when she'd have to pick him up early and explain to his father about Grant's latest screw-up. And then the screaming arguments would start. His father berating Rose for not raising his children correctly. God, his father was such a prick.

Grant cleared his head, focusing on his phone, pushing away the irritation and anger he had toward the man. Today was about the kids and spending as much time with them as he could before he left.

"Hi, I'm here for my daughter's field trip," a very familiar voice said.

His head shot up. What were the freaking odds? He bit back his grin and listened to Lexi check in, wondering when she'd notice him. He hadn't seen her since their sleepover last weekend. After a solid eighteen hours of great conversations, multiple desserts, and amazing sex, he hadn't wanted her to leave.

They'd stayed in bed until their hunger pains got the better of them, and he'd taken her to brunch before she'd had to pick up Abby from her parents. He'd suggested they all have dinner together, with Abby, but she'd balked. Of course, she'd followed that up by pushing him up against his car, planting one long and steamy kiss on him, and then driving away. He hadn't heard from her since, but it was only Wednesday.

"You've got to be kidding me," Lexi said, when she turned around and spotted him.

He chuckled. "What are the odds?" he asked, echoing his earlier thought.

She laughed, sitting down beside him. "The one field trip I chaperone, and you're here."

"Did you have the day off?" he asked.

"No. Took a vacation day. I'm trying to do at least one field trip a year. How did you get roped into this?"

"My pint-sized niece and nephew are well-versed in the art of guilt tripping. Learned that from their mother. Something about how this is the last field trip I can ever go on since I'm moving so far away."

She grinned. "Oh. They're good."

"Learned from the best."

He reached between them, his hand sneaking up under her coat and skimming across her lower back. A shudder rolled through her, and he tightened with need. It seemed to always be like that with her.

She turned slightly into his touch. "You have to stop that. Someone might see."

"I know. If only we could take a vacation day together. When's your next date?" he asked. He wanted to ask her out, but that wasn't what they were about and part of him was afraid she'd say no.

"Nothing lined up yet."

He stifled his groan. That meant she wouldn't need his services anytime soon. "That's unfortunate."

She laughed. "I can't set up dates just to have them bomb so I can have dessert with you."

101

"I know, but at least give me something to look forward to since we are about to spend a few hours with a ton of first graders."

Lexi leaned in to say something, but they were interrupted by another woman.

"Hi, I'm Amber. You're here for the first grade field trip, right?" a stunning blonde asked.

"Yes. Hello, I'm Grant, and this is Lexi," he said, as the woman eyed him up and down, subtlety not her thing.

"Is this your first field trip?" Amber asked, and he nodded. "Ooh, a field trip virgin. I'll make sure to go easy on you."

He could've sworn she winked at him. Was she for real? Lexi coughed, but it sounded more like a weak attempt to cover a snort. He wanted to wrap his arm around Lexi, to show Amber he wasn't interested, but he knew he couldn't.

"Thanks," he said.

"Mr. Parker, Ms. Wells, Ms. Phillips, you can head out to the bus now," the receptionist called out. Grant breathed a sigh of relief as they made their way out to the bus.

They met with both teachers, getting instructions and their assigned groups of ten kids each. The first grade teachers were doing a joint trip, so there were close to fifty kids. He could handle this. He rescued panicked people from the freezing waters of the Pacific Ocean. He could oversee a dozen kids on his own. How hard could it be?

* * *

Two hours later, he was regretting those words. He was a military man, he was known for getting all the details possible before going into a situation, so why hadn't he asked Lily more questions before volunteering his services? He'd heard the word museum and pictured the kids following behind a tour guide as he watched a straggler or two. This was a children's museum and small zoo. With *hands-on* activities. No straight lines walking past paintings and exhibits.

He'd been pulled in more directions than he could count, and his hands were sticky from one of the kids gripping his. How the hell were they sticky? They hadn't even had lunch or a snack. And his shoes were wet. He'd stood too close to one of the activities that involved different liquids. He hoped it was just water on his shoes.

"How are you doing?" Lexi asked, stopping at his side. She was calm. Not a hair out of place as she oversaw her group.

"What's your secret?" he asked.

"What?"

"You don't look nearly as frazzled as I feel."

She chuckled. The husky sound rolled over him, and if they weren't in a room full of kids, he would have pulled her into the closest corner and kiss that smile off her lips.

"Thanks, I think. Just pretend you have it under control." Her eyes darted over their groups before looking back at him. "And they can sense fear," she whispered, and he couldn't stop his bark of laughter.

"You're doing fine. Inside, I'm just as frazzled as you are. It's a lot of things to pay attention to, but no one is crying or hurt, so I say that's a win," she said, nudging his shoulder with her own.

"Well, now you've jinxed us," he grumbled.

She laughed. "You'll be fine. You're a big, strong rescue swimmer. You encounter difficult situations all the time at work. You can handle a dozen kids."

"That's what I told myself, and now I have sticky hands, and my shoes are wet. And, dammit, I sound like I'm whining. Oh God, am I turning into one of them?"

Her shoulders shook as she tried to contain her laughter.

"It's not funny."

"You'll survive."

"Thanks for the pep talk."

"How about we gather our groups and go look at some animals. I think they have a class on habitats. You should be safe." She grinned and called her group to attention like a pro. They followed her out of the room in a perfect line. Not that he could blame them. He'd follow her anywhere.

He shook his head, breaking his gaze from her delectable ass. She should wear jeans all the time. Rounding up his group took a bit longer, and there were a few squabbles, but he wouldn't be deterred. Hopefully there wasn't a petting zoo.

Lexi watched Amber flirt with Grant next to the duck pond after lunch and bit back her irritation. *Not jealous. Nope. Not jeal...* She sucked back a growl when Amber put her hand on Grant's arm and he didn't push her away. Was it

104

just because he didn't want to cause a scene? It annoyed her. Not that she had any claim on him. She clenched her fists, ordering herself to stay put.

She turned back to watch her group of kids as they played with some of the indoor experiments, but she kept peeking over her shoulder at Grant. He flashed her a wicked smile when he caught her looking and heat bloomed in her cheeks. Hell. She was a mess.

"Mommy, come look at this," Abby said, grabbing Lexi's hand.

Lexi followed her daughter, chastising herself for focusing on Grant. She was here to chaperone the kids, not wonder if Grant was lining up a date with overly flirty and ridiculously obvious Amber.

"I wish I could hold it," Abby said.

Lexi looked down at her daughter, who was currently staring at a snake behind the glass. A freaking snake. Lexi tried to hide her shudder.

"He's cute, isn't he?" Abby asked, her eyes pleading.

Oh hell no, they were not getting a snake, and they definitely weren't going to hold one.

Little voices rose around her, asking questions about the snake and if they could indeed hold it. Lexi shot the museum employee a death glare, but he ignored her, and opened the door to the small enclosure, emerging with the snake wrapped around his forearm.

He introduced Wilson to the group, explaining what type of snake it was and that, if they were gentle, they could touch him. The kids rushed over, arms outstretched, and Lexi's heart jumped in her throat, watching her daughter get

105

up close and personal with Wilson. She was going to hand sanitize Abby's entire body after this.

Why couldn't Abby like cuddly animals? Her daughter had a fondness for reptiles that Lexi didn't understand. Of course, Abby's father had been a slimy snake, so maybe she could relate to them. Not that Abby really knew Joe, who'd walked out when Abby was eighteen months and never looked back. He'd also walked out on his job so he could avoid paying child support. Joe was a pro at walking out.

But Lexi couldn't totally regret marrying her ex. She wouldn't have Abby, and even if her daughter were now covered in snake germs, Lexi wouldn't trade her for the world.

"Why'd it have to be snakes?" Grant whispered in her ear, and she jumped a mile, her hand clutching her chest.

She was pretty sure she let out a squeak. She never squeaked before Grant came along. She subtly elbowed him in the stomach. The ridiculous hard stomach that had no give. She'd probably end up with a bruise, but she couldn't hide her smirk at his gasp of breath. She hadn't actually harmed him. She bet he'd gasped just so his breath would feather across her ear and turn her on.

She mentally shook her head. Wow. She needed help.

"Come on, it's funny. Indiana Jones. *Why'd it have to be snakes?*" he said.

"Oh, I got it. It's just not funny," she grumbled. "What if it bites one of the kids? I'll never be asked back to chaperone."

"Wait. That's a bad thing?" he asked.

106

She ignored his grin. "Don't even joke."

"They'll be fine. The museum staff knows what they're doing," he reassured her.

She shuddered again as her daughter got closer to the scaly creature. "Abby loves reptiles and bugs. I don't get it."

"Don't most kids like that stuff? Keira isn't a fan, but Nathan definitely is."

Lexi spotted Nathan right up front with Abby. Lexi wanted to turn away so she didn't have to look at the animal, but she refused to take her eyes off of her daughter.

"Nothing is going to happen. I promise. It's just a small garden snake," Grant said.

"Oh yuck," a nasally voice said.

Lexi glanced over, seeing Amber sidle up next to Grant. Maybe slither up was a better description.

"Those things creep me out. At least we have Grant here to protect us if it gets loose," Amber continued.

Lexi swore she saw the woman bat her eyes up at Grant. Seriously?

Grant shifted away from Amber's tentacle arms and Lexi felt a surge of triumph.

"I'm sure the museum staff will keep a close watch on the animals," he said.

"Well I'm just glad that my little Melody doesn't want anything to do with those creepy crawly things. She's such a perfect little princess," Amber said, motioning toward Melody, who was currently across the room, pinching a little boy.

Lexi let out a soft snort. Yeah, a perfect princess.

One of the teachers walked over to Melody and scolded her. Melody pouted before crying for her mother. Amber rushed right over and told the teacher not to speak to her daughter that way.

"She's something else, huh?" Grant asked.

"Is that your type?" Lexi asked, annoyed that she couldn't help but ask him that question.

"What? No. Definitely not."

She couldn't ignore the thrilling relief she felt.

"Wait. You aren't jealous, are you?" he asked, his dimple peeking out as he smiled.

Smug bastard. "No, of course not. Why would I be jealous? We aren't even a couple."

"No, we aren't." There was a bite in his tone.

"Sorry. I just want to make sure we understand what this is. And that if you wanted to hook up with Amber, we can end this now. We're not a couple, but we are monogamous, right?" This was awkward. Definitely not the conversation she wanted to have surrounded by kids. At least they were out of earshot.

"Don't worry. I'm not interested in her or anyone else right now, except you," he said.

He offered her a tight smile and she hated the tension her stupid comment caused, but she had to make sure they were on the same page. "I didn't want to assume," she said softly.

"Don't assume that I want to hook up with any available female, either." He looked away from her, scanning the grounds, watching the kids.

She grabbed his hand, squeezing his fingers with hers. "I'm sorry."

She couldn't read his expression when he looked at her again, giving her a smile.

"I know," he said, tightening his grip on her hand. "Shall we go check on the snakes?"

"So gross. Why'd it have to be snakes?"

His laugh was warmer—fuller—as he tugged her back toward the kids, and she felt marginally better.

What they had between them was exactly what they'd both wanted. It couldn't be anything more. And it confused the shit out of her.

Lexi: Send reinforcements and cake.

He laughed. She even included cake emoticons. He hadn't heard from her since the field trip, and he instantly wondered if she had a babysitter tonight or if Abby was staying out again. He perked up at the thought of seeing her, his exhaustion from a long day at work fading.

Matt was right. His friend had teased him today that Lexi must think Grant didn't have a social life, since he jumped to rescue her at every chance.

He had a social life. He wasn't sitting around waiting for her call, but he also wasn't actively pursuing anyone else since he was getting regular sex. Honestly, it was the best situation.

Grant: Shocker. Another bad date?

Lexi: At one of those restaurants that serves tiny portions.

Grant: Tapas?

Lexi: Nope. Fancy places designed to make you max out your credit card and then go home and eat a pizza. Or cake.

Grant laughed. He loved that she had a healthy appetite.

Grant: How's the rest of the date going?

Lexi: I think I'm getting hangry.

Grant: That's never good.

Grant: Online match?

Lexi: Yep.

Grant: Aside from being hangry, how's the actual date going?

Lexi: Horrible. He's been talking about alien invasions for the last hour.

Grant looked at his phone twice, waiting for her to fix some obscure autocorrect.

Grant: Aliens?

Lexi: Yes. He apparently binge-watched The X-Files.

Lexi: He asked if I'd ever dreamed of being probed.

Grant: WTF

Lexi: He said he thinks he was, and it was pleasant.

Grant: Seriously. We need to discuss your online date settings.

Lexi: We've talked online for a couple weeks. He seemed normal.

Grant: Maybe he hadn't been probed yet.

Lexi: OMG! I just snorted my wine. Stop it.

Lexi: Are you busy?

Grant: Where are you?

She texted him the address.

110

Grant: I'll be there in twenty. Try to keep the anal probing to a minimum.

Lexi: Umm, what?

Grant looked at his message and choked on a laugh.

Grant: Freaking auto correct. I meant alien probing. LOL.

Lexi: Haha. I just about died. Hurry up. I need cake.

Grant: On my way.

Grant slipped his shoes back on and headed out to rescue his damsel. He shouldn't enjoy her dating misfortunes as much as he did. How could anyone have such horrible luck?

* * *

Twenty minutes later, he pulled into the parking lot and grabbed his phone.

Grant: Here. Still want me to bust up your date?

Lexi: Yes. Hurry. He's currently describing one of his dreams. In detail. If I actually had any food in my stomach, I'd worry about it making a reappearance.

He chuckled and walked in, spotting Lexi. Her eyes met his, and he caught the instant relief as he made his way over to her table.

"Oh, Grant, isn't it awful?" she asked, her eyes still wide, her hand clutching her phone.

He almost asked if she was referring to her date, but held back. The guy looked normal enough.

"Yes," he said slowly, not sure where she was going with this.

111

"Dad told you where I was. Poor Mom," Lexi said.

"Oh no. Was she taken?" alien date asked.

Okay, not normal.

"It's her hip again," Lexi continued, ignoring her date.

So they were going that route again. "Yes, we have to get to the hospital immediately," he said.

Lexi turned back to her date. "I'm so sorry, but I have to go. My mom. She has a bad hip. My dad texted," she rambled, throwing bills on the table and grabbing her coat.

"I hope she's all right. I'll call you," he said.

She nodded, apologizing again, and scooting out of the booth. "I'm starving," she mumbled under her breath, when they reached the door.

"He seemed nice," Grant said as soon as they were next to his car.

"Yeah, definitely not. I can't believe you didn't even bring me a cookie. You know I'm hungry." Her pouting was adorable.

He laughed. "I wasn't going to stop. I wanted to make sure I rescued you before he had a chance to probe you."

She groaned. "So not funny."

"You drive?"

"Nope. I told you, he seemed normal, so I let him pick me up," she said, climbing into his car.

"What time do you have to be home?"

"I have a babysitter for a few hours and I'm starving. Can we order pizza and go to your place?"

He chuckled. "With pleasure," he said, opening the car door for her.

"Let's hope so," he heard her say before the door shut behind him. He tried to ignore his arousal at her comment, but his jeans tightened. He slipped into the driver's seat, trying not to obviously adjust himself.

"Wait. Did you already eat dinner?"

"Yes, but I'm always up for pizza. I'm a growing boy." The last word came out strangled when she reached across the console and ran her finger down his strained zipper.

"I can see that."

"You are so inappropriate." He tried to sound annoyed, but failed.

She laughed. "You bring that out in me."

"Glad to be of service."

"Again. Let's hope." She shot him a grin, and he pulled out of the parking lot, heading home at a slightly over-the-speed-limit pace. He wanted her in his bed now, but getting pulled over would put a damper on that plan.

Two hours later, fully sated with pizza and a chocolate chip cookie pie, Lexi curled up against Grant's side.

"So you want to tell me about your date?" he asked, running his fingers up and down her arm. "Was it a first date?"

"I met him for coffee a few days ago, the day after the field trip. How's Amber, by the way?" She laughed, feeling him shudder against her.

"Very funny. You know she got Lily's number from the class phone list and called asking for my number. Then

Lily accused me of trying to pick up women on a school field trip. That's not what these trips are for," he said, attempting to mimic his sister's voice.

Lexi laughed. "I don't think Lily would appreciate your terrible impersonation of her."

His chuckle rolled through her body, and she pressed deeper against him. Hey. She was cold. *Keep telling yourself that.*

"So did Lily give Amber your number?"

"No. Thank God," he said, and Lexi was annoyed that she felt relief. He wasn't hers, but she didn't want him going anywhere any time soon.

"I take it you won't be signing up for any more field trips," she said.

"Definitely not. And stop changing the subject. I want to hear about this date." He grinned, his dimples taunting her to climb on top for round three. Or was it four? He made her insatiable, and she loved it.

She let out a slow breath. "Fine."

"So, it was a second date, and he picked you up," he prodded.

"Yes. We'd had coffee, and the conversation was pretty good. We talked about work, about Abby."

"Sounding good so far."

"It was, until he launched into a detailed description of what it was like to get probed." She dropped her head on his chest.

Grant let out a bark of laughter. "He was hoping to find a kindred alien spirit."

She swatted his chest. "It's not funny."

"Yes it is. Please tell me you keep a journal or something, documenting all these dates."

She lifted her head up, staring him directly in the eyes, and poked him in the chest. "So not funny. Is it bad that I keep bailing on these dates? I mean, I didn't even make it to dinner this time."

"It's not like you walk out on them without an excuse. They don't know that you've now broken your mom's hip twice and your daughter's arm just to get out of a date."

She dropped her head on his chest, her shoulders shaking. "I'm the worst mother *and* daughter."

"It's fine. People go on horrible dates, and I'm sure you're not the first one to have a back-up plan ready to go."

"Thanks for trying to make me feel better."

"I think we need to grab my laptop and log in to your account," he said.

"Because that's not weird at all."

"What? Just trying to help you out."

"I'm not going to look for possible dates while I'm naked in bed with you," she said, laughing at how ridiculous this conversation was. He couldn't be serious.

"Why not? You know we're just scratching a mutual itch. Not that I want you to stop having sex with me, but we're friends, and you deserve to find your happiness."

Her heart caught in her chest at how sincere he looked, but she pushed it aside. *Itch. Itch. Itch.*

"That's so sweet, but I'm still not logging on to my account." She twirled her fingers in the dusting of hair on his chest.

"I'm actually just curious about your search settings. I'm convinced it's just male. I think you need to be more specific about what you want, aside from breathing."

She punched him in the arm. "Hey, breathing is important, and I did list what I was looking for," she grumbled.

"So far we have gym bathroom selfie man and kinky grandpa who goes through wives like he does latex bodysuits—"

"Eww, that's just gross."

"Sorry, couldn't help myself. Oh, and last but not least, alien man."

She buried her head in his shoulder, unable to stop her snort. "Okay, okay. Yes, it's bad."

"So what are you looking for, since clearly it is not these men?" he asked.

She rolled out of his arms, lying flat on her back, staring up at the ceiling. This conversation was weirding her out, but she knew he was just trying to help.

"I don't know. I want someone with a steady career. Someone who can make me laugh. Who I can talk to, have fun with. Who loves kids and maybe wants more. Someone I can be myself with, and feel safe and comfortable with."

"That seems like a reasonable list," he said.

"And great sex. I demand great sex," she said, adding a fist pump to drive home the importance.

"Totally doable. Great conversations and awesome sex are important, or else all you have are awkward silences and your own hand."

116

Her body shook with laughter. "This conversation is ridiculous."

"No it's not. We're friends, right? And friends talk about this stuff. I bet you talk to your girlfriends about this stuff," he said.

"Of course I do, but I'm not naked in bed with them," she said.

"Way to kill my dreams."

She rolled back into his arms, glaring at him. "I hate to break it to you, but we also don't have pillow fights in our underwear."

"You take that back," he muttered, pulling her closer, and finding every ticklish spot on her body until she was gasping, tears streaming down her face in laughter.

This was what she wanted. Too bad he was leaving soon, and there was nothing she could do about it. She ignored her frustration and rolled on top of him, effectively halting his tickling as she rocked her lower body against his.

She needed to get in all her fun with him while she could. In a few months she might be left with just her hand and BOB, her battery operated boyfriend, and BOB wasn't nearly as bone-melting as Grant.

"Ready," Grant said through his headset a few days later, as he snapped himself into the seat harness on the helicopter.

The pilot responded and headed back to base.

Grant's shift was over, and he wanted his bed and a beer. He hated rescues like this one, but, unfortunately, they were common. He wanted to rail at the guy for taking a small fishing boat out in the blustery March weather. Only an insane person would choose to be out here after the storm warning was issued earlier this morning.

The guy had ended up in the rocks and called for help. This was Grant's fourth call of his shift. Luckily everyone had been pulled out alive. Bruised and banged up, but alive.

Diving into frigid waters to rescue people was part of his job, and he loved the adrenaline rush and the knowledge that he was saving someone, but doing it to rescue people who should've used common sense and stayed home irked him. Not that he'd say anything. No one ever yelled at the victims. It would be like shouting in a vacuum…sucked in and going nowhere.

Grant did one last check of the splint on the guy's arm, then leaned back and rested his head on the seat. The guy was lucky. His boat was totaled but he'd walk away with a few scratches and possibly a broken arm. It could've been a lot worse.

They'd never found those kids from a few weeks back. He wished he could say it was par for the course and he forgot about one case when he moved onto the next, but the unsuccessful attempts stayed with him. That's why he spoke at schools. To get kids to think before they went out. Kids thought they were immortal, but one change of the tides, one brutal storm rolling in, and even the best preparations were for naught.

He didn't know why he was getting all maudlin tonight, but he needed to stop. Today had been a great day.

They landed at base a short while later and Grant ushered the guy inside. Another medic took over and Grant was able to escape to the locker room.

Matt greeted him when Grant walked into the room. "Hey man, what're you up to tonight?"

"Sleep and a beer," Grant said, shucking out of his gear.

"Lame. It's Friday night. Let's go to Crash and Byrne. You go catch up on your beauty sleep for a few hours, then we'll head out around nine?" Matt asked.

"Sure," Grant agreed. "But make it seven. I could go for a burger."

"Sounds like a plan. See you in a few," Matt said, and walked back out to the hanger.

Grant headed for the showers to wash away the salt and stress of the day. As he stood under the hot spray, he thought about Lexi. He did that a lot these days. It'd been just over a week since his last disaster date rescue, and he hadn't heard a peep from her. He wasn't sure how he felt about that.

He'd been tempted a few times to text her something funny or see if she was up for dessert, but he'd resisted. They were nothing more than fuck buddies, not that they'd actually declared that, but that's all it was. Less than three months left before he headed for Florida, and no strings attached was how it needed to stay.

* * *

Grant bellied up to the bar a few hours later, nodding a greeting to Adam Byrne, the owner and one of Grant's oldest friends. Adam was like the brother he'd always wanted, but Grant had gotten stuck with pain-in-the-ass sisters instead.

Adam deposited two local pale ales in front of Grant and Matt. "Burgers with the works?" he asked.

"Yeah. I'm starving," Matt said. "Pretty boy here had to take a nap before we could head out."

Grant glared at his friend. "You want to do a twenty-four hour shift, jumping into freezing water?"

Matt laughed, ignoring him, and scanned the crowd. The guy was always looking for his next hook-up. It was a decently-sized crowd for seven on a Friday, but the place would be packed in a couple hours.

Adam's family had owned the bar for years, and Adam had taken over the reins when his father had died eight years ago. Grant had put in more than a few back-breaking hours helping with renovations when he'd come home three years ago. The place had an old Irish pub feel with a thick dark wood bar and brass fixtures. Grant would miss this place when he left, if only for the mouthwatering burgers they were now famous for.

"He better rest up. Sunday's game is important," Adam said, drawing a pint for the guy on the other side of Matt.

"I'll be ready. How's the hip?" Grant asked, hiding his smirk, apparently unsuccessfully if Adam's glare was anything to go by.

"What happened?" Matt asked.

"Someone decided to ram his captain into the boards at practice this week," Adam grumbled.

"It was a scrimmage. Had to practice all the possible scenarios to be prepared for the game this weekend," Grant said, innocently.

"It's a rec league with no checking," Adam shot back.

Grant grinned. "I know. Just want to make sure you're ready for the game, Captain."

"Keep it up, and I'll tell Sara to burn that burger," he replied.

Grant clutched his chest in mock horror. "Don't even joke."

Adam chuckled and moved down the bar, refilling orders, and thankfully, staying away from the kitchen door. Grant didn't have the heart to tell his friend that everyone came for Sara's food and not Adam's charm, regardless of what his friend thought.

"So how's the family? Looking forward to finally being free of you?" Adam asked when he'd finally moseyed back in their direction.

He ignored the dig. "Doing well. The twins just turned seven last month. You missed the party. Nate asked where you were," Grant said.

"Yeah. Had to work."

Grant didn't buy it. It hadn't escaped Grant's notice that his friend had skipped the last few Lanzi family functions. He was afraid to find out if Adam had hooked up with one of Grant's cousins or something. Grant didn't want to have to kill his best friend.

"So everyone is good? Parents? Maddie? Lily?" Adam continued.

"Yep. Maddie's in her second year at Berkeley. Lily's still working too much. Trying to do everything, be a mom and a dad and sell every property she gets her hands on."

Grant didn't miss the look that passed over his friend's eyes when Grant mentioned his sister. He wanted to think it was because Adam was just as protective of Grant's sisters as Grant was, but he wondered if there was something else. Adam had been livid when he'd found out about Billy's cheating, and Grant had feared he'd have to restrain his friend.

"I'm thinking of opening another bar. Maybe I'll give her a call to look at some properties," Adam said.

"Wow. Another one?"

Adam went on to tell him about new possible locations he was interested in. Grant had to hand it to the guy. When Adam wanted something, he went after it. They talked for another few minutes before the bar started filling up, and Adam had to go back to slinging drinks.

* * *

An hour later, sufficiently stuffed with the best burger Grant could remember having, he nursed his second beer. The few hours of sleep he'd had after his shift had only relieved some of his exhaustion. He wanted to call it an early night, but Matt would never let him live it down.

Grant's mind wandered to Lexi again. Did she have a date tonight? He'd hold off sleep if she called him for dessert. He glanced down at his phone. Still nothing from her. Not that he was waiting or anything.

"Any texts from the damsel?" Matt asked, smirk in place.

Shit. He'd thought he'd been subtle with that check. "Nope."

"You have plenty to pick from in this bar. You two aren't exclusive now, are you?"

"Of course not. We aren't dating." Not that Grant had any interest in hooking up with other women since he'd met Lexi, but that was just because he was getting sex on a semi-regular basis, nothing more.

"Wait. Grant's got a girl?" Adam asked.

Grant spun around. He hadn't realized his friend was right behind them. "No. There's no girl."

Grant ignored Adam's raised brow.

"Just someone he keeps rescuing from bad dates and then banging," Matt chimed in, and Grant wanted to slug him.

"Really?" Adam said, blatant interest, with a hint of mischief, in his eyes.

"It's nothing. I've helped her out a few times, and it's just sex. Nothing more." Who was he justifying his actions to? He didn't need to explain himself to his friends.

"Does this damsel have a name?" Adam asked.

"It's Lexi," Matt said.

"It's nothing. Just some fun before I go," Grant said at the same time as Matt.

"No, it's actually Lexi," Matt said, gesturing toward the door where Lexi stood with some guy.

What was she doing here? She looked around the bar, but didn't see him. He wanted to know who the guy was.

Probably a date. She turned back to the guy, gesturing toward a small high top table in the corner. Grant couldn't take his eyes off her, and then he felt like a creeper.

Clearly, it was a date. Was it going well? Did she need his services?

"The redhead?" Adam asked.

"Yep," Matt said. "Looks like she's on a date. You better keep your ringer on."

"Very funny," Grant deadpanned, ignoring Matt's grin.

"She's hot. Too bad she's taken," Adam said.

"Give it time," Matt said. "I bet she'll be texting Grant within thirty minutes."

Grant bristled. "Don't be an ass." As much as he wanted that to be the case, he didn't like what Matt was insinuating.

"Dude, she has a pattern. Date sucks then she gets you to rescue her."

"It's not like she purposely picks horrible dates. She just has really bad luck." He ignored their grins at his defense of her.

"We'll see," Matt said, clearly not believing him.

"I'll send Paula over there to get their order. Maybe she can get some dirt on this one," Adam said. "Or maybe I'll go over there myself. Paula looks pretty busy."

"How about you not," Grant grumbled.

"I want to get to know your damsel. You keep sticking up for her," Adam said.

"Yes, because she's a friend, and you can be a total douche."

"Ouch. That hurts, man." Adam clutched his chest, pretending to stagger back.

"Whatever."

Adam enjoyed riling Grant up, they had a twenty-year friendship based on mutual tormenting.

Grant tried to not focus on Lexi across the room. Her hair was pulled up in some twisty style, her neck, that he'd grown attached to, bare and begging for his lips. She looked stunning, as usual, her V-neck top drawing his attention to her cleavage. Not that she was out on display, but he knew what was under that shirt. How pink her skin turned when he kissed her chest, scraping his scruffy beard against her creamy flesh. His jeans tightened. Dammit. Every time with her. He needed to get control over his body.

His phone remained soundless in his pocket. He refused to take it out and put it on the bar, knowing Adam and Matt would tease him endlessly if he did. *Bastards.*

Chapter 8

Lexi drummed her nails against her thigh and sipped her second martini of the night, wishing she'd ordered a shot, or three. Another disaster date. At least this one, she'd only agreed to drinks. She'd messaged back and forth with Brian for over a week. They had so much in common. He worked for an accounting firm, had a ten-year-old son, and was recently divorced.

Too recently.

He'd spent the last thirty minutes going on and on about his ex-wife, who he wasn't over. And who apparently used their child like a pawn to get more support out of him. At least he paid child support. One point for him.

"That's unfortunate," she said, trying to sound supportive. It definitely wasn't a topic she'd planned to discuss on a first date.

"I know. And my therapist said I should try online dating. Get back out there. She's so smart. So I figured I'd pick someone who'd been divorced longer than I had. Pick your brain for how you moved on."

"Umm." Great. So this was a fact-finding mission for him. She sure could pick them.

He sighed. "Yeah. I see my therapist three times a week. I don't know what I'd do without her."

"Oh. That's nice." What the hell else was she supposed to say to that?

His phone dinged on the table and he grabbed it, swiping it on.

"Everything okay?" she asked.

"Yes. Just had to text my mom to tell her I got here okay," he said, setting the phone down, only to have it ding again. "She says hello."

"What?"

"My mom wanted to see how it was going, and she says hello," he repeated.

Seriously. He was in his mid-thirties, and he had to text his mom.

"You must be really close with her."

"Yep. I talk to her every day when I'm at work, and of course, I see her every night since I moved back home after the divorce."

Wait. What? "You've been divorced for a year, right?"

"Yes," he said, munching on a pretzel from the bowl the waitress had dropped off.

"And you moved back home?"

"Yes. Why would I leave? I'll move out when I find my next wife," he said, completely sincere.

Red flag. Red flag. Holy hell, Grant would have a field day with this one. She didn't want to keep relying on his services, but this date was turning into another winner, and she could go for dessert.

She'd give it one more drink. That was a respectable time to end a drinks-only date. And then she was calling a cab. Not that she wouldn't mind seeing Grant again. It'd been a week since her alien date.

127

She focused on possibly seeing Grant as Brian continued to talk about the joy of living at home with his mother.

Ten minutes later, her phone vibrated in her pocket.

"Oh. Do you need to get that? Is your mother checking in?" Brian asked. Like that was freaking normal.

Yep. Time to plan her escape. She glanced down at her phone, trying not to laugh when she saw the text.

Grant: Date tonight?

How the hell did he know?

Lexi: How do you know I'm on a date?

Grant: Lucky guess.

Lexi: Maybe I'm spending a night in with Abby, watching her favorite movie.

Grant: Are you? What movie? Is it a scary one?

"Tell your mother I said hello," Brian said.

Lexi jerked her head up. She'd forgotten about him.

Lexi: A freaking nightmare.

"It's not my mother. Sorry about that. You were saying," she said, keeping her phone in her lap as Brian continued on about his mother and his therapist. The latter, he'd met through his mother, not that his mother went to the same therapist. Same office. Conflict of interest and all.

Her phone vibrated in her lap.

Grant: Ditch the guy, and come have a drink with me.

Grant: Or I could keep sending messages so your phone can vibrate in your lap.

Lexi: How did you know my phone's in my lap?

Grant: Lucky guess.

Grant: He looks like a real winner.

128

Lexi: How do you know that?

Grant: I know your type.

Lexi: Ugh. Yeah, it's bad. His mother texted to check on him.

Grant: Seriously? On the date?

Lexi: Yep. He had to let her know he arrived.

Grant: How old is he? You going for much younger after kinky grandpa?

Lexi: Not funny. 35 and lives at home.

Grant: I'd say bad hip again, but he'd probably offer to take you to the hospital and have his mother meet you there.

She tried to muffle a snort laugh, but it came out strained.

"Is everything okay?" Brian asked, his eyes filled with concern.

She really was a terrible date once she started talking to Grant. She should feel bad about that, but she didn't.

"Sorry about that," she said, dropping her phone in her lap and trying to focus on him.

"No problem. So then my therapist suggested…" he continued to rattle on, and she tuned him out and drained the rest of her glass, looking around for the exit.

She could do this. Escape without Grant's help. Especially since Brian just mentioned her meeting his mother, and she didn't want to wait the twenty minutes it would probably take Grant to get here.

And then she saw him. Sitting at the bar. He looked up from his phone, a grin spreading across his lips as he tilted his beer bottle toward her in greeting.

Her fingers flew over the screen.

Lexi: Hey stalker. You following me now?

Grant: And good evening to you, too.

He followed that with a winking emoticon, and she bit back her own grin.

Lexi: How did you know I was here?

Grant: Maybe it's just fate.

Lexi: Or maybe you're a creeper who's following me.

Grant: I'm going with fate. So, what reason am I coming up with to get you out of this one?

Lexi: I'm going to handle it myself.

Grant: So you don't want dessert?

She attempted to ignore the heat spiraling through her. She definitely wasn't skipping dessert if he was willing. She shifted in her chair and looked up, catching his grin before he tipped his beer back to take a long swig.

Shit. She was mesmerized by his throat moving as he swallowed. She needed help.

"Lexi, are you okay? You look flushed," Brian said, pulling her away from her fantasies. Except Grant was real, and everything he did to her was beyond her fantasies. Hell, she needed cake.

"What? Oh, I'm fine," she said, focusing back on Brian. Her date. And not the man who was driving her to distraction, sitting a short distance away, with his scruffy jaw that felt amazing on her skin....

"I hope you're not getting sick. It's flu season. My mother is getting older, and if I bring home a cold and she catches it, then she won't be able to make me dinner."

Wow. He was crazy *and* an asshole. She was beginning to understand why his wife left him. She let out a small cough.

"My throat has been a little itchy today. I really hope I'm not getting sick. I didn't get a flu shot this year. I never do." She was probably laying it on thick, but desperate times and all.

Brian pushed his chair back, sat up straight, and eyed her throat like something was going to come out of it and attack him. He reached for his wallet, flipping open the billfold in seconds.

"It's getting late. Maybe we should call it a night. I'll go pay the tab," he said, sliding off the high stool.

"Oh, yes. I really hope I'm not sick," she said, reaching for her wallet. "Let me give you some money for the tab." She held out a few bills, watching Brian swallow but not take it from her hand.

"Don't worry about it. I'll pay tonight. You can get it the next time," he said, backing away from her diseased cash.

"Thanks. I'm going to run to the ladies' room. I had a great time," she leaned toward him as if to hug him, and his eyes widened in panic. She bit back her chuckle. Men were so ridiculous when they feared getting sick. She wasn't passing around the plague or anything.

"Yes. I hope you feel better. I'll call you," he said, turning toward the bar before she could get in another word. She'd hang out in the bathroom for a few, until he was gone, and then tell Grant that she was perfectly capable of rescuing herself while they celebrated her freedom over cake. And sex. A shiver rocked through her. Yes, definitely sex.

131

* * *

A sharp rap sounded on the bathroom door a few minutes later, Grant's voice coming through the wood.

"The coast is clear."

She heard the laughter in his voice, and she yanked the door open. "Did you see that? Looks like I'm learning how to rescue myself from my own dates."

He grinned at her. That dimple peeking out from his scruff. She wanted to lick it.

"What did you tell that guy? He ran out of here like he was on fire."

Lexi couldn't fight her laugh.

"Wait. Did you tell him that his mother was in the hospital? That's just mean," he said, his eyes twinkling with amusement.

"That's not even funny," she said, shoving him. He barely moved. He was a solid wall of hot, hard male. She may have let her fingers linger over his chest, internally cheering at his quick inhale.

He gripped her hand, pulling her close, and brushed his lips against hers. "Let's get out of here," he breathed against her mouth.

She rocked against him. "Yes please, but you promised me cake first."

His shoulders shook. "You're killing me, you know that?"

"All in good time," she said, patting his chest before brushing past him and heading toward the bar. "I need cake after that one."

He chuckled behind her, his hand grazing across her lower back. She tamped down the urge to turn around and shove him toward the door. It'd only been a week since they'd had sex. After four years of going without, a one-week absence should be nothing. She needed to get a grip on her need for him. He wasn't going to be available to her in a few short months.

"So are you going to tell me what you told your date?" he asked.

"That I had the plague," she said, sliding onto a barstool.

"What?"

"My skin might've been flushed, so he asked if I was sick. I told him my throat had been scratchy, and..." she trailed off as he leaned away from her. She couldn't stop her bark of laughter.

"I can't get sick," he said.

"For the love of...what is it with men and their fear of the common cold, which I don't have, by the way. I saw my opening to get out of the date and took it." She laughed as he visibly relaxed.

"That's a relief."

"And they say women are the weaker sex. You can't handle the thought of a measly little cold."

"I can handle it, but who wants to get sick. And, we are definitely stronger," Grant said, puffing out his chest. Lexi caught his grin, or she might have slugged him in the stomach for that comment. Although, she'd probably hurt her hand trying that. Damn solid, ripped bastard.

"I'm telling your mother you said that the next time I see her," the bartender said.

"You wouldn't dare," Grant said, taking the seat next to her.

"Hi, I'm Adam. You must be the damsel," the bartender said. He was slightly taller than Grant, and just as fit, if his tight black t-shirt was anything to go by. His green eyes crinkled as he grinned at her.

"Damsel?" she asked, raising her eyebrow to Grant.

"Ignore him," Grant grumbled next to her.

"I'm pretty sure I rescued myself tonight, thank you very much," she huffed, turning back to catch Adam stifling his laughter. "I take it you two know each other. Or do you just share my secrets with everyone?"

"I've known Grant for years…since we were kids. I'm the brother he never had."

"And never wanted," he muttered.

"Ah man, you're breaking my heart," Adam said.

Lexi laughed. "So you grew up together? I bet you have great dirt on him."

Adam turned to Grant. "I like her," he said before facing Lexi again. "Let's get you a drink and then the stories I can share…"

"No stories," Grant grumbled.

"So you get to hear about all my embarrassing dates, and I don't get any dirt on you?" she asked Grant. "Oh, and I'll take a glass of Chardonnay, and what are my dessert options?" she asked Adam.

"We'll have the chocolate chip cookie bomb, and don't you have other people to serve?" Grant said to Adam.

"Don't go anywhere," Adam said, making his way down the length of the bar.

"Chocolate chip cookie bomb. That sounds amazing," Lexi said.

"You'll love it," Grant said, running his finger along her knuckles. "I missed you."

Lexi felt his words in her belly, and she shifted close to the edge of the barstool. His knees bracketed hers, surrounding her. She didn't want to miss him, and she refused to tell him she had.

"So, what are you doing here?" she asked, still unbelieving that they happened to come to the same bar tonight.

"Matt and I stopped by after work," he said.

"Where's Matt?" She turned away from Grant and looked around before spotting him chatting with a woman. "Ah, there he is."

"Looks like he found someone to hit on. Always someone new."

"Is he usually like that?" she asked, ignoring the fact that Grant probably thought the same thing about her since almost every time he saw her she was on or escaping from a different date. Ugh, she really needed to work on her search qualifications.

"Pretty much."

"So he's not having luck on eMatch, either?"

"If he comes back over here, just ask about dolls," Grant said, and she didn't miss the mischief in his eyes, the corners crinkling in amusement. Why did he have to be so adorable? And where was that dessert?

"Dolls, huh? Okay. So, do you come here often?"

His grin spread, and she wanted to reel those words back in.

"You don't have to use lines on me. I'm a sure bet." He dipped his head closer, his eyes darkening as he brushed a soft kiss across her lips.

"Shut up." Shit. She sounded breathy. She pulled back. "You know what I meant."

He chuckled. "Yes, I try to stop by at least once a week. Adam and I have been friends for twenty years. I helped him renovate the bar."

Of course he did. Was there anything he couldn't do? Oh right, stay in town. She pushed that thought aside. *We're scratching an itch. We're scratching an itch.* She wondered how many times she would have to tell herself that before she finally believed it.

"And here we are. Hope I'm not interrupting," Adam said, dropping off their drinks and a decadent dessert that she wanted to dive into immediately. Gooey fudge covered a deep-dish chocolate cookie that looked warm and inviting.

She scooped a bite into her mouth, not caring about her groan as warm, melty chocolate and sugary cookie exploded on her tongue. "Holy crap, this is amazing," she said, looking up and catching both men staring at her. She licked the fudge from the corner of her mouth. "Sorry, but it is."

"Sometimes I think you're more turned on by dessert than me," Grant said, shifting in his seat.

She grinned. "No, it's about a fifty-fifty split."

"I'm in competition with a cookie," he grumbled, then took a bite. "Wow. This is good."

"Glad you like it," Adam said, grabbing another beer for Grant out of the cooler and depositing it in front of his friend.

"Now, tell me his most embarrassing story," Lexi said to Adam, ignoring Grant's protests.

"I'm going to kill him," Grant grumbled when Adam finally walked away, hopefully for good, to check on something in the kitchen. Adam had filtered in and out of the conversation, sharing a few stories between grabbing drinks for other patrons. Even Grant's pleading looks hadn't swayed his friend from telling Lexi a few memories that he'd rather not relive. Not that they'd been horrible, just embarrassing. Stupid lifelong friends always had the best dirt.

But hearing her laugh was worth it.

"You must've looked adorable in a tiara," she said between giggles, her cheeks flushed, her eyes filling with tears of laughter.

"Last tea party I ever attended, no matter how much Lily begged," he muttered.

Lexi grinned. "But if Keira asked you?"

He sighed. "Yes, I'd put the damn tiara back on for her. Just don't tell her that."

"I make no promises," she said, laughing, her eyes sparkling.

He shifted to trap her knees between his, her eyes widening when he ran his thumb across her palm. Damn, he'd missed her this week. He'd wanted to text her to check in. Maybe send a funny meme. But his hand refused to hit send every time.

"You want to get out of here?" he asked, leaning in and nipping her earlobe, her indrawn breath tightening his belly.

"I thought you'd never ask." Her eyes darkened, her desire clear and matching his.

"Is your car here?"

"I took a cab," she whispered, her breath fanning over his jaw.

"Even better," he said, taking her hand in his and pulling her up from the barstool. They bid Adam good night, and Grant caught Matt's eye, giving him a quick nod before Grant hustled her out the front door and into his car. He opened the door for her, and she climbed in.

"So chivalrous," she murmured, buckling herself in.

He shook his head. "Who the hell do you date? They don't open doors for you?"

"Umm. No," she replied, nibbling on her lower lip.

"Idiots," he grumbled, making his way around the front of the car and getting in. "So where am I going?"

It was a quick drive, and he was pulling into her driveway in under ten minutes. He may or may not have been speeding. And it would've been completely her fault if he had since she'd decided to run her nails from his chest to his belt while he listened to the robotic sounds of his GPS. She was going to be the death of him.

He hopped out of the car and took a steadying breath. The crisp night air washed over him, cooling down some of his desire. He refused to think about pressing her against the car and kissing the life out of her.

In his attempt to control his need, she was already out of the car and fumbling with her keys. She pulled him into the house and pressed him against the door that had just shut behind him. "I've wanted to do this all night," she growled, sealing her lips with his, her hands sinking into his hair.

Control was overrated. He groaned against her mouth and pulled her tighter, slanting his head to get a better angle as he devoured her, and she returned with equal fervor.

She fiddled with the top two buttons of his shirt, slipping them through the holes before yanking his shirt up over his head.

"What's the rush? We have all night. When does Abby get back?" he asked, his voice husky.

"Tomorrow afternoon," she said, pulling on his belt loops.

"Plenty of time," he said, plunging his hands into her silky hair and gripping her skull before his lips met hers again.

Her hand slid up his chest, her nails scraping against his flat nipples, and his muscles clenched in need. He wanted her more than any woman he'd ever been with and that should freak him the hell out, but he couldn't stop.

He walked backwards, his mouth still fused with hers, hoping he was moving in the direction of her couch. He winced when his calf met what he assumed was the coffee table. At least that meant he was getting closer.

He broke the kiss and pulled her down on the couch. She fell into his lap with a laugh, and shifted to straddle his hips. They both groaned as she grinded against his erection, pushing him deeper into the cushions, where something sharp poked him.

"Umm, there's something sticking me in the ass," he mumbled against her lips.

"What?" she asked, sitting back on his thighs.

"Something's poking me," he said, reaching behind him and pulling out a superhero figurine.

"Sorry, I thought I got all of Abby's toys," she said, grabbing the offending item and setting it on the side table. "So are you telling me you don't want Captain America near your ass?"

"Think I'll skip that," he said against her lips. He wrapped his arms around her waist, and she fell against his chest.

Her eyes sparkled with humor. "Superheroes don't do it for you?"

"I mean, if you want to dress up as Wonder Woman, who am I to stop you?" he asked, running his hands up and down her spine.

She pulled back, swatting his chest. "Wonder Woman? You're such a cliché."

He laughed. "Is this really what you want to talk about while you're straddling my lap?" He swiveled his hips, pressing his cock against her.

She ran her hands over his belly, and he gritted his teeth as white-hot desire rushed through him. She brushed kisses along his collarbone, her teeth nipping his shoulder.

Her hands travelled down his chest, tracing each of his muscles along the way. He wanted her to trace them with her tongue like she had last week. His body tightened in remembrance, and because she was now palming his aching cock.

"I need to be inside you," he groaned, lifting his head to watch her.

She ignored him, slowly lowering the zipper of his jeans. The sound of the teeth parting rang in his ears. Her hand dipped inside, gripping him, stroking him once, then twice, pulling his cock free of his boxer briefs. Her thumb rolled over the tip, collecting a drop of moisture before bringing her thumb to her mouth.

He wanted her plump lips wrapped around his cock. He'd beg for it if he had to.

She scooted off of his lap, kneeling between his spread thighs, and stroked his erection. Her thumb traced the large vein below the tip. Her gaze locked with his as she lowered her head, taking him into her hot mouth. Her lips closed around him, and he fought the need to shout as she started to suck him, her tongue darting out, swirling around his cock as she took him in, inch by painstaking inch.

He groaned, torn between throwing his head back in pure bliss and continuing to watch her.

The pressure built as she continued to move up and down his shaft, her hand cupping him, squeezing lightly, moving in perfect rhythm with her lips.

She pulled up so only the tip was still in, her tongue darting out to lick the slit, gathering everything he had to give her, then taking him back into her mouth as far as she could.

He lifted his ass off the couch, moving with her, and trying not to shove his cock down her throat.

"I'm so close," he groaned. "You have to stop."

She ignored him again, continuing to torment him. She reached up, scraping her nails along his nipples, and his self-control vanished.

He threw his head back, his orgasm exploding through him as he came with a shout. "That was amazing," he groaned, staring at the ceiling, and trying to slow his galloping heart.

Chapter 9

Lexi sat back on her heels, her gaze roaming over Grant's body as he tried to catch his breath. She loved that she did that to him.

He lifted his head, his chocolate gaze latching onto hers. He was better than any dessert. He tucked himself back into his briefs and pulled her to standing, his hot breath seeping in through her shirt, warming her belly.

She sunk her hands into his hair, the soft strands sifting through her fingers as he pressed kisses along her stomach. She didn't think she could be more turned on if she tried, and she wanted nothing more than to strip naked and sink down on top of him.

She gripped his arms, pulling him to standing. "Bedroom, now."

He toed off his shoes and removed his socks and pants, leaving him in just his boxer briefs. He had those lines on his hip. That perfect V that made women lose their minds.

She ran her fingers down the lines, and he shuddered beneath her hands.

He gripped under her arms, lifting her, and she wrapped her legs around his hips. He strode with purpose, and no shortness of breath, as he carried her down the hall. His eyes locked with hers, her entire body heating at his passion-filled gaze.

She guided him toward her room, hoping she didn't have laundry strewn about since she hadn't anticipated having a sleepover tonight.

"Shit," he bit out, his arms tightening around her.

"What?"

"One of your heels just gouged me," he grumbled.

"But I have boots on."

"I'm pretty sure it wasn't a shoe that you are currently wearing, unless you are super flexible."

She caught a twinkle of laughter in his eyes through the thin streak of moonlight coming in through her curtains. "Sorry about that."

"I'll survive," he said, pressing a kiss to her nose.

She was impressed that he hadn't dropped her when he stepped on the shoe. "Glad to hear it," she said.

They reached the edge of her bed, and he lowered her down, following her onto the comforter, their bodies still linked together. She sank her hands into his hair, pulling at the strands as he kissed the spot where her shoulder and neck met. She shivered at the pure desire that rippled through her, from her scalp to the tips of her toes. Would she ever get enough of him?

His lips skimmed along her collarbone, just visible above the neckline of her shirt. He pulled her up into a sitting position and whipped the shirt off over her head, tossing it over his shoulder.

"Much better. You had way too many clothes on."

Her laugh turned into a husky moan when he traced his tongue along the edge of her bra before latching onto her nipple, sucking her through the flimsy fabric. Heat pooled low in her belly, and she squirmed against him, his chest hair rubbing against her stomach.

144

He reached behind her, unclasping her bra, and pulled the fabric away. His thumb rolled over her nipple, and it pebbled into a hard bud under his touch.

"So beautiful," he murmured against her skin before taking one of her breasts into his mouth again, his hot breath surrounding her tender flesh.

"Yes," she moaned when he lightly bit down on her nipple, her back arching, wanting to push her breast fully into his mouth.

He released her with a pop, kissing down her chest and across her belly. He sat back, stripping her of the rest of her clothes until she was completely bare in front of him.

"I've been thinking about tasting you since the last time I had you spread out in front of me," he said, his pupils fully dilated as he ran his finger along the crease where her thigh met her core, brushing along her lower lips.

She closed her eyes and shuddered when he swiped his finger through her wetness, his thumb grazing her clit. He was going to tease her to the brink of insanity.

"I need you inside me," she moaned. She'd never been so vocal with a partner before, but he wiped away any self-consciousness she had, and she felt free with him.

"Not yet," he murmured.

She heard him shifting, his shoulders brushing against her thighs. She opened her eyes, her gaze locking with his as he pressed kisses to her trimmed curls, then swiping his tongue along her lips.

"Oh yes," she gasped, her hands clenching the sheets around her.

His tongue traced a lazy circled around her clit sucking her into his mouth, her hips lifting, giving herself up to him and whatever he wanted to do to her. He hummed against her clit and she gasped, squeezing her thighs around his head.

Her body was a molten ball of desire, and she couldn't get close enough to him.

He continued to torment her, sucking on her clit and licking along her lower lips. His scruffy jaw rasped against her thighs, sending bolts of pure need coursing through her body.

His eyes locked with hers, and he plunged his finger inside her, curling it up, hitting that spot that drove her crazy.

"Don't stop," she cried out, her body tensing up, her back arching off the bed. She released her grip on the sheets, her hands cupping her breasts, tweaking her nipples between her fingers, her breath coming in pants.

She felt his groan against her core, and raised her head, catching his eyes locked on her palming her breasts. She bit her lip, her head dropping back on the bed as he sucked her clit. A second finger joined the first, moving in and out of her. Her inner muscles clamped down as the pressure built.

Her orgasm ripped through her, her body shuddering as he continued to lick along her lower lips. Her hands dropped to her sides, her heart racing.

He rose, shucking his boxer briefs, his cock standing at attention. It really was beautiful, and if she had any strength left, she would have sat up and wrapped her hand around it.

"I think you killed me," she said, her voice husky, her breaths shallow.

He shot her a cocky smile. "I aim to please."

She giggled. "You're aiming at something." She couldn't move, but she wanted him inside her.

"So you're saying you just want to cuddle?" he asked, grabbing a condom from his jeans.

"No. I want you inside me. I might just lay here, though," she said, watching him roll the condom over his erection. She'd wanted to do that.

"I'd rather have you on top," he said, moving between her spread thighs, and kissing his way up her body.

"I guess," she said with a grin, pushing him flat on the bed and straddling his hips. His cock pressed against her core, and she rocked against his hardness. Her exhaustion faded when his cock touched her clit, and she gripped his erection, stroking him slowly.

His eyes locked with hers, molten chocolate and pure desire in his gaze. He swiveled his hips beneath her, and she lifted her body, sinking onto him in one downward move.

Their gasps intermingled as he settled into her heat, up to the hilt. Her inner muscles clamped around his cock, their bodies melding into one. She moaned at the fullness, her legs squeezing his hips as she moved up and down.

"Yes. Oh, Grant. Yes," she moaned, her hands gripping his chest, her nails grazing over his flat nipples.

His hips rose from the bed, meeting her downward motion each time she sank down on his erection. She dropped her head, swallowing his growl of pleasure when she sealed his lips with hers. His tongue darted in her mouth, tangling and twisting with hers, plunging in and out of her mouth, mimicking the rhythm of his cock moving in and out of her body.

"You feel incredible," he panted, breaking the kiss.

She ground her pelvis against his, the friction applying the perfect pressure on her clit. The stimulation was overpowering, and she closed her eyes, focusing on the pleasure rolling through her.

Her hair fell in her face, and he reached up, tucking it behind her ear, and running his hand along her jaw, pulling her down into another kiss. She ignored the shot to her heart at his tender gesture, giving herself over to his kiss as he moved in and out of her body.

"Yes. Oh, yes," she moaned, breaking the kiss and leaning back. She lifted her hips, pulling almost off of him, squeezing her inner muscles on the tip of his cock, then sinking back down. She rocked against him, the new angle hitting the perfect spot, intense desire building in her belly.

She reached behind her, gripping his thighs, and moved up and down his cock, her entire body shuddering when his thumb grazed her clit. Her orgasm ripped through her, bolts of pleasure rocking through her body as she came.

She rode the waves of her orgasm, his thrusts quickening. His ass lifting off of the bed, her inner walls clamped around his cock. He gripped her hips, holding her in place as he moved within her. She felt his shudder when his own orgasm took over his body.

She collapsed down on top of him. Their chests plastered together, her labored breaths intermingling with his.

He ran his hand up and down her spine, and she shivered under his touch.

"Now I really can't move," she groaned.

He chuckled, pressing a kiss in her hair, and wrapping his arms around her.

She burrowed into his warmth. She could stay there forever. *No.* She had to push that thought from her head. They couldn't stay like this forever. She lifted herself up, his cock slipping free of her body, and she rolled onto her back next to him.

"Stay put," he whispered, squeezing her hand before he rose from the bed and walked into her bathroom.

She focused on his ass, his muscles shifting as he walked. She had to concentrate on that, and not on the feelings rolling through her. Feelings she could not have. This was sex. Pure, wonderful, super-hot sex. It was nothing more. It couldn't be anything more.

Grant cracked his eyes open the next morning, turning away from the bright light coming in the window. He forgot to shut the damn curtains. No. Wait. This wasn't his bed. *Lexi.* He ran his hand over the sheet next to him, reaching for her, but the bed was empty, the fabric cool.

He distinctly remembered falling asleep, snuggled behind her like perfect spoons. A flash of disappointment rolled through him at waking in an empty bed, and he wished he could blame that disappointment solely on his morning wood, but he wanted to wake up with her wrapped in his arms.

That train of thought needed to end. They were hooking up, and that was it. Yes, he considered her a friend, a hot friend that he enjoyed in and out of bed, and he'd miss her when he left, but that was it. *Just friends.*

He grimaced, wondering how many times he'd have to tell himself that before it stuck. He pushed the unwelcome thoughts aside and got out of bed, slipping on his pants. He was almost positive that Lexi's daughter wouldn't be back until later in the afternoon, but he got dressed just in case.

He walked into the kitchen and spotted Lexi at the stove. His stomach grumbled at the smell of eggs and bacon.

"Morning," he said, his voice still scratchy from sleep.

She let out a shriek and spun around, spatula waving in the air, her hand on her chest. "Holy crap, you scared me."

"Forget I was here?" he asked, fighting back his grin.

"Of course not," she said. "I'm just not used to strange men in my kitchen at nine in the morning."

He walked over to her, slipping his hands around her waist and pressed a kiss below her ear. "I woke up and you were gone," he said.

"I thought I'd make breakfast," she said, pulling free of his arms. "Do you want coffee?"

"Sure." He eyed the mark on her shoulder, under her tank top strap. "Shit. Did I do that?" he asked.

"Do what?" she asked, handing him a steaming mug.

"You may have a hickey on your back," he said, trying not to laugh as her eyes widened.

She grimaced, shaking her head. "Oh my God. I haven't had one since high school. How visible is it?" He caught the small smile on her face so he knew she wasn't totally pissed.

"Just don't walk around without a shirt on, and no one will see it," he said, taking a sip of coffee.

"There goes casual bikini Fridays," she said, turning back to stir the eggs.

"What?" he sputtered, choking on his coffee that had just gone down the wrong pipe.

Her shoulders shook. "Couldn't resist. It's winter, I should be safe, but maybe keep the sucking to a minimum."

He set down the mug and snaked an arm around her waist. "I thought you liked my sucking skills."

She spun in his arms, running her hands up his chest. "They're not bad." Her eyes sparkled with humor.

"Maybe I need to work on them," he said, lifting her up, pressing her core against his erection.

She moaned, rubbing against him. She licked her lips, her cheeks flushed.

He dipped his head, sealing his lips with hers, swallowing her gasp, darting his tongue in her mouth to twist and tangle with hers.

He deepened the kiss, and she sunk her hands into his hair, her fingers tightening on his scalp. His hands trailed down her back, and she arched in his touch. He palmed her ass, lifting her up onto the counter, and stepped between her spread thighs.

She broke free from his kiss. "Wait, what about breakfast?"

He turned the knobs on the stove to off, and pushed back the pan filled with sizzling bacon. "I'd rather have you for breakfast," he said, kissing her again. He hardened thinking about her spread out before him like a feast, but he waited for her response before taking her on the cool marble.

"Eat up," she said, before covering her mouth. "I can't believe I just said that," she mumbled through her fingers.

He couldn't stop his bark of laughter. At least he knew she wanted this just as much as he did.

They ripped their clothes off in a flurry, and he couldn't stop staring at every creamy inch of skin she revealed. Her blush spread over her throat and across her rose-tipped breasts. He pulled up the barstool and dove in.

Chapter 10

"When are Auntie Penny and Manda going to be here? I want my pizza," Abby said a few days later, her arms crossed over her little chest.

"They should be here any minute," Lexi said, keeping the annoyance out of her tone. She did want to see them—well, for the most part. They'd invited themselves over again, and she could've said no, but hadn't. They were still curious about Grant, and they would probably grill her as soon as Abby went to bed. She didn't know how to explain the fact that she was okay with how everything was going. That she didn't think about what it would be like in ten weeks when he left.

What a total lie.

She thought about that more than she wanted to admit, but she'd never tell them that. They'd want her to get out now, so she wouldn't get hurt, but she craved him. Her self-control and logic vanished as soon as he appeared.

And they definitely hadn't conserved water last weekend. She tried not to think about being braced against the shower wall, his strong arms supporting her as he ravaged her body. No. She was not going to think about that. She was sitting in a room with her daughter. She should not be thinking about Grant right now. And his amazing body. And the things he could do with it.

Good God. The things he could do with it. Hell, she was turning into a sex-starved crazy person. She internally shook her head, pushing aside all thoughts of him in the shower. The water coursing down his body...*stop. Just stop.*

"Mom, they're here," Abby's little voice intruded on her inappropriate thoughts. Get your mind out of the gutter, she scolded herself, and rose to answer the door.

"What are you thinking about?" Amanda said as soon as she walked in, with Penny trailing behind her, pizza boxes in hand.

Was she wearing a freaking sign or something?

"Oh, I'm starved," Lexi said, grabbing the pizza from Penny and ignoring Amanda's comment. She caught Amanda's inquisitive stare and ignored that as well.

"Thank goodness you guys are here. I thought I would starve," Abby declared, hugging her honorary aunts and eyeing the pizza box.

Penny chuckled. "I'm sure you would've survived," she said, ruffling Abby's blonde curls.

"We got Penny's favorite, veggie supreme," Amanda said, flashing Abby a grin.

Lexi couldn't stop her laughter at Penny's shudder. The woman had yet to meet a vegetable she liked, not that veggie supreme was Lexi's choice, but at least she was willing to eat it.

Amanda and Penny slipped off their shoes and plopped down around the coffee table. Abby loved having them over for dinner because she felt like a big girl, being included in a special dinner.

Lexi loved her friends. They'd been there through the worst with Joe, coming over in the middle of the night to help with Abby when Joe had first walked out and Lexi had been left with an infant to raise on her own. Amanda and Penny didn't have kids of their own, but they were surrogate mothers to Abby, and Lexi would be forever grateful for their support.

Lexi sat back, watching her daughter interact with her friends. There was no irritation at the incessant questions of a six-year-old, and after pizza, one of Abby's favorite movies, and freshly painted fingernails and toenails for everyone, Penny volunteered to put Abby to bed. There were no tantrums to stay up late since Abby had passed out about thirty minutes ago. Lexi had tried to keep her daughter up, knowing a grilling was coming, but Abby hadn't cooperated. *Mother of the year.*

"Who needs another glass of wine?" Amanda asked when Penny returned to the living room.

"I'll take one," Lexi said. "And thanks for putting her to bed, Penny. You didn't have to."

"Just getting in some practice for when I have my own."

Lexi laughed. "She was already asleep. I wouldn't call that practice."

"I have to start somewhere," Penny said, plopping down on the couch.

"You can always come over and babysit one night," Lexi offered.

Amanda grinned. "Right, so Lexi can go out with her boyfriend."

"He's not my boyfriend," Lexi said, taking a gulp of wine. Abby had been in bed point five seconds, and they were already starting.

155

"What exactly is he, and when do we get to meet him?" Penny asked.

"It's just physical. Just sex until he leaves. That's it." Had that sounded as rehearsed to her friends as it had to her?

"You sure about that?" Amanda asked, clearly not buying her response.

"Yes. It can't be anything else." She took a sip of wine to give her something to focus on other than the slight sadness she'd heard in her voice.

"Why can't it be anything else?" Penny asked.

"I've already explained this. I'm not going to move Abby, and it's not like he's asked."

"She's only six. She'd survive. She might even like it," Amanda said.

"She's almost seven and has friends and family here."

"It's not like you'd be moving halfway around the world, and there are these things called planes and FaceTime and Skype," Amanda said.

"I'm assuming he's aware of your refusal to move, right?" Penny asked.

Lexi fiddled with her wine glass. "We haven't actually talked about it. I mean, I've only known him for two months. It's way too early for that conversation. Not that it matters," she muttered.

"But he's leaving in two months, so it does matter," Penny said. "And even if he asked, you'd say no, wouldn't you?"

"Of course. It's not a relationship. It's sex and cake. That's it."

"As amazing as that sounds, is it really just cake and sex? You've now had at least two sleepovers with him. Is he horrible in the morning? You two aren't talking to each other in between moans and groans?" Amanda asked.

"We have fun together, but it's just physical. We don't even date. He just crashes mine," Lexi said, draining the rest of her wine.

"Are you picking horrible dates just so he can show up and rescue you?" Amanda asked.

"No. Of course not," Lexi bristled, but paused. No. No, she definitely wasn't doing that. She picked terrible dates because she had horrible luck when it came to men. Except for the man that had basically fallen into her lap. She pushed that thought away.

"I'm not sure I believe you. We just don't want you to get hurt," Amanda said.

"I know."

"Or push away someone that could be perfect for you because of a small distance issue," Penny said.

"He's moving to Florida. That's not close by," Lexi said.

"Yeah, Florida. Not Australia," Amanda said.

"It's still far, and I'm not moving, and he didn't ask," Lexi repeated. "You know I have my reasons." Lexi officially hated this conversation. She didn't want to argue with her friends, but they didn't get it. They hadn't moved around as kids so many times, and Lexi's oldest friends were people she went to college with. She didn't even have the excuse of being an Army brat. Her father just liked to up and move, whenever he wanted.

157

Lexi wanted friends she'd known all her life. She wanted to live in a town where she grew up and could run into people she went to elementary school with. Her family had moved to San Francisco when Lexi was seventeen. Aside from her senior year of high school, she'd only lived in her parents' current home during her summer breaks from college. She wouldn't do that to Abby. Abby had enough instability in her life already.

Not that Abby really remembered Joe, but it could be something niggling in her self-conscious that affected her as she got older. Lexi wouldn't add to any future stress by uprooting her. She would provide her daughter with safety and stability, even if it meant saying goodbye to the one guy she could actually develop feelings for. She refused to believe she already had.

Penny scooted closer to Lexi, wrapping her arm around Lexi's shoulder. "We just want you to be happy. Don't throw this away if it could be more. He sounds like a great guy, and you know you've never connected with another man like this before."

"I know," Lexi said, not sure how else to respond.

"Just think about it. Don't make a decision now," Penny said.

"I won't." But she already had.

"Okay, no more depressing talk. Tell us what you guys did this weekend. He stayed over, right?" Penny asked.

Lexi felt her cheeks heat as she looked over at her kitchen counter, and she heard Amanda snicker.

"Spill it," Amanda said.

Lexi shared almost every detail with her friends. She also promised Penny that she'd disinfected the kitchen counter before they'd arrived tonight.

But she didn't share everything. She didn't want to tell them how she'd felt waking up in Grant's arms. Feeling warm, safe, and secure when he'd tightened his hold on her, brushing his lips across her brow, and murmuring in his sleep.

Nope. It was purely physical, and if she had to make that her mantra, she would.

Lexi: Are you busy?

Grant: Another winner?

Grant looked at the time. It wasn't even six o'clock.

Grant: Bailing fast, huh? That bad?

Lexi: Maybe I'm not on a date.

Grant: I know. But last weekend you didn't, so I assumed tonight you did.

He refused to tell her she had a pattern of dating every other weekend. Not that he'd paid attention or anything. He snorted. That was just sad.

Lexi: I'm not sure I like that implication and you know what they say about assuming?

He laughed at her throwing his words back in his face.

Grant: Okay, no assumptions. And, no, I'm not busy. What's up?

Lexi: My car was making weird noises this morning and now it won't start.

Grant: Where are you? Is Abby with you?

Lexi: Off of Main Street, near Lanzi's. You know that place has the best tiramisu. And no, my mom took her to dinner and a movie. I was running errands and it died on me.

Grant: I'll be there in ten.

Lexi: Thanks.

Grant grabbed his keys, already dreading bringing her to his family's restaurant. They would grill the shit out of him.

He'd probably regret it, but he could go for some tiramisu, and he knew that if his family got word of him eating at another Italian restaurant, that'd be worse than the knowing looks he would receive walking in there with a date. Not that Lexi was a date.

Within ten minutes he spotted her leaning against her car, and he pulled into the spot behind her.

She straightened, brushing aside a wayward strand of hair, and grimacing at her car.

"Thanks for coming," she said.

"Of course."

"I hate this car. It's old and I'm sure it needs some repair, but it definitely wasn't smoking when I left the house a few hours ago."

"It probably overheated. I'm not sure how I can help," he said, eyeing the hood where white smoke was slowly emerging. His knowledge of cars was limited, but plumes of smoke was never good.

"I called my roadside service and they are on the way."

"So you didn't need me to rescue you."

She smiled. "Well, I figured I'd be stuck here for a while and Lanzi's is just around the corner, with that amazing tiramisu."

He let out a bark of laughter.

"Plus my mom is watching Abby as long as I need her tonight, and roadside assistance doesn't provide the full service that you do."

Her cheeks flamed dark pink and he couldn't stop his grin. "So that's what I'm good for? Dessert and a good time?"

She grinned. "Oh, like you're offended."

He tugged her close. "I'm completely offended," he whispered in her ear before nipping the lobe. Her indrawn breath punched him right in the gut, and he'd rather take her home instead of to Lanzi's.

She tugged free, brushing her hand down her jeans, her breathing choppy. "The tow truck should be here in fifteen minutes. Have you ever been to Lanzi's? The food is amazing," she said.

He hesitated. "Yeah. I've been there before. And their tiramisu is pretty good." Especially since it was his grandmother's recipe.

"You don't sound like you want to go there. We could try some place else."

"No. It's okay. It's just that it's my family's restaurant," he said.

Her eyes widened. "Really? Would that be weird? You know, since this isn't an actual date. We don't have to go there if you don't want to," she said, but her disappointment was clear.

"No. Let's go. They do have the best food. Not that I'm biased or anything," he said, shooting her a smile.

* * *

Within an hour her car had been towed and Grant was pulling into the parking lot behind Lanzi's. The repair shop said they would give her a call as soon as they knew exactly what was wrong with it, so they had time for dinner and a grilling he'd been dreading since he agreed to bring her to the restaurant.

"I can't believe I didn't know they owned it," she said, walking in.

"It's been in my step-father's family for almost sixty years, but I don't have the same last name, and neither do Lily, Keira, or Nathan, so it makes sense. I actually worked here until I joined the Coast Guard."

"Really?" she asked.

"Grant, are you on a date?" Sophia, the hostess, and his cousin, interrupted them.

Great. And so it begins...

"Hi Soph, this is Lexi. She's a friend." He made the introductions. "Looks busy tonight."

"Lexi. Lexi," Sophia drummed her nails on the hostess stand. "I know that name. Auntie Rose mentioned. Just a friend, huh?" she asked. That gleam in her eyes made him nervous.

"Yes." His tone brooked no argument. "Can we grab that booth?" he asked, pointing to the corner. It was tucked away under shadows, not that it would matter. Sophia would tell the entire kitchen he was here on a date, and yet he'd agreed to bring Lexi here. He was a glutton for punishment.

"Sure, sure," she said, grabbing menus.

Grant said hello to everyone who greeted him, which was almost everyone in the restaurant. It was extremely popular with the locals, and he'd spent all of his teen years here.

Lexi laughed. "Do you know everyone?"

He grinned. "Maybe."

"Here you go. Becky will be over shortly," Sophia said. "Along with the rest of the family," she muttered just to him.

Yep. Definitely a mistake.

Lexi slid into the booth and he took the opposite side. No need to make it look any more like a date than it already did. Her hazel eyes twinkled in the dim lighting as she looked at him over her menu.

"Maybe we shouldn't have come here?"

He heard humor in her voice and hoped that his family wouldn't embarrass him too much. It was a fruitless hope. "No. It's fine. Just ignore everything my family says and we'll be okay."

"I knew this evening was looking up," she said, her smile huge.

"Very funny," he grumbled, focusing on the menu, even though he could recite the thing in its entirety.

"So you worked here all through high school? Can you cook?"

"I'm not too bad."

163

"You cook, you're pretty decent in bed, and you have a steady job. How are you single?" she asked.

"Hey. I'd like to think I'm more than just decent in bed. Unless you need me to show you again." He wiggled his brow at her. He caught her grin and wanted to reach over across the table to show her just how good he was.

Chapter 11

"I don't need a demonstration," she scolded him, sipping her water. This was so not the place for this conversation. She wasn't sure any place would be acceptable for this conversation—and with his entire family in the restaurant—definitely not. She shook her head, swearing her brain stopped functioning around him.

"What should I get?" she asked, trying to focus on the menu, and not on his eyes twinkling at her, or that damn dimple she wanted to lick. Hell, she was hungry.

"What are you in the mood for?" He wiggled his eyebrows at her again and she laughed.

"You're terrible."

"That's not what you said last time."

"Stop it," she said between laughs. "You're distracting me, and I'm starving."

They perused the options, Grant made a few recommendations, and then they placed their order with Becky, another one of his relatives. While they waited, no fewer than three cousins and an uncle stopped by to chat. Lexi loved that he was so close with his extended family. Family was very important to him.

"Are you related to everyone who works here?" she asked.

"Just about," the hostess said, stepping up to the table.

"Soph, don't you have people to seat?" he grumbled. Lexi couldn't stop her smile.

"Nope. It's slowing down, and I'm training Izzy. She can seat anyone who comes in. It'll be good for her," Sophia said, slipping into the booth next to Grant.

Lexi could've sworn she heard his groan at his cousin's intrusion.

"So how long have you two been dating?" Sophia asked. "Did you bring her to Sunday dinner yet?" she asked, directing the question at Grant, but keeping her eyes on Lexi.

Lexi tried not to squirm under Sophia's gaze. "Oh, we aren't dating. Just friends," Lexi said.

"Yes, just friends," Grant echoed, holding Lexi's gaze. The heat crackled around them. *Just friends.*

Sophia eyed both of them. "Really? You sure about that?"

"Yes," Lexi and Grant said at the same time.

"Auntie Rose said something…" Sophia trailed off with a yelp, and Lexi had the distinct impression that Grant had pinched his cousin to get her to stop.

"Rose said what?" Lexi asked, ignoring Grant's gaze.

"Oh, just that you were lovely, and your daughter is best friends with our Keira," Sophia said.

Lexi knew that wasn't what Sophia was going to say, but she let it go, for now. "That's so sweet," Lexi said.

"Oh, and I don't blame you for not dating this one. He's a pain in the ass," Sophia said.

"Thanks a lot squirt," Grant grumbled.

"Don't call me squirt. You might be bigger than me, but I have tons of stories I can share with *your friend*," his pint-sized cousin said, her brown eyes filled with mischief.

Lexi didn't miss the emphasis on "friend."

166

"I think they need you back up front," Grant said, lightly nudging Sophia in the shoulder. "Izzy's got it." Sophia nudged him back and smiled at Lexi.

Lexi grinned. "So what was Grant like when he worked here?"

Sophia settled back against the bench. "When he was a teenager, he was all arms and legs. So gangly. Not like the brick wall he is now. I swear every time he walked into the kitchen, we were afraid he'd fall over his own feet and into the flat top grill. And the number of trays he dropped in the beginning." She shook her head, chuckling. "Let's just say that Uncle John had to foot quite a few dry cleaning bills for a while."

"Hey, I wasn't born into the restaurant. It took me some time, but I was a fantastic waiter toward the end. Customers loved me," he said, his chest puffed up with pride.

He was adorable.

"Yeah, because you flirted with every woman who walked in here. From babies to grandmas," Sophia said. "He's a horrible flirt."

"I'm not that bad," he objected.

"You flirted with me right away. After your stupid rescue comment," Lexi said, wanting to kick herself for opening her mouth when she saw the grin spread across Sophia's face.

"I thought you were just friends? How exactly did you two meet?" Sophia asked.

"Umm," Lexi stalled, wondering what Grant had told his family about her. If he'd told them anything.

"Oh look, our food is here," Grant said, eyeing Becky like she was a lifesaver as she approached the table with the loaded tray.

Lexi's stomach grumbled at the smells emanating from the tray. She was starving. She would never agree to a fancy restaurant with bite-sized portions again.

"Uncle Frankie says he needs you up front," Becky said to Sophia before setting their food in front of them.

Lexi wanted to inhale her food, but the steam coming off the lasagna stopped her. As much as she wanted to dive right in, she was attached to her taste buds, so she held back.

"Fine, but we're not done here. I need the rest of that story," Sophia said, pointing a finger at Grant.

"There's no story. Now go help Izzy."

Lexi caught the relief on his face when his cousin left. "She's so annoying," he griped, and Lexi laughed.

"How many cousins do you have?" Lexi asked, still patiently waiting for her dinner to cool. She deserved sainthood for waiting because the smells coming from her plate had her salivating.

"Too many," he said, cutting into his steak pizzaiola and blowing on it before shoveling it in his mouth. "I come here just for the food," he groaned around the mouthful.

"I think it's great that you are close with your family. When did your mom marry your step-father?"

"When I was fourteen, almost fifteen, I think. Yeah, so that was twenty years ago," he said.

"Wow. And you seem to get along."

"Yeah. John's great. I definitely was a punk kid to him when my mom first started seeing him, but I was pretty

168

much a pain in the ass through my entire teenage years." He let out a sardonic laugh.

"Do you still see your dad?" A shadow passed over his face. "I'm sorry. I don't mean to pry."

"No. It's okay. I haven't spoken to him in years. He was a horrible father. Having John come into our lives was the best thing that could've happened."

He focused on his plate, and she itched to grab his hand. "That bad?"

"My father was an asshole. He had a drinking problem and liked to take it out on us."

She gave in, reaching across the table and linking her fingers with his, giving him a soft squeeze. "I'm sorry."

"He never beat us, mostly just verbal abuse, a lot of threats and yelling. As I got older, I started yelling back at him. I hated how he treated my mother. I remember him raising a hand to me once and my mother stepped in, ready to take the blow. He tried to apologize, said it'd never happen again, but of course the next time he drank, he started up again, and she left him."

"Your mother is very strong. A lot of women just stay," she said, like she had. She focused on their linked hands. His engulfed hers, but she knew in that moment that he would only protect her, and never raise it against her.

"My mom is amazing."

The pure love on his face warmed her heart. "Yes, she is."

"Then they divorced when I was ten, and Mom got a job here. She went to high school with Sophia's mom, and they'd remained friends. My mom never met John when they

169

were in school since he was a few years older. She started working here, and the rest is history."

"That's so great. I'm glad everything worked out. So when did you start working here?"

"Fifteen."

"Really? And you were all gangly legs and arms, crashing into everything?" She grinned, trying to add some levity to the conversation.

"Sophia is a pain in the ass. Don't listen to her," he grumbled.

She laughed. "I need those stories. It levels the playing field to get dirt on you from your friends and family. It wouldn't be fair for you to get to hear about, *and witness,* my dating horror stories and for me to get nothing in return."

"Oh, I think you're overly compensated, without my stories."

His grin was devilish, and she swallowed hard. "Stop distracting me and let me enjoy my meal," she muttered.

"Just wait until we get to dessert. It'll blow your socks off," he said, his gaze still locked with hers.

"Let's hope," she said, no longer interested in the food in front of her.

"Are you almost done packing?" Grant's mother asked that Sunday night as they sat around the large dining room table at his parents' house. Sunday night dinner was a requirement, unless he was on an overnight shift or had a hockey game. He was going to miss her cooking when he left. Maybe she'd ship her sauce to Florida.

170

"I have almost two months left, so nope," he said, popping half a meatball in his mouth. He was going to miss this.

"I'll come over and help you pack," Rose continued.

"Thanks, Mom, but I've got it covered. I'm pretty good at packing after all my moves," he said. He loved his mom but she'd drive him crazy, questioning his packing methods and repacking everything.

"You'll tell me if you need help, right?" she asked, dropping another meatball on Maddie's plate. "You need to eat more," she said, turning her attention to her youngest.

"I'm fine, Mom," Maddie grumbled, before eating all the food on her plate under Rose's watchful eye.

"So, how's Lexi?" Rose asked, glancing back over at Grant, her expression nonchalant. Grant almost choked on a ravioli.

"What?"

Rose smiled. "Lexi. I heard from a little birdie that you're seeing her."

Of course she knew. He was going to kill Soph. He loved his family, but part of him was excited to move. He doubted his mother had spies in Florida, but he wouldn't put anything past her.

"Lexi? I'm not seeing her," he said, avoiding her gaze. He was pretty sure his mother was a mind reader as well.

"Don't lie to me, Grant William," Rose scolded.

He hated when she used his middle name.

"You took her to the restaurant last weekend," she said.

171

He shouldn't have taken her to Lanzi's.

"We ran into each other, and she was hungry," he said, trying not to squirm under his mother's gaze.

"Sounds like a date to me."

"I thought you weren't dating anyone because you're leaving?" Lily asked.

"We're not dating. We're just friends," Grant said, eyeing his family around the table, catching the gleam in his mother's eyes that told him she didn't believe him for a second.

"But you like her. I can see it in your face," Rose said.

"I knew something was going on. I could tell at the kids' birthday party. How did you even meet her? It's not like you pick up the kids from school that often," Lily said. He could see the wheels turning in her head.

"Who are we talking about?" Keira asked, staring between Grant and Lily. Grant loved his niece, but she got her curiosity and nosiness from her mother, who'd gotten it from Grant's mother.

"Abby's mom. The one who yelled at Uncle Grant that one time," Nathan piped in. The kid forgot nothing.

"First of all, there was no yelling. Just a misunderstanding," Grant said, eyeing his nephew, trying to relay the message that Nathan was supposed to be on his side. Guy code and all.

"She was yelling," Nathan repeated. So much for a telepathic connection.

"She thought I was someone else, and she apologized for that," Grant grumbled.

"So that was the first time you met her?" Lily asked, clearly doubting him.

"Of course. And we had a laugh and that was it."

"You seemed very close at the party. I saw you two talking in the corner," Maddie piped in.

"You should marry her, Uncle Grant. Then Abby and I would be cousins. She's one of my bestest friends," Keira said.

"I'm not marrying her. We aren't even dating," Grant said. This was getting out of hand. The women in his family were like the damn Spanish Inquisition.

"She's such a nice girl, and Abby is a dear. You should date," Rose said.

"Mom, I'm leaving in two months. I'm not dating anyone."

"So ridiculous. I saw the connection you two had. And how could she not love my son. Maybe she'd move with you," Rose continued.

Great, now his mother had him married and moving his new family.

"She wouldn't move," Grant said, instantly regretting his words when his mother perked up. Damn it. She was too observant.

"You've talked about it? I thought you were just friends," she said.

"We are. It was an offhanded comment on her part. We were just talking about me moving and…"

"But if you were dating, and you seriously asked her, she might move," Rose interrupted.

"Again, just friends. Nothing more," he repeated, wishing the conversation would end. He didn't want to think about asking Lexi. It was too soon. The whole discussion was ridiculous.

"Don't push away the possibility just because of your job."

"Stop reading into something that isn't there," he said. He wasn't sure if he was telling his family or if he was trying to tell himself.

"And don't ignore what is right in front of you," his mother said.

Grant held back his groan, looking to his step-father for help.

"Let's leave the poor boy alone," John chimed in. Grant wanted to hug the man right then and there.

"I just want him to be happy," his mother said.

And he loved her for that. His mother supported her kids in everything they wanted to do, but she wanted to protect them and see them as happy as she was with Grant's step-father. He couldn't fault her for that, even if she did drive him insane at times. Wasn't that what mothers were for?

"I know, but let's stop interrogating him," John said, smiling at his wife. "So how's school going?" John asked, turning the attention toward Maddie.

Maddie talked about her current classes. She would graduate when he was in Florida, and his family would kill him if he didn't make it back to watch her walk across the stage.

"Uncle Grant," a small voice said beside him, and he looked down at his niece.

"Yes?"

"Can we play with your guitar tonight? I have a new song I'm working on," Keira said.

"Of course we can," he replied.

"And if you wanted to marry Abby's mom, so we could be cousins, I promise to love you forever," she whispered.

"I'll keep that in mind." He bit back a chuckle. The women in his family were relentless, even the youngest at age seven.

⌒

"Thanks for agreeing to meet me for drinks tonight," Lexi's date, Scott, said after the waitress dropped off their cocktails.

"No problem. Penny mentioned that you had a huge caseload, so I figured drinks would be easiest." And it limited the time she had to spend with him if the date sucked.

"Yeah, it's crazy at the office. I'm working on a few big cases right now, so I barely have time to eat," he said with a laugh. "I think I've had dinner in my office every night this week."

She took a sip of the martini, the tart lemon and sweet sugar bursting on her tongue. The alcohol rushed to her head and she was glad that she'd had dinner before she left the house. "So you're a workaholic," she said.

"Definitely. But it will be worth it if I make partner soon."

175

He definitely looked the part. Very slick. Maybe a little too slick. She internally shook her head. She needed to stop assuming. He came across like a very nice guy in the five minutes she'd known him. Was she this bad with all her dates? Ready to write them off within seconds just so she could see Grant?

She needed to stop thinking about him. She needed to focus on Scott. She bit back a chuckle. Another "S" guy. Grant would tell her she was pushing her luck after Sean and Steve hadn't worked out. Why did he have to always pop into her mind? Why couldn't she just go out with one guy without thinking about Grant? Even if they never measured up to Grant. She had to get past that.

Focus on the nice guy in front of you.

"Wow, partner. I think Penny mentioned that Michael is going for partner, too. Have you been with the firm long?" That could make double dating awkward if Scott was promoted before Penny's fiancé.

"Yes, we are both going for it. We've both been there for about five years, and some healthy competition never hurt anyone. It's a great firm."

He had beautiful blue eyes and a ready smile that she couldn't help but return. "I promise not to report anything back to Penny if you want to tell me what it's really like to work for her father," she said.

He laughed. "No. I actually like working for Mr. Connor. He's taught me so much in such a short time."

"I don't know him very well. We've only met once or twice," she said. "So, when you do have free time, what do you do for fun?"

176

"I'm a huge baseball fan. I have season tickets and try to get to as many Giants' games as I can. The season just started a few weeks ago, so I've had to give away my seats for more games than I wanted to, but I couldn't miss opening day. Are you a fan?" he asked, before taking a sip of his Scotch.

"Not a big sports fan, to be honest." In fact, baseball bored her to tears.

"You have to go to a live game. You'll love it," he said.

"Maybe."

"And you have a daughter, right?"

She smiled, impressed that he'd asked. Very few of her dates asked about her daughter. Not that she wanted to go into gushing mom mode on her dates, but he got points for asking. "Yes. Abby. She's six and she's amazing. Right now she has a fascination with snakes that I'm fully opposed to."

"Then I won't tell you about the pet snake I had growing up," he said, his eyes crinkling when he smiled.

She shuddered. "Please don't."

"So aside from a reptile fear, tell me about yourself. You work with Penny, right?"

"Yes. I'm the office manager. Not nearly as fun as I'm sure your job is," she said.

"I'm sure I have to handle just as much paperwork as you do," he said.

Lexi smiled, sipping the rest of her martini, listening to him talk about his job and answering his questions about the joys of working for an accounting firm. Penny had high hopes for this date. Double date hopes. And he had yet to do

177

or say anything alarming or weird, which was much better than any of her eMatch dates had gone. She wasn't even reaching for her phone to text her way out. That had to count for something.

An hour passed in easy conversation. No hairball pictures or discussions about aliens or her diet plan. She internally shook her head. Man, she really sucked at online dating.

"I hate to bail like this, but I have to be in court early tomorrow morning," he said after they finished their second round of drinks and he settled the bill. "But this was fun."

"Yes, it was," she refused to acknowledge the awe in her tone.

"My friend just opened a new wine bar in the Tenderloin district. Maybe we could make plans for dinner one night?" he asked.

"Sure. I'd like that," she said, grabbing her purse and sliding off the bar stool.

His hand rested against the small of her back as he guided her from the bar and into the crisp night air.

"I'm just over here," she said, motioning toward her car a few spots down from the door.

"It was really nice meeting you," he said, shifting to face her, the corners of his mouth turned up in a slight smile.

"You too. Thanks again for tonight, and enjoy court tomorrow."

"I'll call you," he said, before dipping his head and brushing a kiss across her cheek.

"Goodnight," she said, watching him walk away. Sure his kiss hadn't set every one of her nerve endings on fire, but it'd been nice. Nice was good. Nice was a start.

She slipped into her car and turned up the radio, humming that stupid song by some former tween heartthrob that she wasn't supposed to like. She let out a laugh. She'd successfully gone on a date tonight. That was a feat unto itself. Maybe she could actually do this?

Chapter 12

Lexi's phone pinged.

Grant: How's the car?

Lexi: Seems to be running fine now. Thanks.

Grant: Any hot dates planned this weekend?

Grant: Just need to know if I have to clear my schedule.

She couldn't stop her smile. It'd been a week since she'd seen him, and aside from a few sporadic texts, they hadn't really spoken. She hadn't even mentioned Scott.

Lexi: Very funny. One day I'm going to have a successful date.

The other night had been a successful date. A short one, but still a success. She hadn't heard from Scott, but it'd only been two days.

Grant: You'd leave me to eat cake alone? What kind of friend are you?

He followed his statement with a crying emoticon. He was ridiculous.

Lexi: Guess you'll just have to send me cake to share with my date.

Grant: That is NOT how this relationship works!

She chuckled.

Lexi: No dates this weekend, except with Abby. Exploratorium tomorrow.

Grant: That's a shame. I could go for some cake this weekend.

Lexi: Me too.

Wait. Did he really mean cake? She sure didn't. Well, she always wanted cake, but she also wanted what followed it. Her need for him never waned. She thought about him when she was supposed to be working. When she was home. He was too much of a distraction. But they only had two months left. Two months. She wasn't sure how she felt about their rapidly approaching expiration date.

Should she tell him about her date with Scott? Just end everything with Grant right now? But she knew she wouldn't. Part of her knew she should end it now, but her body ignored her brain. She was too selfish to let him go.

Lexi: I have to go. Have a good weekend.

Grant: Sure. You too.

Lexi tossed her phone into her desk drawer. She needed to figure her shit out. This had recipe for disaster written all over it.

* * *

The following afternoon, Abby pulled Lexi along from exhibit to exhibit at the Exploratorium in the city. The place was amazing, with hands on experiments for kids and adults. She'd read about it online for top things to do with kids on a rainy day, and April was blustery as ever.

"This place is so cool," her daughter echoed her thoughts.

They were walking along a gravel path in the sound gallery. "I know. What do you hear?" she whispered to Abby. The goal of the exhibit was to try different walking techniques, like tiptoeing, to hear the different sounds her feet made on the gravel. Abby wanted to stomp, but Lexi kept telling her to move gently.

"Mom, stomping is a sound," Abby replied with a huff.

Lexi chuckled. Sometimes Abby was the sweetest little girl and sometimes she was six going on sixteen. "I know."

They moved further into the gallery, and Lexi laughed, watching Abby make funny faces in the massive mirror that turned everything upside down.

Abby squealed with delight and spun around, dashing off.

"Abby," Lexi shouted, panic coursing through her, along with confusion. Abby was pretty good at staying by her side when they were out.

When she spotted her daughter, Abby's arms wrapped around her best friend, Kiera, Lexi felt a different type of panic set in.

"I told you she yells," Nathan piped in, looking up at his uncle.

Why was he here? And why did he have to look so adorable giving her an embarrassed smile at his nephew's comments?

"Hi Grant," she said, acting like she wasn't mesmerized by his chocolate brown eyes. Why did they have to be chocolate? They just reminded her of dessert and what happened after dessert. Hell. His eyes were basically liquid sex.

"Hi Lexi. Funny seeing you here." His dimple peeked out. Damn dimple, always taunting her.

"Yes. Funny," she replied, as three sets of children's eyes followed their interaction. Kids were way too observant.

"Did you just get here?" she asked, trying to not let his mere presence affect her.

"Yes," he said.

"We've never been here before," Abby chimed in. Had her daughter sensed the tension?

"Really? Never?" Nathan asked. "It's so cool here."

"I know," Abby said. "We just did that gravel walkway, and Mom didn't like me stomping, but it's a sound."

"The light room is my favorite," Keira said, tugging her friend along.

Lexi and Grant walked behind the kids. He brushed his fingers along her wrist, and she attempted to ignore the heat spiraling through her at the brief touch.

"What are you doing here?" she whisper-demanded.

"What? The kids wanted to come today, and I wasn't working, so I told Lily I'd take them."

"Was this before or after I told you I was bringing Abby here?" she asked.

He turned his innocent eyes on her. "I totally forgot you mentioned coming here today."

She scoffed, not believing him for a second. But her heart sped up at the thought of him being here because of her.

He placed his hand on the small of her back, his thumb lightly pressing. "What? Is it so bad that I showed up?"

"No. It's just confusing."

"Why? Aren't we friends?"

183

"Yes, we are. Friends who have sex, not spend the weekend out with our kids together."

She ignored the brief flash of hurt in his eyes. It was only there for a second before his smile was back in place. This, whatever *this* was, was getting complicated.

"I'm sorry. I sound like a total bitch." She hated that she couldn't define what they were. That they didn't fit in a nice, neat box.

"No, I get it. I thought it would be fun for the kids to hang out together. I know Keira and Abby are the bestest of friends. Keira told me last weekend," he said, leaning in as if it was a secret.

She laughed, unable to stop herself. "Then let's go join the bestest friends," she said, heading toward the kids.

"I still can't believe you've never been here before. It's like a rite of passage for all school kids and families."

"Oh, I didn't grow up here. We moved to the area when I was seventeen," she said, watching the three kids play with a light display, their giggles heard over the crowd.

"Seventeen. That's a rough time to move," he said.

"Yep. I grew up in a small town outside of Boston. We moved around locally a few times, and then out here when I was in high school," she said, schooling her features.

"Army brat?"

"Wish I could explain it with that, but nope. My father would get annoyed with where he was working, or the town we lived in, and he'd want to move. I guess he was a believer in the grass is always greener." She hated how bitter she sounded and knew she should get over it, but it pissed her

184

off that her mother always went along with what her father wanted. Her mother still did.

"And your mom went along with this?"

"She never wanted to ruffle any feathers," Lexi said. It made her sad to think of her mother catering to her father's every need, giving up on dreams she may have had, just to appease him. "It's why I want to stay here. I don't want Abby to go through what I did. Constantly trying to find new friends, to find her place in each school. It's a lonely existence." She hated sounding like a petulant child.

Her grabbed her hand, giving it a light squeeze. "That's understandable. And your family is here, right?"

"Yes. They moved around a few times when I was in college and when I was married, but then they moved back here a couple years ago, after my dad retired. They wanted to be close to Abby, and I'm grateful that they moved back, so Abby has her grandparents here."

"Do you like living here?" he asked.

Her heart irrationally sped up at his question. Amanda and Penny's voices were in her head from the other night, but she pushed them away. He was making conversation, not asking her to move.

"Yes, I do. I love my town, and we're so close to the city, so we never run out of things to do. We have the benefits of a huge city, without the crazy hustle and bustle of actually living there."

"Yeah. I am going to miss being this close to my family. Well, for the most part," he scowled. "They do enjoy being up in my business."

185

She loved how close he was to his family. He may think they were a pain, but she only saw pure love and affection when they were together.

"I guess one of the positive sides of all my moving is that I can't run into someone I grew up with. I pretty much kept to myself my last year of high school, so there are no old boyfriends or former best friends that I'll cross paths with here."

"Did you leave a heartbroken boy behind in Boston when you moved?"

She laughed. "Definitely not. I didn't really date until college, and that turned out just awesome," she grimaced.

"Again, your taste in men is awful," he said, his lips turning up in a smirk.

"What does that say about you?' she asked, thankful for the change in topic.

"I pretty much fell in your lap. Or was it you falling into mine? It's not like you picked me," he said.

"Very funny," she grumbled.

"I still think you need to give me your eMatch login. I bet I can find you a guy who won't have you running for the hills before the appetizer shows up," he said, that damn dimple peeking out.

"Again, not funny." Silently wondering if she should give in. Maybe he could find the perfect guy for her. And how fucked up would that be? She mentally shook her head. "But I actually had a successful date the other night."

He stopped short. "Wait. What?"

She couldn't, for the life of her, explain his expression. She could've sworn she caught a brief glimpse of sadness before he masked it with a smile.

"Yes. Made it through a few drinks without any alarm bells going off." She shot him a smile and nudged his shoulder, a total friend-zone move. "Maybe I can do this?"

"Was it an eMatch date?" he asked, and she couldn't ignore the slight tension in his tone.

"No. He works with my friend's fiancé. Secretly, I just think she wants to be able to double date," she said.

"Do you have another date planned?"

"Not yet. But he said he'd call soon. It was only two days ago."

Something passed over his gaze, and she wanted to kick herself for bringing it up, but they were friends and he was leaving. Eventually, she was going to find someone else. Not that Scott was necessarily that guy. She'd liked him, but she barely knew him. He'd been nice and attentive. Was that all it took? She internally shook her head.

"Well, that's great, Lexi. But if you ever need me, I'm just a text away," he said.

"Thanks," she replied, not sure what else to say.

"Sure," he trailed off.

"Mom, we want to go to the other room," Abby said.

Lexi was grateful for the interruption for she feared she and Grant were about to enter into an awkward silence. Something that had yet to happen.

"What?" Lexi asked.

"Keira and Nathan didn't see that funny clock yet. Can we go to that room again?" Abby asked.

187

"Of course."

"Awesome," Nathan piped in, leading the way to the other gallery.

They spent the next hour exploring every room, their attention focused solely on the kids. Grant would kneel down at their level to try an experiment with one of the kids, giving them his complete attention before turning back and smiling at her.

He was so good with them, his niece and nephew clearly loved him, and it was great seeing him get along with Abby. She and Keira were giggling at him as he played with one of the exhibits, making funny faces at them through a glass.

She wanted this for Abby. A strong male role model. A father figure Joe would never, and could never, be. Her heart fluttered every time he did something sweet with the kids, and she cursed herself for caring more about him than she'd planned. Amanda and Penny's warnings to not get hurt echoed through her head, but Lexi couldn't stop herself from wanting to continue seeing him. She'd pay the consequences later, but for right now, it was worth it.

Grant plopped down on his sofa Friday night, propping his feet on the coffee table, taking a swig from his beer, and settling in to watch the game. The Strikers, the local hockey team, was on, and he tried to never miss a game. He was exhausted from his shift today and the extra practice Adam had demanded tonight. They had a big game on Monday, but they were just a rec league. Not that Grant didn't want to beat the smug bastards they were up against.

188

After a beer and one period, he glanced at his silent phone, the game not holding his attention. Aside from a random text or two, Lexi had been radio silent since he'd crashed her date with Abby at the museum last weekend. Did she have a date tonight? Maybe with that guy again?

She'd eventually go on a date with a guy she actually liked, but selfishly, he'd hoped that wouldn't happen until after he left. God, he was an asshole. They were friends and he should be happy for her.

She'd thrown him for a loop when she'd told him about her successful date. That conversation had been awkward and they'd spent the rest of the afternoon focused on the kids and not whatever they hell they were at this point. Had her radio silence been because of his response? He wasn't ready to let her go, even if they could only be just friends.

He swiped his phone on before he could stop himself.

Grant: How's the date going?

He watched the three dots pop up and then disappear, only to pop up again. He hated those damn dots as he waited for her to reply. Dammit. He should've left his phone alone and concentrated on the game.

Lexi: How did you know I was on a date?

Grant: It's Friday.

Lexi: I don't have a date every week.

That was true. He hadn't received a date rescue text in weeks, actually.

Lexi: Yes, I'm on a date.

Grant: Make it through dinner?

Lexi: Yes. We're at a club downtown.

189

Grant paused. Her normal humor was missing.

Grant: Is everything okay?

Lexi: Not really. He's much more of an asshole than I expected.

Grant: What? Did he do something?

Lexi: I asked him to take me home, but he keeps saying after the next drink.

Grant shot up off the couch, slipping on his shoes and grabbing his keys. His phone vibrated in his hand.

Lexi: I'm just going to call a cab. Don't worry about me.

Grant: Where are you?

Lexi: I'm good, Grant. I'll grab a cab.

Grant: Just tell me where you are and I'll come get you.

She gave him the address.

Grant: I'm on my way.

Lexi: Sorry to be a pain. Thanks.

Grant made it to the bar in under twenty minutes. It was after ten. Miraculously, traffic hadn't been horrible, and he'd sped the entire way. He hated the completely different tone of her texts tonight. The missing sarcasm made him nervous.

Grant: I'm here. Where are you?

He wasn't sure she'd hear her phone over the noise of the crowd so he headed deeper into the bar, the mass of bodies swallowing him up. His phone was on vibrate since he figured he'd feel it if she texted a lot easier than trying to hear it ding.

It buzzed in his hand.

Lexi: I'm in the lounge section, with his friends. Toward the back.

Grant headed in that direction, finally spotting her auburn waves under the dim light. She looked uncomfortable and his chest seized. Her drink was full on the small table in front of her, her legs crossed away from the group as they laughed loudly around her. She was the only woman in the group.

"Lexi, baby, you haven't touched your drink," one guy said, scooting way too close to Lexi for Grant's comfort.

Grant bristled at the endearment coming out of the douchebag's mouth.

"Thanks. I'm good for now. I think I'm just going to go grab a cab," she said.

Space invader wrapped his arm around her shoulder, tugging her closer. "Come on, babe. You said you were free all night. Let loose. Have some fun?" He lifted her glass, offering it to her, a lascivious smirk on his face, and Grant had seen enough.

"I don't think she's interested," Grant growled.

Lexi's eyes shot up, crashing with his. He read both anger and relief in her gaze.

"Who the hell are you?" space invader asked. Grant resisted the urge to peel the guy's hands from Lexi's shoulder and break each and every finger.

"Lexi, you ready?" Grant asked, ignoring the douche. Was that her date?

Lexi started to stand, but the idiot gripped her hand, holding her in place. "You're just going to leave? You didn't

191

even finish your drink," the guy said, his words slightly slurred.

Seriously, if this was her date, she needed to rethink online dating.

"Yes, she is," Grant said, trying to keep from grabbing Lexi, even when every instinct in his body told him to pull her into his arms and escape.

"I should go," she said, shaking free of the guy's hold and stepping toward Grant.

"Come on, babe. At least finish your drink," the guy said, pulling her down into his lap.

Lexi yelped, trying to stand back up, and Grant lost it. He yanked Lexi out of the creep's arms and sucker-punched the guy in the nose. The sound of crunching bones gave Grant more satisfaction than it should.

"Grant," Lexi gasped.

"You broke my fucking nose. I'll sue you, you asshole. I'm a lawyer." The guy's words were muffled as he cupped his face.

"Let's go," Grant said, linking his fingers with Lexi's and squeezing. She slung her purse over her shoulder and followed him out of the bar into the cold night air. He tried to calm his breathing and pulled her against him. She stiffened in his arms. Fuck. He'd let his anger get the better of him and he'd manhandled her, which had never been his intention.

"I can't believe you hit him," she muttered against his throat.

"He pissed me off," Grant growled.

She pulled out of his embrace and leaned against the concrete wall next to the bar. "Do you always hit people when you're pissed?"

Her eyes narrowed, waiting for his response. He had a temper, but he usually kept it in check, and he'd always been careful around her. "No. I'm not a violent person, Lexi, but that guy had it coming. You believe me, right?"

"Right before you punched him, you looked ready to kill him," she said, her fingers twisting together. "I've never seen you look at anyone like that."

"I'm sorry. I didn't mean to scare you. He just wouldn't let you go and then he pulled you into his lap, and I saw red." Why did he have to justify this to her? Hadn't it been obvious that he only wanted to protect her? "Come on. Let me take you home."

"No. I should probably call a cab and just go home," she said, grabbing her phone.

"Lexi, wait. I'll take you home," he said, linking his fingers through hers and rubbing his thumb along her knuckles, trying to soothe her without pulling her into his arms, which is what he desperately wanted to do.

"I'd rather just call a cab," she said, her head dropped, focusing on her phone screen.

"Please. Let me take you home. We don't even need to talk if you don't want to." He tucked his finger under her chin, tilting her head up. He hated the freaked out look in her eyes. He was such an ass for his reaction to her date because it clearly affected her more than he'd anticipated. Not that he'd thought it through before punching that asshole.

"I'm so sorry. I promise I don't go around hitting people. You've never seen me angry before tonight, right? My reaction to him basically restraining you was to hit him and protect you." He pulled her into his body, pressing a soft kiss to the top of her head, and he felt the shudder roll through her.

"I know. It's just that my ex had a temper, and he acted on it a few times," she mumbled against his chest. He felt the overwhelming desire to find her ex and do more than break his nose.

"I cannot apologize enough," he murmured against her hair. "But I can promise that I would never do anything to harm you, but if I ever run into your ex, I'd probably punch him, too."

He felt her smile against his chest. Apparently, violence against her ex was acceptable.

"Is Abby with your parents tonight?"

"Yes."

"Will you come to my place for a while? Then I can take you home whenever you want, and you won't have to kick me out," he said.

"I don't know," she whispered.

"I promise that we will just talk," he said.

"I guess," she said.

His heart rate sped up. Not at the thought of getting her home and in bed with him, but more with the knowledge that she had forgiven his outburst. He was usually pretty good about his temper, but that asshole had provoked him.

"And I have cake at home," he said.

"Well, if you have cake," she trailed off with a soft laugh.

He was grateful for that laugh. He guided her to his car, opening the door for her.

He got into the driver's seat and took her hand in his, giving it a small squeeze. She squeezed right back, and relief rolled through him.

* * *

Fifteen minutes later, they pulled up to Grant's house, and he ushered Lexi inside.

"Have a seat and I'll grab dessert. Do you want any wine?" he asked.

"Just water, thanks," she said. She walked into the living room and settled into the couch. It swallowed her up. Why did she look so much smaller than before?

He grabbed some tiramisu his mother had dropped off and glasses of water, setting it down on the coffee table in front of her. He sat down next to her, pressing his thigh along the length of hers, wanting to wrap his arms around her, but he held back.

"Do you want to talk about it?" he asked.

"Talk about what?" She took a sip of her water and pulled a plate of tiramisu into her lap, taking a large bite. "Oh my God, this is amazing. Just like Lanzi's," she said, clearly wanting to focus on dessert and not the elephant in the room.

"It should be. My mother made it. Dropped it off yesterday," he said, keeping his gaze on her eyes, imploring

195

for more information without actually asking a question. He didn't want to pry, but he needed to know.

"It's amazing," she said around another bite.

A bit of mascarpone clung to the corner of her mouth, and he swiped it away with his thumb, sucking the combination of sweet cream and her off his finger.

"The best," he said, grabbing his plate, so he didn't grab her.

She turned to face him, color back in her cheeks. "Thank you for coming tonight."

"Of course. Better now?" he asked.

"What isn't better with this dessert?"

He grinned, wrapping his arm around her shoulder and tugging her closer. He needed to feel her heat beside him.

"So do you want to talk about it?"

"The ex or the date?" she said.

"How about the date? Another online match?" He wanted to know about her ex, but he figured it was a stickier topic than her date.

"No. Penny's fiancé works with him. He's the guy from the other night that I told you about." Her voice merely a whisper.

"Are you serious? That guy was a total douchebag and you went out with him twice? You made him seem like a nice guy last weekend."

"I know. He wasn't like that at all when we just met for drinks before. And he wasn't that bad at first. He took me to a nice dinner; the conversation was fine. We were getting along great."

"Then what happened?" he asked tightly, his anger barely held in check, but he didn't want to frighten her again. She squeezed his hand and he took in calming breaths.

"He asked if I wanted to meet up with some of his friends at the bar a few doors down, so I agreed. They just kept drinking and getting louder. More obnoxious. I told him I wanted to go home, but he kept saying we could leave after one more drink. He didn't start getting all handsy until after you texted me."

Grant bristled at the memory of the guy's hands on her. "I'm glad I was on my way, then."

"Me too. Guess the guy couldn't handle his booze." She shrugged, taking a sip of water.

"That's no excuse. Especially since you told him no," Grant stated.

"I know. I should've just left, but I knew you were on your way at that point, so I waited."

"Next time don't wait," he said.

"I won't," she said. "And thanks, if I didn't say that before."

"No more dates with that guy," Grant said, trying to lighten the moment.

"Yes. No more dates with him. I just hope he doesn't cause you any trouble, but if it comes to that, I'll talk to Penny. I'm sure the threat of getting him in trouble with his boss will shut him up."

"I'm not concerned about me, but if he causes you any trouble you need to let me know," he said.

"I will. So did I interrupt your plans tonight?" she asked, peering up at him through hooded eyes, clearly trying to distract him from asking for more information about her date and her ex.

He wanted her to talk about it, to feel comfortable confiding in him, even if he had to pry it out of her.

"Nope. Just relaxing after a long day. I'm glad I get to spend the end of it with you. Not happy with the turn of events, but I'm glad you're here." He flexed his right hand. His knuckles were bruised but they weren't too bad.

"What are you doing?" she asked, leaning over him, her hair brushing against his throat. "Oh my God. Does that hurt? You should ice that," she said.

He ran his battered hand across her cheek. "I'm fine." He pulled her tighter against him. "Just happy you're here."

Chapter 13

Lexi snuggled into Grant's side. She felt horrible for his bruised hand and wished she'd just left Jeff at the bar and called a cab when he'd started drinking heavily. Penny would ask about the date, and Lexi had no plans to hold back. Drunken asshole was definitely not her type. He'd seemed so normal on their first date that she'd been shocked by his change in behavior tonight.

"Anything else you want to talk about?" he asked.

"Not really," she drew out. He wanted to hear about Joe, but she didn't want to rehash that nightmare. She looked up at him, his chocolate eyes brimming with faintly banked anger and clear concern. Joe was out of her life, and good riddance, but she hated how he'd made her feel. She wished she could forget everything about him, but she saw him in Abby's eyes every day.

"You had a very strong reaction to me hitting that guy. Not that you shouldn't react to me punching someone, but you were afraid, and I don't ever want you to be afraid of me," he said, running his finger along her cheek.

"It just shocked me. I hate violence," she said.

"Tell me about him," he prodded. "Did he hurt you physically? And Abby?"

She pulled away from his chest, looking him square in the eyes. "He never hurt Abby. He only hit me a few times."

"That's a few times too many," Grant said, shifting his body so they faced each other on the couch. He took both of her hands in his, gently squeezing, his eyes imploring her to continue.

"I know. And that's why I kicked him out. Abby was only eighteen months old when he left, and he never looked back," she said, breaking his gaze, not wanting to see the pity that would be there. It was always there when she told people about her husband leaving when Abby was just a baby. She didn't want their sympathy.

"Good riddance," he murmured, and she looked back up at him. There was no pity in his eyes.

"Yes. It'd been a long time coming, and I've held back on telling Abby about her father, but she's almost seven and very inquisitive. I just don't know what to tell her."

"Were you together a long time?"

She nodded. "Yes. Seven years. Started dating halfway through college and then a few years after we graduated, I got pregnant, and we got married."

"Wow. That's a chunk of time."

His expression was open, with no judgment, just encouraging her to continue. Aside from Amanda and Penny, she'd never been this transparent and honest with anyone. She felt safe with him. And that excited and scared her at the same time.

"Yes it is. The pregnancy wasn't planned, and neither was the marriage. My parents are old fashioned and demanded that we get married, so we did. Shotgun weddings rarely work out, but we'd dated for over four years at that point, so I thought we could last." She shrugged against his chest. She'd been so naïve. So stupid. Babies never fixed a bad relationship.

"You were so young. Did your parents know about the abuse?" he asked, tilting her head back to look at him, anger glittered in his eyes.

"No. And he wasn't always like that. When we were first dating, it was perfect. We had very few arguments, I didn't even know about his temper. It wasn't until we'd been dating a few years that I really saw it. He would yell at me, but never in front of our friends and family. I told myself he was just venting and it never meant anything."

He squeezed her hand again, and she needed that connection right now. Dammit. She would not cry in front of him; she hated looking weak.

"I will admit to having a temper, but I'm usually good at controlling it. I can promise that I will never lash out at you," he said, complete sincerity in his gaze.

"I think I know that. It was just unexpected tonight," she replied.

"I cannot apologize enough. My need to protect you and get you out of that guy's arms overshadowed my common sense. I swear it's not my normal behavior." His thumbs grazed her knuckles again, his hands in constant movement against hers, like it was second nature to soothe her, and she believed him.

She gave him a soft smile. "Thank you for wanting to protect me."

"I protect those I care about," he stated matter-of-factly, and a flutter spread through her chest at his words. She cared about him, too. More than she should.

"I know."

"And just so you know, verbal abuse, is still abuse," he said.

"I know that, too. I just pretended that he was stressed at work." She really didn't want to talk about this.

"So, this was all before Abby came along."

"Yes. I thought we were on the same page. Eventually get married, have kids, buy a house. You know, all the typical stuff. But, I got pregnant by accident, a momentary lapse and I forgot that antibiotics cancelled out birth control. I know they warn you, but I forgot. He was pissed, but I refused to make our mistake go away. His words, not mine. I thought, we'd both finished college, had decent jobs, in our mid-twenties, and had been dating for so long that marriage and kids wasn't so far-fetched an idea. I mean, we weren't eighteen."

"He sounds like a grade-A asshole," he bit out, his hand squeezing hers. "And how could he not want to marry you?" he asked.

She refused to acknowledge the flutter in her stomach at those words.

"And he didn't want kids. At least not at that time. But I dragged him to the first ultrasound appointment, and he listened to Abby's heartbeat. He said, we can do this, and I wanted to believe him. I wanted our daughter to have her father. To have a complete family. We were going to raise her and not get married right away, but then my parents found out and guilted us into marriage." Was it possible to sound wistful and bitter at the same time? But it felt good to get this off her chest. He really listened to her, his eyes had yet to glaze over as she told her story.

"Parental guilt. My mother is awesome at it," he said, and she bit back her smile.

She'd only met his mother once and had loved her instantly. That was a family she wouldn't mind being a part of. *Shit.* She couldn't have those thoughts.

"So we got married and had Abby. He started resenting the lack of attention I gave him because I was taking care of our daughter, and he would lash out."

"You had a baby. I'm pretty sure they require tons of attention," he said, his tone incredulous.

"I know," she shook her head, remembering Joe pouting. "He'd yell about how his life was ruined and that he never wanted kids. I'd yell back. It was awful. He hit me twice, and the second time, I kicked him out. I told him that I wanted a divorce. The next day, he walked out on his job so he wouldn't have to pay child support."

"What a fucking douchebag," Grant barked out, his hand clenched in a fist. Lexi wrapped her fingers around his.

"It's fine. He didn't want her or us, and we don't need him. He probably has a job now, but, to me, he's just a sperm donor, and I'd rather pretend he doesn't exist. Eventually Abby will ask questions that I don't want to answer, but for right now, we are good."

"You're better off without him. How did your parents react?"

She let out a choked laugh. "Oh, they were pissed. My father especially. He has archaic views of a woman's place. Thought I couldn't raise Abby on my own. We still don't have the best relationship, for multiple reasons, but they both love Abby."

"You should've told them about the abuse," he said.

"I didn't want to tell them." She dropped her head, focusing on their linked hands. "It's embarrassing that I let it get as far as it did. It makes me weak."

He placed his finger under her chin, tilting her head up. She hated that he could see the unshed tears in her eyes, but more than that, she hated those wasted years. Not seeing Joe for who he really was and letting him get the better of her.

Grant brushed a tear away with his thumb. "You are not weak. You could never be weak. You're raising your daughter on your own. When I look at you, I see a strong and amazing woman. Never doubt yourself."

She wanted to melt into a puddle at his words. At the sincerity in his eyes. "Where did you come from?" she whispered.

He let out a soft chuckle. "I'm just stating the facts. And thank you for telling me about him. I know it wasn't easy."

"I've only told Penny and Amanda about the abuse, but I trust you." And she did. She felt comfortable confiding in him, which should make her panic because he would be out of her life in two short months, but she couldn't stop herself or her feelings.

He tugged her closer and she shifted, snuggling against his chest. He ran his hand down her spine.

"I'll never let anyone hurt you again," he whispered against her hair.

How she wished that was true. She pushed that thought aside, knowing that the next man to hurt her would probably be him.

Grant continued to stroke her hair, the strands slipping through his fingers like the softest silk. Her breathing was steady against his throat, and he hated his body's reaction. She'd just poured out her soul to him, and he wanted to drag her to bed and ravish every inch of her body. He was a horny asshole.

Anger gripped him at the memories of the guy in the bar and now knowing about what her ex had done to her. He hadn't lied. She was strong and amazing, and he hated that his actions tonight had scared her and brought up a time she'd rather forget.

Her fingers trailed up and down his chest, fiddling with the button at the top of his shirt, and he shifted around, trying to get comfortable, trying to get his desire for her to chill out. Now was not the time, but tell that to his hardening erection.

"Can I get you anything? More dessert?" he asked, anything to step away and gather himself before he pulled her into his lap.

She sat up, her hands trailing south, reaching the button on his jeans. "I'm not hungry for dessert," she said, her voice husky. "I just want to forget about tonight, forget about every shitty guy I've dated or married."

She straddled his lap, pressing her heated core firmly against his denim-covered cock, and his heart stopped. She was using him to wipe away the bad memories, and he was happy to oblige.

"Whatever you need," he whispered, cupping her face in his hands and crushing his lips to hers. He let her lead the kiss and take control of the seduction. She had power over him, and he wanted her to know that.

She tilted her head, their mouths fitting like perfect puzzle pieces, and he groaned against her lips. Her tongue darted out, tracing along the seam of his lips, and he opened his mouth, tangling and twisting his tongue with hers, swallowing her moan as she ground against him.

He slowly ran his fingers up and down her spine, pressing his thumbs to her lower back, and she arched against him.

She deepened the kiss, sinking her hands into his hair, pulling at his scalp, and he felt her touch down to his toes. She continued to rock against his body, his cock hardening to the point of pain, and he broke free of her kiss with a groan.

"I'm not trying to rush you, but I need you naked now," he panted.

Her laugh hit him right in the gut. "The feeling is mutual." Her hazel eyes sparkled with humor and desire, and he was glad to hear that laugh. To see her smiling.

He pushed the thin sweater from her shoulders, and she yanked it down her arms, throwing it behind her.

"Anxious?" he asked, cocking a brow.

"Shut up," she said, pulling her blouse over her head, tousling her wavy hair in the process.

He cupped her full breasts through the silky bra, her nipples pebbled against his palms, and he lowered his head, taking one distended tip in his mouth, sucking her through the fabric.

She gripped his hair again, holding his face to her body, and pushing her breast into his mouth.

He reached behind her, popping the clasp open. She pulled the straps down, and the thin fabric pooled between their bodies.

Her skin was flushed pink, and he ran one finger down her chest, scraping a nail across her nipple. Her stomach muscles clenched as he treated the other nipple to the same torment.

She tugged on his head, and he fought his grin, knowing exactly where she wanted his mouth. His tongue traced a circle around her nipple, before nibbling on the pebbled point.

"Oh yes," she moaned, her lower body rocking against his.

He released her with a pop, blowing a breath over her wet skin, then pulled back, watching her body shudder with need. He'd never needed anyone as much as he needed her.

Her hands slipped under the hem of his shirt, yanking it up over his head, her fingers skating down his chest, scraping across his flat nipple. He sucked in a breath at her touch, wanting to feel her hands on every part of his body.

She leaned in, spreading kisses along his collarbone, sucking at his pulse point, then traced his flat nipples with her tongue.

His hips lifted, rubbing against her, and he cursed the clothes between them. He squeezed her hips, kneading the flesh of her ass through her jeans.

Her hand slipped under his waistband, gripping his cock, and he couldn't stop his groan. Her thumb rubbed over the tip, and he pulsed in her palm. She squeezed lightly, moving up and down his shaft, and he threw his head back, taking in a quaking breath.

He put his hand over hers, stopping her movement, knowing that if she kept that up, he'd come in her hands. He needed to be in her body, clenched in her heat, when he came.

"What?" she asked, her voice husky, her lips plump and glistening with moisture from their kiss.

He groaned at the image of her lips around his cock, of him sinking into her mouth, but tonight was solely about her.

"Wrap your legs around me," he said, pressing a hard kiss to her lips, tasting the sweetness of their dessert. Tasting pure Lexi.

He scooted to the edge of the couch, and she wrapped her legs around his waist. He stood, palming her ass, and her arms tightened around his neck, her body pressed flush against his.

"Holy shit, that's hot," she gasped.

He chuckled and kissed her nose, then headed down the hall to his bedroom. He intended to ravage every inch of her delectable body until she couldn't move or remember any man had ever done her wrong.

Lexi clung to Grant's hard body as they entered his dark bedroom. How was his breathing still normal? Desire shot through her as she rubbed against him with every stride.

This was what she needed. Tonight, and every night she could have him. Expiration date be damned.

She gripped his shoulders, his back muscles shifting under her hands, pure strength undulating beneath her touch. Unlocking her legs, she slid down his body, feeling his cock pressed against where she needed him most. She needed to see him and moved to the side of the bed, turning on his bedside lamp, flooding the room with soft light.

He reached for her again, his eyes glittering, his dilated pupils telling her he wanted her just as much as she needed him.

His gaze held hers as he toed off his shoes and shucked the rest of his clothes. His rock hard erection begged for her touch, her mouth. She ran a finger down his shaft and wrapped her hand around him, giving him a few slow strokes as he pulsed in her palm. She loved the power she held over him.

"You have to stop," he groaned, slipping out of her touch.

"I don't want to," she grumbled, reaching for him again.

He chuckled, pulling her against his body and silencing her protests with a bone-melting kiss.

She met him kiss for kiss, tongues tangling and twisting.

His hands cupped her face, holding her like she was a precious treasure. Her heart clenched at his tenderness in a moment when all she wanted to do was get naked and attack him.

He lowered her to the bed, following her down, his body shifting against her curves, pressing her into the mattress. He braced himself up on one elbow, trailing a finger down the center of her chest and belly and flicked open the button on her jeans.

"So beautiful," he murmured. He dropped his head to her chest and worshipped her breasts, the wet heat of his mouth surrounding her sensitive flesh.

He spread kisses down her chest, his tongue tracing a lazy pattern over her belly while he slid down to kneel between her parted thighs.

She propped herself up on her elbows, her gaze locking on his, his eyes ablaze with pure need. He reached for her, the combination of their whispered pants and the sound of the teeth parting on her zipper made her heart race.

"Hurry up," she moaned, annoyed by his soft chuckle when he paused and licked along the top edge of her panties.

He was driving her insane, and she was tempted to kick him away and finish stripping herself. If he wasn't inside of her in the next two minutes, she wouldn't be held responsible for the bodily harm she'd inflict. He wouldn't be laughing then.

"I need you," she moaned, just as he divested her of the rest of her clothes in one fell swoop.

"Patience."

"Is a virtue I'm missing," she muttered, grabbing his shoulders in an attempt to move him up and over her body, but he didn't budge.

He stared at her core, his fingers tracing over her trimmed curls, getting closer and closer to that little bud that ached for his touch. He lowered his head, his tongue licking at her lower lips, gathering her need. He drew her clit into his mouth, sucking gently.

She arched against him, her heart galloped, her breath coming out in desperate pants while he tortured her with his tongue. Her arms fell out from under her, and she dropped back onto the bed, her hands tangling in her hair as his tongue tangled inside of her body. His mouth was amazing, and she never wanted it to end.

Her hands moved down her body, one settling in his soft hair while she cupped her breast with the other one, tweaking her nipple.

He growled against her core, and she felt it down to her toes. She lifted her head, catching him staring at her hand currently cupping her breast. Pure lust filled his gaze, and her heart raced. Before Grant, she never touched herself during sex, always afraid the guy would think he wasn't getting the job done on his own.

But with Grant, he encouraged her, with words, and with the complete desire in his eyes whenever she touched herself. She felt safe with him. Confident in herself.

He traced a lazy circle over her clit with his tongue and plunged one finger and then another into her core. Her muscles clenched around him, tension coiling tight in her belly as he continued his torment, alternating between tracing the tip of his tongue around her clit with sucking the tender bud in his mouth, while his fingers moved in and out of her body, mimicking what his cock would hopefully be doing in the very near future.

He hummed against her core, sending bolts of desire through her body. Her orgasm rocked through her, and she shouted her release, her body clenching around his fingers and tongue.

Her hands dropped to her sides, and she took in deep breaths. He spread soft kisses up her body, before linking his lips with hers.

"Oh Lexi," he murmured against her mouth.

He pulled a condom from underneath her pillow and sat up, quickly sheathing his cock. He gripped his erection, dragging the tip through her wet folds.

She shuddered, her head rocking from side to side on the pillow before he sank inside of her, one slow inch at a time, until he was seated to the hilt. Her muscles clenched around his cock, and they both let out a trembling breath.

He moved in and out of her languidly, gently, taking his time to drive her insane when all she wanted was for him to take her hard and fast. Leaning down, he locked his lips with hers, wiping away her every thought with his kiss. His tongue moved in and out of her mouth in perfect rhythm with his cock.

He took her hands in his, intertwining their fingers and pushing their linked hands above her head as he rocked against her. Their pelvic bones pressed together, creating the perfect friction that drove her insane, and she begged for more.

The tension in her body built up, and she gasped against his mouth as their bodies shifted against each other.

She broke free of the kiss. "Harder," she moaned against his lips. She squeezed his hands, arching her hips to meet his every thrust.

He dropped his forehead to hers, groaning when she squeezed her inner muscles around his cock. She wanted to torment him just as much as he was tormenting her.

He looked into her eyes, his passion-filled gaze stole her breath, and he ground his pelvis against hers. He slowed again to torturously, languid thrusts, his eyes never leaving hers, and she wanted to ignore the feelings rising in her chest. Lust and passion she could handle. Anything else was too much.

She broke the stare, arching her head back into the mattress, and he picked up the pace, driving into her.

"Oh yes. Don't stop," she moaned, her legs locked around his hips, squeezing him.

"Are you close?" he asked, his voice husky with desire.

Before she could respond, her orgasm overtook her, her words a jumbled moan, her heart racing like she'd run a mile.

His orgasm followed hers, and he came with a groan. He released her hands and cupped her face, giving her a quick, deep kiss before collapsing on top of her and burrowing his face where her shoulder met her neck.

He pressed a kiss behind her ear and her entire body clenched.

"You're amazing," he mumbled, his breath tickling her over-sensitized skin.

"You're not so bad yourself," she whispered, running her nails along his spine.

"I'm just going to pass out right here," he said.

"I'm sort of a fan of breathing. You know, once I actually catch my breath."

He chuckled against her neck, and she felt it clear down to her toes. She already wanted him again. How was she ever going to give this up?

Chapter 14

"Dude, what the hell happened?" Adam gestured to Grant's hand before Grant was able to slip the glove over his bruised knuckles. The pain had rapidly diminished the morning after he'd punched that asshole, so he'd hadn't paid attention to the fading bruises in the last two days.

"It's nothing. Doesn't even hurt," Grant said, grabbing his stick and making his way out of the locker room. Adam lumbered behind him and Grant knew the conversation wasn't over.

He hit the ice, smelling the clean crispness as his blades sliced through, hearing the sounds of his skates gliding across the perfect surface. Some people did yoga to relax, he skated. Of course, not many would say that playing hockey was relaxing, but it was a rec league so the full checks were minimal, and the fights were few and far between.

With the stress of his job and the intensity it required, playing hockey was almost calming. He chuckled at how ridiculous that sounded, but it was true. Yes, he was intense when he was on the ice, but it was just different.

"You're really not going to tell me what happened?" Adam asked, skating the length of their side of the rink with him, as the opposing team circled their half.

"I may have punched one of Lexi's dates this weekend," he said, taking off to shoot a warm-up puck into the net.

"What?" Adam asked, when he caught back up to him. Adam propped his stick up, leaning against it, while he watched the rest of the team. "Why the hell did you punch him?"

"You would've done the same thing. The guy was all over her, refusing to take her home, pushing drinks on her. Total douche." He had little concern that the guy would actually sue him. He'd hit him again if needed. *Damn asshole.*

"So she called you to rescue her again. What's she going to do when you're gone? She sounds clingy and weak. Always depending on you. The sex must be stellar," Adam said. Grant felt the overwhelming desire to punch his friend.

"She's not weak, and don't you ever talk about her that way," he growled, advancing on Adam.

"Calm down, man. I'm just telling you what I'm seeing. I work in a bar. I see chicks like this all the time. I'm trying to look out for you."

"You know nothing about her. And she didn't ask me to rescue her this weekend. I texted her first. She said she was going to grab a cab, and I offered to pick her up," Grant bit out, only noticing the rapidly increasing grin on Adam's face after his confession. Fuck. He hadn't meant to say all of that, but Adam had forced Grant to defend Lexi. She wasn't fucking weak.

"I knew it. Shit. You really like this one. You know you're leaving soon, right?"

He was tempted to punch that grin off Adam's face. "I know. And we're just friends. I protect my friends," Grant said, shooting another puck toward the net with more force

216

than he'd intended, the vulcanized rubber rebounding off the pipes with a clang.

"Just friends, huh? Keep telling yourself that," Adam said, skating to the other side of the ice to stretch before Grant could say anything else.

He needed to hone his frustration into winning tonight, not getting distracted by thoughts of Lexi. He lined up another shot, sailing the puck into the back of the net, attempting to ignore Adam's words. He and Lexi were just friends. Not that he hadn't thought about what would happen if he weren't leaving. He wished he could do more. Take her out on an actual date. But what was the point? He was leaving, and he knew her thoughts on uprooting Abby. She was so stubborn, but he also understood her reasons, which aggravated the shit out of him.

He needed to ditch those thoughts. They weren't even a couple. They weren't even dating.

But last weekend...last weekend had been different. He was invested. She'd opened up to him more than before, and he was in awe of her strength, leaving her ex, raising her infant daughter alone. Grant felt a surge of rage rush through him at the thought of her ex. He'd never wanted to hunt a man down and beat the shit out of him until she'd told him about Abby's father.

And the sex...the sex was amazing, but even he knew it'd been more than just sex last weekend. He was screwed. They were just scratching an itch, and he shouldn't be thinking about Lexi in Florida.

It wasn't an option.

217

Not to mention that he was sure she was avoiding him. He'd thought they were good after that night, but her responses had been minimal to the few random texts he'd sent over the past week. Just a smiley face or LOL. Not that they had long, in-depth conversations over text, but something was up.

Ah hell. How had he let this happen?

He shook his head, clearing the thoughts he couldn't have and skated over to Adam. Grant dropped down next to his friend and finished his final stretches, his focus on the ice and not on the woman who had him in knots. There was plenty of time for that later.

Adam eyed him skeptically. "You good, man?"

"Yeah, let's do this," he said. With one last hip stretch before he rose, he skated back to the bench, trying to prepare his head for the game. They had to win tonight to make it into the post season that started in two weeks. It's not like there was a Stanley Cup at the end, but he was determined to win it all before he left. At least that was a realistic goal.

"Girls night, finally," Amanda said, clinking her martini glass to Lexi and Penny's glasses.

Lexi laughed. "It hasn't been that long." She took a sip of her Lemon Drop. The tartness tickled her tongue. She'd been looking forward to a fun night with her girlfriends ever since her mom had asked to take Abby for the night. Aside from that night a few weeks ago when Penny and Amanda had shown up at her house with pizza and an interrogation, Lexi hadn't had a girls' night in so long.

"Lexi's too busy going on horrible dates so she can have tons of glorious sex with Grant," Amanda said, smirking at Lexi.

And it was already starting. "Hey, that sex is reward for getting through those dates."

"One of which, I set her up on. I'm so sorry about Scott and what an asshole he turned out to be. He's always so nice at the company parties," Penny said, remorse in her tone.

"You've already apologized multiple times," Lexi said, reaching out and squeezing Penny's hand. "You didn't know how awful he was. And he wasn't bad on our first date."

"I'm still sorry," Penny grumbled. "I can talk to my dad about him."

"No. It's fine." As long as Scott didn't try to sue Grant for defending her, she was just going to pretend it never happened. She'd spent the last two weeks thinking about that night. How tender Grant had been, soothing her panicked nerves, anticipating her every need before she even realized it. God. It was just supposed to be sex, but it was turning into so much more, and she was freaking out.

"Hey, what's that face?" Amanda asked.

Lexi looked up. "What?"

"You just looked sad for a minute. Is it because of our lack of girl time, or because the sex isn't as good as you claimed?"

"Very funny. It's not that. The sex is awesome. It's just…" she trailed off.

"It's just that you're going to miss him when he leaves, and he means more to you than you thought he would," Penny said.

Ugh. Penny was a damn mind reader.

"Yes. And I'm not even going on dates anymore. I'm done with eMatch, but I don't want to give Grant up, so I haven't told him," she said, shaking her head. "I cancelled my account last week.

"Wow. Really?" Amanda asked.

"Yes. I didn't hit your required five," Lexi said.

"I don't care about that. I just wanted you to get out there. And you did," Amanda said, nudging Lexi's shoulder. "Sure the dates were awful, but you had fun afterwards, right?"

"Yes, but it doesn't matter. I like the guy that's leaving. Dammit. I wasn't supposed to like him," she lamented. And yet, here she was at Crash and Byrne, wondering if Grant might show up. She was screwed.

"Have you told him that you aren't trying to date anyone?" Penny asked.

"No. I don't want to put pressure on him. On whatever this is. Make him think that I expect things now that he isn't just a rescue bang."

Amanda giggled. "A rescue bang?"

"What the hell else should I call it?"

"I don't know. How about a relationship?" Penny asked, trying to hide her smile.

"It can't be a relationship. He's leaving, remember? It was just supposed to be some fun before he leaves. But it's not just sex anymore. A few weeks ago, we ran into each other at the Exploratorium. Actually, I told him I was bringing Abby and he showed up with his niece and nephew. And it was fun," she said, taking a long sip of her drink.

"And that's bad?" Penny asked.

"Of course it's bad. I don't want Abby to get used to having him around. He's leaving in like six weeks." She took a large gulp of her martini, focusing on her drink instead of her friends. She didn't want to see the pity in their eyes. She'd known this would happen, but she'd jumped in feet first, ignoring the consequences.

"Again, he isn't moving to the middle of nowhere. Or halfway across the world. Why can't you see what happens?" Penny asked.

"I don't want Abby to get hurt when it doesn't work out and I don't want to get hurt, either." But she already knew it was too late for her.

"Have you talked about what happens when he leaves?" Penny asked.

"Not really."

Penny reached over, squeezing her hand. "Would you even think about it, if he asked you to move with him?"

"I'm not moving. He knows that. Not that he'd ask. We were very clear about what this was."

"Yes. But things change," Amanda said.

"No they don't, and I don't want to talk about it anymore. We're supposed to be having a fun girls' night," she said, pushing Grant from her mind. Not that he was ever very far from it. Especially since she was still glancing around the bar hoping he'd show up. She was hopeless.

She hadn't seen him in two weeks and, hell, she'd missed him. Time and again her fingers had hovered over his number, funny texts she wanted to send not flowing from her head to the keys on her phone. It was a cop-out just responding to his few texts with emoticons and not opening up to the conversations she wanted to have.

"We just want you to be happy and not ignore what you could have with Grant if you'd just let it happen," Penny said, the sincerity in her eyes clear.

"I know. But no more talk of what-ifs. We need to talk about the wedding. Less than a month to go. Aren't you excited?" Lexi asked, taking a sip of her martini and focusing on Penny.

"Ooh, yes. Bachelorette party in three weeks. You better not have plans for the following day. You'll need recovery time," Amanda said, her grin almost scary. Maybe Lexi shouldn't have let Amanda do the bulk of the planning.

"Oh God. Please don't make me regret agreeing to this," Penny grumbled.

Amanda laughed. "I promise. Nothing totally crazy. Just a fun night out with lots of booze and dancing. Maybe a stripper or two."

"No strippers. I already told you that," Penny bit out, glaring at Amanda.

Lexi giggled. The bachelorette party didn't include strippers, but Amanda couldn't help herself.

Amanda barked out a laugh. "Your face. Oh man. You're too easy. Don't worry. There'll be no strippers."

"There better not," Penny said.

"I promise. Just a fun night out. But if you change your mind about some man candy, you just let me know."

"Don't hold your breath," Penny snapped.

"Whoa. Okay, I'm sorry. What's going on with you?" Amanda asked.

"Sorry. Just wedding stress," Penny said, draining the rest of her glass.

"How are you holding up? I know you have everything booked already, but the last month can be super stressful with the anticipation of the actual day and making sure everything is perfect," Lexi said.

"I'm fine. It's just stressful, and I can't wait for it to be over. Then we can get back to our normal lives," Penny said.

"Totally understandable. Is Michael helping?" Lexi asked, watching Penny carefully, looking for anything that would point to more than just standard wedding stress.

"Not really. He's working a lot. I completely get it. It's sometimes nice to have the condo to myself at night. Michael doesn't need to see my stupid freak-outs about flowers or the cake, or all the little things that don't really matter," Penny said.

"But it's important to you, and he should be there, even if he doesn't know the difference between a gerbera daisy and a regular daisy," Amanda said.

"It's fine," Penny said.

Lexi heard something in Penny's voice but chalked it up to stress. She'd been there before. "Well, if you need help with anything, or want to talk about anything, you'll let us know, right?"

"I know. And everything is fine," Penny said, giving them a bright smile. "I'm getting married in a month and honeymooning in Italy. It's going to be awesome."

"Yes it is," Lexi echoed.

"No more about my crazy wedding," Penny said, turning her focus to Amanda. "I want to know what's up with you. We haven't heard anything about your dating life recently."

Amanda grinned. "It's still ongoing, but now that Lexi's finally getting some, I thought it would be nice to focus on her."

"Hey," Lexi exclaimed. "Not funny."

Amanda smirked. "Kinda funny."

"I'm ready for another round," Lexi said, holding her empty glass out to Amanda. "And you have to get it since you're such a pain in the ass."

Amanda laughed. "Whatever. You love me."

"I'd love a drink," Lexi replied.

Amanda grabbed the empties and walked over to the bar.

Grant nursed his beer that night and watched Matt lay a line on the unsuspecting woman who had just walked by. They'd been at Crash and Byrne for twenty minutes. The man moved fast. Grant bit back his laughter as the woman shut down his friend.

"How many times do I have to tell you lines don't work?"

Matt tipped back his bottle of beer, draining it, before turning to Grant. "Lines work. You just have to find the right

224

one for the right girl. It's like a puzzle, and I'm excellent at puzzles."

Grant laughed. "Yep, keep telling yourself that."

"I've had three dates already this week, and you're pining. I'm not taking advice from you."

"Whatever, man. I'm not pining."

"Really? When was the last time you went out with someone other than Lexi? Instead, you wait by your phone for her to call. It's just sad," Matt said, shaking his head.

"Except I'm getting sex regularly with no messy strings that I'd have to cut when I leave. How's that not a win-win?"

"You sure there aren't any strings? Didn't you take the kids and meet up with Lexi and her daughter the other week to go to a museum? A freaking museum. With kids," Matt said, horror on his face. "Sounds like more than just sex to me."

"Keira is best friends with Lexi's daughter, and they wanted to go to the museum. Lily asked me to take them. She had showings all morning."

"Sounds like strings to me," Matt said.

Grant ignored him, grabbing his beer. Maybe there were a few strings, but they were loose, and he didn't mind them. What he didn't like was the fact that she was avoiding him. Two weeks of ignoring his texts, and it was starting to piss him off. Okay, she wasn't actually ignoring him, but stupid emoticons were not responses.

"Shouldn't you keep your phone out, in case she calls?" Matt taunted.

Grant glared at his friend and kept his hands on the bar, refusing to take his phone out of his pocket. Not that it mattered, since he had it on vibrate, just in case.

"Grant. Didn't expect you tonight," Adam said, the kitchen door swinging behind him, two plates of food in his hands.

Grant's stomach grumbled just seeing those burgers even though he was still stuffed from dinner.

"You want one?" Adam asked, nodding toward the plates.

"I'm good for now," Grant replied. He wasn't actually hungry.

"Be right back," Adam said before walking away, tempting burgers in hand.

"Man, I could go for one of those, and I'm not even hungry," Matt echoed Grant's thoughts.

He chuckled. "I was thinking the same thing."

"Your damsel's here," Adam said when he returned, depositing fresh beers in front of them.

Grant's head shot up, and he craned his neck around, searching.

Matt barked out a laugh. "Yep, definitely not pining."

Grant turned to glare at his friend. "Shut it."

"Hey, maybe she's following you. She knows you're friends with the owner and that you like to show up here. She probably didn't have a date tonight but was looking for some action," Matt said.

"And you're looking for a punch in the face," he bit out.

"Whoa. Whoa," Matt said, hands raised. "Sounds like strings to me."

"Don't be an ass," Grant said, finally spotting her at the other end of the bar. She was with two other women, her face lit up as she laughed with her friends. She was stunning. Her laugh got him in the gut every time.

Adam laughed. "I bet she's back for my cookie."

"What?" Matt asked.

"He's talking about the dessert. We had the cookie bomb the last time we were here," Grant said, ignoring his friends' chuckles. *Idiots.*

"Oh right, dessert and sex is her MO," Matt said.

Matt was just trying to get a rise out of him, but he was beginning to hate the guy.

"You ready for Monday's game?" Adam asked. Grant wanted to hug his *true* friend for changing the subject.

"Yeah," Grant said. They were inching closer and closer to winning their season. Every year he'd played, they'd lost in the post season. Last year they made the league final but lost the game by one damn goal. He was determined to go out with a bang next month.

They moved on to talking about the team, and Grant tried to not look over at Lexi every chance he got, ignoring his friends' smirks when they caught him. He didn't think she'd spotted him yet, and he wasn't going to crash her girls' night. Well, not right this second. He'd give her an hour. Maybe thirty minutes. Shit, the strings were tightening.

"Well he's yummy," Amanda said over the rim of her martini glass, nodding her head toward the bar.

"Who?" Lexi glanced over her shoulder, her eyes meeting Grant's. His grin widened and she felt her cheeks flush.

How was he here? Was he following her?

She held in her snort. Hell. She was pathetic. She'd known the odds were good that he'd show up tonight. That's why she'd picked it. She couldn't believe she hadn't noticed him as soon as she'd walked in. His gray henley stretched his broad shoulders, and her fingers itched to trace every muscle she'd finally traced with her tongue just a few weeks ago. Her body flamed to life, and she wouldn't need any alcohol to feel warm and fuzzy tonight.

"That's him, isn't it?" Amanda asked over Lexi's shoulder, but Lexi didn't turn to face her friends, or even acknowledge their comments.

"Did you know he was going to be here tonight? You did suggest this place," Amanda continued.

Still ignoring.

"You totally knew he was going to be here," Penny said, her voice laced with humor.

Lexi turned to face her friends, shrugging her shoulders. "I had no idea he'd be here, but his friend does own the bar." Amanda's grin widened, and Lexi wished she'd kept that last part to herself.

"What about sisters before misters?" Amanda pretended to sound offended as Penny snickered.

"Shut up. I'm not ditching you for him. And I really had no idea he'd be here." Just secretly hoped when she'd spent two painstaking hours picking out every stitch of

228

clothing she currently had on, down to the matching bra and panty set in deep green. He loved that color on her.

"But it was a possibility. A very good possibility," Penny said.

"Maybe," she said, focusing on her friends.

"I can't wait to finally meet the sheet warmer," Amanda said.

"Nice, Amanda. Real nice," Lexi muttered. She turned back to see Grant walking toward them, a half smile on his lips, that dimple peeking through the scruff on his jaw. God, she wanted him.

He moved with a leisurely gait, completely aware of what he did to her. She couldn't hide anything from him, and right now, she wanted to peel the soft denim from his lean hips and climb him like a damn tree.

Jesus. She was having a hot flash.

"Of all the bars, she had to walk into mine," he said when he stopped in front of her, his grin deep.

His Bogart impression was terrible, but she couldn't stop her smile. "What is it with you and old movie quotes?" she asked.

"It seemed fitting," he said, sliding next to her in the booth, his thigh pressed against hers, his heat branding her. Yep. Totally having a hot flash. Dammit.

His breath washed over her cheek, and she froze. Was she supposed to kiss him? Pretend they were just friends? God, she was hopeless. Their friends all knew what was going on. This was the one time they weren't a secret.

She gave him a quick peck on his cheek before pulling away and tucking a strand of hair behind her ear. "Hi."

He chuckled lightly, clearly aware of her embarrassment. "Introduce me," he said.

"Umm. Oh, so, Grant, this is Amanda and Penny," she said, turning to face her friends and attempting to ignore the smirk on Amanda's face. It was totally going to be misters before sisters if Amanda kept this up.

"Nice to meet you," he said, giving them a smile that was slightly less panty-melting. She'd like to think he saved that particular smile just for her.

Lexi greeted Matt, who'd wandered over, and introduced him to her friends.

"So nice to meet you, too," Amanda said. "And how exactly do you two know each other?"

Lexi groaned as Penny laughed. She really needed to reevaluate her friends, because right now they sucked.

Grant wrapped his arm around Lexi, and she sucked in a startled breath, a shiver shooting through her to her toes.

"We're old friends. Dessert buddies, actually," he said.

Lexi ducked her head down, knowing her cheeks were a brilliant shade of red. She was going to kill all of them. *Slowly.*

"So nice to meet you," Penny said.

Okay, she'd keep Penny. At least Penny wasn't going out of her way to embarrass her. Amanda, though, was questionable, as she asked what Grant's favorite dessert place was.

"Did you have dessert yet? I know you're partial to the cookie bomb," he said, before grunting when she elbowed him in the ribs.

He shot her a smile when she finally looked up into his face. "So violent."

"Don't torment me," she replied. "At least not in public."

His eyes widened, and desire shot through her at her suggestive comment. Where had that come from?

"I haven't heard from you in a while. Are you surviving your dates without me?" he asked.

"Umm. I haven't had any dates," she said. "I can't drop Abby off with my parents all the time, so my dating life isn't that busy." And she was done with dating. Not that she was going to tell him that. She grabbed her martini, took a healthy sip, and coughed.

"I don't think you're supposed to chug it," he whispered, rubbing his hand over her back.

She pushed down the shiver that threatened to roll through her.

"Pace yourself. I want you completely sober so you'll remember everything I do to you later tonight," he said. Her body turned into an inferno.

"You know what they say about assumptions."

He chuckled. "Oh I know all about them, but this isn't an assumption, it's a promise," he shot back. A shiver raced down her body before she could stop it.

Everyone bustled around her, but she heard nothing except the roar of desire coursing through her. Grant squeezed in next to her on the bench seat. He had more than enough room to stretch out, but she wanted him this close. His denim-covered thigh pressed against hers, his heat seeping in through her jeans. She didn't want to throw herself in his lap, but she scooted closer, subtly burrowing into his side.

His arm wrapped around her waist, his fingers tracing up and down her hip. She gave herself over to the sensation and tried not to purr like a contented cat. Clearly, they weren't going for a secret relationship. She might not know exactly what they were, but she had no desire to fight it or question it tonight.

"Are you both rescue swimmers?" Amanda asked.

"No, I'm a Flight Mechanic. I'm the mechanical and electrical specialist that makes sure everything is in perfect working order before Grant has to jump out of the helicopter," Matt said.

Matt went on to answer all of their questions about his job. Lexi had a pretty good idea of what Grant did, but she was still curious about the why. Not many people chose to jump out of helicopters into frigid water. Was it the adrenaline rush? They'd briefly talked about his job, in between bouts of crazy sex and plates of dessert, but she'd held back on asking him why.

"So you guys have worked together now for over three years, right?" Lexi asked.

Grant and Matt both nodded.

"Is Grant known for rescuing other women from horrible dates or is it just our Lexi?" Amanda asked, and Lexi growled at her.

"That growl is sexy. Do that again," Grant whispered against her ear, before nipping the lobe with his teeth.

Matt laughed. "Nope. I'm pretty sure Lexi is the first."

"I can't help that my dates have been the worst. What about you?" Lexi asked, trying to turn the attention away from herself.

"You're on eMatch, too?" Amanda asked.

"Yeah, but I don't think he's using it for its intended purposes. And he keeps dragging me along to the meet-ups" Grant said.

"Hey, if I hadn't, you never would've met Lexi," Matt said.

"Very true," Grant murmured, his eyes locked with hers, and she shifted in her seat.

"I think I'm ready for another drink," she said, focusing on the empty glass in her hand, and not Grant's heated gaze. She didn't want to read anything into the glimpse of emotion she'd seen there. This was purely physical.

Grant pulled his arm from her waist and grabbed her empty glass. "I'll grab the next round. Anyone want anything?"

They gave him their order, and Matt went with him to the bar to grab their drinks.

"Wow. He really likes you," Amanda said, leaning in after Matt and Grant left.

Lexi looked at her friends who were both nodding and had huge grins on their faces.

"Yeah, he likes the sex. It's nothing more," she said. Hell, she was tired of that statement, knowing she could repeat it ad nauseam and her heart would still want more.

"You sure about that?" Penny asked. "He couldn't keep his hands off you."

"Exactly. Just physical," she replied.

"I don't know about that," Amanda said.

"Don't start. Don't put ideas in my head that can't happen. He's leaving in less than two months," she said, trying to keep the pleading tone from her voice.

Penny reached out and grabbed her hand. "Why couldn't it be more?"

"Because he's leaving and he's made no comments about what happens after. And it doesn't matter. He's going to be gone for at least four years."

"Maybe he'll invite you to go with him," Penny said.

"I'm not uprooting Abby. You both know I would never do that. She deserves stability in her life, something I've tried desperately to give her." Lexi rolled her shoulders and looked her friends straight in the eyes. "Now, no more of this. We're having fun tonight, right?"

"Right," Amanda replied. "But just think about it. I've never seen you happier."

Lexi snorted. "I would hope not since we've only known each other since right before my divorce."

"That's true, but don't ignore what is happening here out of fear," Amanda said.

Before Lexi could reply, Grant and Matt were back, drinks in hand.

234

"Were you girls gossiping about us while we were gone?" Matt asked, squeezing in next to Amanda and handing her a drink.

"Nope. But we want to hear some of your online dating horror stories. We get all of Lexi's, but we want them from the male point of view," Amanda said.

Grant chuckled. "Why don't you tell them about the dolls?"

"What dolls?" Penny asked.

Matt launched into his story and Lexi leaned back, sipping her martini. Grant's ever-present arm was wrapped around her again, but she resisted the urge to snuggle into his body. She tried to focus on Matt's tale and not the questions that swirled in her mind.

Chapter 15

"Mommy, they're here," Abby shouted Saturday morning before the doorbell could finish ringing. Lexi took a deep breath, rolling her shoulders as if to prepare herself for battle. She could do this. She could spend another day with Grant that was outside of their initial agreement. Why couldn't they have just stuck to the rules? It was getting too complicated.

She hadn't seen him since last weekend when he'd whisked her into his bed after meeting her friends. That was the first night they'd spent together that hadn't started with a disaster date, but, as per usual, it'd been toe-curling amazing. Ugh. This wasn't supposed to be happening. They were marching toward that expiration date at lightning speed, and she was going to end up with a battered heart and sexually ruined for all other men.

Okay. That might be a touch dramatic, but she couldn't help it.

"Mommy, hurry up," Abby yelled, pulling Lexi out of her crazy thoughts.

She took one last look in the mirror, fluffing a wave of auburn hair and tossing it over her shoulder before trudging down the stairs, her new hiking pants softly swooshing with every step. Abby had demanded new hiking clothes—not that they had old hiking clothes—when Keira had invited them for a day of exploring Muir Woods.

Lexi shouldn't have agreed. Spending more time outside of the bedroom with Grant would only lead to more trouble in the end, but her daughter had begged, and Lexi had caved. She told herself it was because she shouldn't keep Abby from spending time with her best friend, but Lexi wasn't fooling herself. Her motive wasn't completely selfless. Not that Grant could ravage her on the side of a mountain with the kids around. Wait, were they climbing a mountain? She definitely should've done some homework on their destination.

"I'm coming, I'm coming," Lexi muttered, yanking open the door.

"Oh I'm so excited, look at my new hiking shoes," Abby said as Keira rushed through the door, their excitement infectious as they hugged.

"Good morning, Lexi." His voice rolled over her, and she tamped down a shudder before looking up to greet him. Why did he have to look so mouth-watering? Khaki pants rested on his lean hips, the material molded to his thighs. She took a deep breath, willing him to both not turn around and to turn around, because she could only imagine how great his ass looked in those pants.

Her gaze travelled up his body, briefly stopping at the dark green shirt that stretched the breadth of his chest, and met his gaze. His smirk told her he knew exactly what she was thinking. *Damn him.*

"Good morning. Are you guys excited?" she asked, turning back to the kids. Luckily, they were chattering about their destination and hadn't noticed the tension.

"Yes. We've been to Muir a bunch of times. Uncle Grant likes to take us on outdoorsy adventures to wear us out," Nathan said, grinning up at his uncle.

Grant shrugged. "You have a lot of energy."

Lexi chuckled. "Abby's been talking about it for days. Even made us go shopping for hiking attire."

"Looks good," Grant muttered, his gaze making a quick trip over her body.

Heat fluttered in her belly. She needed to get a grip around him.

"You should've gone with a different color," he said.

"What?" She looked down at her pants. "Black goes with everything."

"Yes it does. Including ticks."

"Ticks?" This is why she preferred staying indoors. The shudder that rolled through her had nothing to do with him.

"They blend in with black clothing."

"Ugh. I only have black workout pants and the pants I'm wearing. Is it really bad? Should we stop by one of those outdoorsy stores for me to get something else?" Just not khaki, she hated that color.

He let out a soft chuckle, and she wanted to punch him.

"Don't make fun of me," she said.

"Sorry. Couldn't help it. You'll be fine. Even if I have to check you for ticks later." He wiggled his eyebrows at her. It was both disgusting and hot. How was that possible?

"Is she yelling at you again?" Nathan asked, coming to stand between them and looking up at both of them.

She ignored Grant's laugh. *One time*. She yelled at him one freaking time.

He shot her a grin before ruffling Nathan's hair. "Nope, buddy. We were just talking about what trail to take."

"We've never been there," Abby said.

"We can walk along the water or in the forest. It's so pretty. I love it there," Keira said, spinning around.

"Just don't try to climb any of the trees. Uncle Grant will get mad at you," Nathan said.

"You can't climb the trees, Nathan. This is a national park, and they have rules. We could've been kicked out," Grant said, giving his nephew a stern look.

"Well how was I supposed to know? I'm a kid, and I like climbing trees," Nathan replied. Lexi bit the inside of her cheek to halt her laughter at Nathan's look of pure innocence.

"And now you know, so no climbing trees unless you ask first."

Lexi didn't miss the smile he tried to hide, and she'd bet anything that Grant had been as mischievous as a kid as Nathan was. Hell. Grant still was.

"Can we go?" Keira asked.

"Yes. Are we all ready? Maybe one last bathroom break?" he asked, holding their coats as both kids agreed and followed Abby down the hall.

He was going to be a great dad. Ugh. That was a train of thought she needed to derail, immediately.

He grabbed her hand, pulling her close, and brushed a kiss across her lips. She sunk into his arms, deepening the kiss before breaking free at the first sound of little feet headed back in their direction.

She took in a shuddering breath, willing her heart rate to slow. "Hi."

He grinned back. "Hi." The sparkle in his eyes punched her right in the gut. Why had she agreed to this?

"You know, I forget how short you are," he said, tucking her under his arm.

"I'm average height. You're just a giant. And this isn't the first time you've seen me without heels," she replied, pulling free of him.

"Yes, but usually you're horizontal when your shoes finally come off."

Dammit. She'd walked right into that one. She would not look at his darkening eyes. Nope. Definitely not. Warm dark chocolate enveloped by his pupils. Shit. Don't look. She took a deep breath and focused on the sound of the kids coming down the hall toward them.

"Ready," Nathan yelled, grabbing his coat from the couch where Grant had dropped it when he'd wrapped his arms around her.

Lexi grabbed coats, towels, and a small cooler.

"I don't think we're going to swim in the ocean. Too cold," Grant said, motioning toward the towels and grabbing the cooler from her hands.

"I know that. Kids are messy. I like to be prepared. Everyone ready?"

The kids chorused "yes" and they headed out, Lexi snagging Abby's booster seat on the way. Once the kids were loaded into their seats, Grant held the door open for Lexi, squeezing her hand as he helped her in.

She ordered herself to ignore the tingles. Her traitorous body refused to listen.

Stupid body.

"No tree climbing," he said an hour later when Nathan eyed a particular sturdy tree at the front entrance of the park. He knew that look. He definitely had that look when he was Nathan's age. It was a perfect climbing tree, but Grant was the adult in this situation, and if he brought his nephew home with a broken arm, Lily would skin him alive.

Grant stayed back with Lexi as the kids wandered ahead of them on the wide dirt trail.

"I think I stepped in something," Lexi grumbled.

"What?"

She shifted on her feet, lifting one heel and then the next. "Nope. It's just nature."

He laughed as she wrinkled her nose adorably. "So hiking isn't your thing, huh?"

"That obvious?"

"Well, this park is perfect for you. Nice wide trails. You didn't think I was going to take you up the side of a mountain or something, right?"

"I had no idea. Abby really wanted to come and, even if I'm not a fan of it, I know the outdoors is good for you."

"Wait until you see the coastline views. You'll want to come back every weekend," he said, linking his fingers with hers.

"Yeah, let's not get ahead of ourselves," she replied, not pulling free from his grasp.

He ignored the pure contentment that rolled through him while he held her hand and watched the kids in front of him. This was what he wanted. Just not right now. Timing was everything, and right now, it was not working in his favor.

He could still picture Lily's smirk from a few days ago when Keira had mentioned a visit to Muir Woods with Abby, and Grant had jumped to volunteer. He'd played it off as just an excuse to spend more time with his niece and nephew before he left, but Lily hadn't bought it. And then she'd grilled him, reminding him of his rapidly approaching moving date. Sisters could be such pains in the ass, and he hated that she was right.

Not that it had stopped him from showing up today, ready to spend another day with Lexi and her adorable daughter. If only it was four years from now, and he was home for good, settled. The strings were getting sticky, and his desire to fight them off diminished each day.

"So, how was your week?" he asked.

"Not bad, I guess," she said, tucking a strand of hair behind her ear.

"You've gone three weeks without a horrible date. That's impressive."

"You're an ass," she said, swatting his chest. "And I haven't been on any dates recently, so nothing terrible to report."

"I think we found the answer to avoiding horrible dates. You just can't date," he said, grinning.

She glared at him. "Sure. That's the answer. Just be single forever."

Or just for four years. He kept that thought to himself. It would help no one if he voiced it.

"I'm kidding. I'm sure the right guy will show up eventually. You know, once you change your search settings to more than just breathing male."

"That's not what it's set at. People just aren't honest on their dating profiles. I don't want to date anyone I work with, and I don't want to meet some random guy in a bar, so Internet dating is the only other option."

"Maybe I could introduce you to some of the guys on the base?" Why had he offered that?

"Umm. That could be a little weird. But they don't know about us, right? Not that there's really an *us*, but you know what I mean," she babbled, her cheeks flushed

"Nope. Only Matt," he said. He wanted out of this conversation. "So, nature…"

"How's work…?" she cut herself off with a laugh. "Yes, new topic, please."

"Work is work."

"But you love it, right?" He nodded, and she continued. "You know you never told me why rescue swimming."

"Because deep down I'm just a little boy who likes jumping out of helicopters."

She eyed him.

"Of course that's not the reason. A lot of people think it's just for the adrenaline rush, or the God complex of saving lives, but it's not. And I'm not going to say it was just something I fell into."

"But of all the possible careers, you went with this. It's a little extreme. Hot, but also crazy."

He grinned. "Yep, the ladies love when I talk about my job."

She punched his shoulder. "Shut up. I want the real reason."

"I didn't know what I wanted to do when I got out of high school, but it definitely wasn't college right away. My father's a firefighter, and while I knew I wanted to help others, I also knew that firefighting wasn't for me." Not to mention that he hated his father, so he refused to follow in his footsteps.

"After high school, I wasn't ready for college, so I researched my options and joined the Coast Guard. I spent a few years as a shipman and, I guess rescue swimming called to me." That sounded cheesy. "It's the elite of the elite in the Coast Guard, with a huge dropout rate in training, but I was determined. Only two other guys completed the training class I was in, out of a dozen. I still love it, after fourteen years."

"But don't you ever worry about the risks? It's such a dangerous job," she said.

"Our training is extensive and constant. Yes, there's a risk every time we jump into the water to pull someone out, but the number of rescue swimmer casualties is very small. For what we do, it's an amazing statistic. And the number of people I've helped over the years well outweighs the risk. Sometimes we're too late or someone gets lost at sea, but the number of successful rescues I've helped with makes me keep going." He reached for her hand, staring at their intertwined fingers.

"What is it?" she asked, clear concern in her voice.

"I always remember the ones we don't find. Especially the kids. It's definitely the part of my job that I hate."

"I can't imagine," she said, running her thumb along his knuckles.

He never talked about this with anyone. Even his family. It was the ugly part that no one wanted to hear about, but the look in her eyes urged him to continue.

"A few months ago we were searching for two teens. They went out early one morning. A storm came in and we never found them. When kids go missing, I always think about Keira and Nathan. If something ever happened to them..." he trailed off.

"You'd be there to protect them. To rescue them if need be," she assured him. "And I'm sorry about the missing kids."

"Sorry. Didn't mean to get all gloomy on you," he said, giving her a small smile.

"I want to hear about your job. It fascinates me," she said.

"It's a new adventure every day. I can say that. I was never going to be a guy who sat behind a desk. It's not who I am," he said.

"What are you going to do in four years when you retire? Will you really just give it up and move on to something else?" she asked.

"I guess. I hadn't really thought beyond the next assignment." He watched a shadow pass over her eyes, but he was being honest. He had no idea what the future held. "There are other jobs within the Coast Guard that I could take if I wanted, or jobs completely out of the Coast Guard. I have a lot of training that I can carry over into other fields. I'll figure it out in the next few years."

He could feel the tension with every word, and he hated it, but he would never lie to her.

"We should catch up to the kids before they disappear," Lexi said, pulling her hand free of his.

He nodded, following after her, not sure what else to say.

They spent the rest of the day exploring the park, stopping for a brief picnic overlooking the shoreline. They looked like the perfect family, but Grant shoved that notion aside. He never should've let this get so out of hand.

"What the hell was that," Lexi screeched as a loud crash echoed through her house. She pressed her hand to her chest, willing her racing heart to slow.

"Mom," Abby cried out. Lexi ran down the hall to her daughter's room.

"Abby, are you okay?" she asked, sliding into the bedroom.

"Yes. What was that? It scared me," Abby cried.Lexi scooped her up, hugging her tight.

"I don't know, honey. But we're okay," she said, glancing around her daugher's room to see if anything was amiss.

"It was so loud," Abby whispered.

"I know. Let's go see what happened." Lexi stood up, keeping Abby tight in her arms, and made her way through each room in the house, finding nothing.

"Mom, look," Abby said when they reached the living room. "The tree fell over. The one I'm not allowed to climb."

Lexi's eyes widened. The old oak tree that used to stand tall in the far corner next to the house currently lay across her front yard. She grimaced imagining the damage to her car parked in her driveway. *Son of a bitch.* At least it hadn't hit the house. It was right next to Abby's room. One directional change and… She shook her head. She wouldn't play the *what if* game. She knew that tree needed to come down. With so many dead branches, leaves hadn't grown in a handful of spots in years.

"That's not good," she said, trying not to freak Abby out but already assuming her car was probably totaled or close to it. And she'd just gotten it repaired last month.

She wrenched open the front door to evaluate the damage and breathed a huge sigh of relief. The tree just missed her car, only the thinner branches scraped across the hood of the car. Hell. That could've been a disaster. Not that removing a tree of that size was something she could do on her own. Who was she supposed to call for something like this?

She set Abby down, pulled her phone from her pocket, and swiped it on. She knew she shouldn't rely on him, but he was here and he'd told her to call him whenever she needed anything.

Lexi: So if a tree falls…

Her phone dinged back almost immediately. She refused to focus on the thrill she felt at his quick response.

Grant: in a forest and no one hears it?

Lexi: Oh, I heard it.

247

Grant: Where are we going with this?

Lexi: You busy?

Grant: Nope. Getting ready to grab some dinner.

Grant: Wait. Do you have a date tonight? On a Monday?

It annoyed her that her dating was his first response, but what else did she expect?

Lexi: Very funny. And no, not on a date.

Grant: Is everything okay?

His concern made her belly flutter. She should call a tree company, and her insurance company, but her first thought was to call him. She had to wean herself out of that mindset.

Lexi: A rather large tree fell in my yard.

Grant: The oak in the front? The half dead one?

She stared at his response. How did he know that? Was she adding tree expert to his long list of skills?

Lexi: Yes. That one.

Grant: Are you both okay?

Grant: Anyone hurt? Abby freaked out?

Grant: Any damage?

Lexi: Whoa. Calm down. We're both okay. It didn't hit the house and it just missed my car, but it is blocking a good portion of the driveway.

Grant: I'm on my way over.

Lexi: You don't have to. I was just texting to see if you could recommend anyone to call.

Grant: I'll be over in ten.

Lexi: Okay.

"So I can't climb it now, right?" Abby asked.

248

"What? No, you can't climb it," Lexi said, shaking her head.

"But it's on the ground already, so if I climb over it and fall, I won't get hurt," Abby continued, a pleading look in her eyes.

Lexi bit back a laugh. "No climbing. Mr. Parker said he would come over and figure out what we can do."

"Really? Is Keira coming, too?" Abby clapped her hands in delight.

"No. Just Mr. Parker."

"That's okay. I like him."

"You do?" She shouldn't have invited him tonight. Not that she'd actually issued an invitation, but she didn't want Abby getting attached to him. It would only make everything worse when he left.

"He can have dinner with us, but he better not take all my chicken nuggets," Abby declared, her arms wrapped around her skinny chest as she stared at the tree she wanted to climb.

This time Lexi did laugh. "We aren't even having nuggets for dinner. I'm making chicken parm." Although she probably shouldn't cook Italian food for Grant. There was no way she'd measure up to his mother's cooking.

"Oh, that's my second favorite," Abby said. Lexi guided her toward the kitchen so they could start dinner and she could focus on something other than the fact that Grant was coming over for dinner and she had a damn tree blocking her driveway.

* * *

249

"He's here," Abby shouted from the living room ten minutes later, before the doorbell could finish chiming.

Lexi took in a calming breath and rubbed her palms down her hips before opening the door. She expected a snarky quip when he walked in, but his eyes only held concern and relief.

"I'm glad you are both okay," he said, gripping her shoulders and squeezing. He turned and dropped to his knees. "Was it super scary?" he asked Abby.

And Lexi melted. Dammit. Watching him show equal concern for her and Abby was unfair to her well-being.

"Super scary. It was so loud and then mom was yelling for me. I didn't know what happened," Abby said, her eyes wide.

"I bet. Shall we go and take a look at the damage?" he asked, still looking at Abby.

"Yes," Abby said, placing her small hand in his as they walked outside.

Lexi bit back the emotion that threatened to overtake her at that small gesture. She was so screwed.

Grant didn't want to think about what could've happened as he walked out to her car. She'd been extremely lucky that the tree hadn't hit the house.

"So how bad is it?" Lexi asked.

"Could've been a lot worse," he said, hating how nervous she looked. Was it just because of the tree?

"And now the tree is on the ground. I asked if I could climb it but mom said no," Abby pouted.

"Why would you want to climb it now? It's laying flat on the ground," he said.

"But it's safer now. If I fall off, I'm already almost on the ground," Abby said, and he couldn't fault her logic. Not that he would agree with her, judging by the glare Lexi was currently shooting at him.

"But it's not safe because it fell over, and we don't want you to get hurt," he said, dropping Abby's hand so he could walk around the car. He lifted up a few branches, pushing aside what he could. "It's not that damaged. Just some scratches to the paint. You were lucky that the leafy part hit your car and not the larger branches."

"I know. So what do I do now?" she asked, playing with the tie on her hoodie.

"I'm going to remove the smaller branches so we can try to clear your driveway enough for you to get your car out tomorrow. You should call your insurance company and call Ben's Tree Removal. Ask for Ben. He used to date one of my cousins and I went to high school with him. Give him my name and he'll get out here quick to remove the rest of the tree."

"You're going to remove part of this tree on your own?" she asked, her eyebrows raised.

"Sure. I'm handy with a chainsaw," he said, shooting her a grin.

"Of course you are. And thanks for coming over. You'll stay for dinner, right?" There was a wary hopefulness in her gaze.

This was new territory for them. A family dinner.

Abby looked back and forth between them. "Yes. We are having chicken parm. It's my second favorite."

"Not your first favorite?" he asked.

She shook her blonde curls. "Nope. Chicken nuggets are my favorite, but I don't like to share them."

He laughed. "I completely understand. Good thing chicken parm is one of my favorites, too." His mother's recipe was the best he'd ever had, but he'd never tell Lexi that. He wanted her to keep inviting him back.

"Abby, let's go back inside and make dinner so Mr. Parker isn't out here all night," Lexi said.

"Okay. Unless I can help you, Mr. Parker," Abby said.

"Absolutely not," Lexi said. "The last thing I want is you around a chainsaw." She tugged Abby toward the door. "I'll call those companies now."

"This shouldn't take too long," he said, grabbing the chainsaw from his car.

* * *

In under an hour, he'd cleared enough branches for her to get her car in and out of the driveway, then he headed into the house. His stomach grumbled at the enticing smell of golden baked chicken with bubbly cheese and tomato sauce. Probably from a jar, but he'd never tell.

"Smells amazing," he said, entering the kitchen and spotting Lexi in front of the stove, stirring pasta. He refused to focus on the feelings stirring inside him. How homey this scenario was. How he wished it was four years from now and

252

that he didn't have to leave. He pushed those thoughts aside. He couldn't dwell on the impossible.

"It's just about ready. Someone from my insurance company is coming to look at the damage tomorrow and Ben said to call him when I'm ready for the tree to be removed. Thanks for his name." she said, smiling at him over her shoulder as she drained the pasta.

"No problem. Need any help?"

"Nope. Just wash up and we can eat," she said before turning toward her daughter, "You too, Abby."

"I'm washed up," Abby said.

Lexi chuckled. "Maybe one more time, and you can show Mr. Parker where the bathroom is."

"Okay," Abby said, hopping down from her chair. "It's this way."

She held her hand out to him and he grasped it. It was so small in his and the feelings churning in his belly as she walked with him down the hall were similar to holding hands with Keira, but different. He needed to derail this line of thought.

A few minutes later, they were all seated at the table. Food passed around and conversation flowed. Abby was hysterical and adorable. Her little voice filled with excitement when she talked about a nature show she'd watched. The girl loved her reptiles. Grant chuckled at Lexi's every shudder.

After dinner, they made their way into the living room, Abby snuggled into Lexi's side, still talking. In fact, Abby was mid-story when she fell asleep in Lexi's arms.

Grant laughed softly. "Did she just pass out in the middle of talking?"

Lexi grinned. "She was just so excited. I'm going to put her to bed." She stood up with Abby in her arms and walked down the hall.

Grant rested his head back against the sofa, listening to the soft sounds of Lexi wishing Abby good night, then she was walking back toward him.

"Glass of wine?" she asked.

"Sure."

"I can't thank you enough for coming over tonight. I don't know what I would've done," she said, setting their glasses down and tucking her feet under her on the couch.

He tugged her close and she fell against his chest.

"I know how you can thank me," he said, wiggling his eyebrows at her, loving the flush that flooded her cheeks.

"Stop. We can't. Abby is just down the hall," she said, pulling back.

"Yes. Asleep."

"I know. I just don't think it's a good idea," she said.

"That's fine. We'll cuddle until you change your mind," he said.

She laughed. "So sure of yourself, are you?"

"It's called confidence."

"Sure. Sure. Thanks again for coming over tonight. You do love a good rescue," she said, before pressing a kiss to his cheek.

"Stop that. We're just cuddling," he admonished, grinning at her.

"Right, cuddling." She rested her head on his shoulder. "This is nice."

"Mmhmm," he murmured, running his fingers down her arm. She shuddered under his touch and he bit back his grin. "We could watch a movie. Something funny with no reptiles."

She pulled back, looking up at him. "Just had to throw that in there, didn't you?"

He chuckled, grabbing the remote and flipping through the channels.

They decided on an old comedy and he sunk deeper into the couch, her arm resting on his chest.

Halfway through the movie, he heard her soft snores. He pulled her into his lap, brushing a kiss across her brow and let her sleep until the final credits rolled.

He stood up, Lexi still in his arms, and carried her into her bedroom. He lowered her to the bed, sitting down on the edge. She stirred when he pulled a blanket over her.

"Crap. I fell asleep, didn't I?" she asked, pushing her hair from her face. Her cheeks flushed from sleep. "I'm terrible company."

"I had your snores to keep me entertained," he said, then gasped when she elbowed him in the gut.

"I do not snore."

"So violent. And it's cute. More of a whistle than a snore."

"So not funny," she protested.

"It's adorable," he said, brushing a kiss across her lips. He hadn't really kissed her in over a week, and he craved her taste.

She wrapped her arms around his neck, pulling him into the kiss, and he pressed closer with a groan.

His tongue traced the seam of her lips, sinking in to tangle with hers, swallowing her soft moan.

He shifted on top of her, their bodies perfectly aligned. She sunk her fingers into his hair, holding his body to hers, her curves molding around him. He shifted his weight to one hand while the other skated up her hip and to the outside of her breast. He wanted to strip her bare and sink into her heat more than taking his next breath.

She broke the kiss, pressing her forehead to his. "Grant, we have to stop," she whispered, her voice strained with a need that echoed his.

"Why?" he groaned, rocking his erection against her lower body.

"Abby…"

"Is asleep."

"We can't."

He rolled off of her, lying beside her, watching her chest rise and fall as rapidly as his currently was. She wanted him just as much as he wanted her. It was clear.

"I'm sorry, but you should go. I can't have Abby see you here in the morning. It would be confusing, and I just can't…"she trailed off.

He shifted onto his arm, facing her. Her eyes were filled with too many emotions to name, saddness being one of them, and he hated that. "I understand." He pressed a final kiss to her lips, pulling her into his arms one last time. "Thanks for dinner."

"Thanks for moving that damn tree." Her chuckle was watery.

"Any time," he said, shifting off the bed. "I had fun tonight, and you make a pretty good chicken parm."

"Better than your mom's?" she asked, scooting off the bed to stand next to him.

"Umm."

She laughed. "I'm kidding. I know I can't compete with the your mom's food."

"It was really good. Promise," he said, loving the sparkle in her eyes. The sadness from moments ago, gone.

He kissed her one last time, molding his lips to hers and leaving them both breathless, before pulling away. "Call if you need anything. I'm up for any type of rescue. Tree, date, reptile." He laughed when she shuddered at the last one.

"Good to know."

"Night, Lexi."

"Night."

He headed home, wondering when he'd hear from her again, and hating the fact that in a month he'd be on the other side of the country, unable to drop everything to rescue her. He never should've gotten in so deep, but now that he had, he'd stretch this out for as long as he could.

Chapter 16

"Good morning, sleepyhead." Lips brushed across her brow, and Lexi burrowed deeper into the warmth, ignoring the headache between her eyes.

"Ugh. No talking," she muttered against his shaking chest. "And stop shaking the bed with your overbearing laughter." Which only caused him to laugh more. "You know, it's not nice to make fun of the ill."

"Man, how much did you drink last night?"

She lifted her head, slowly, taking in his scruff and that dimple. Stupid dimple. She hated that thing. Such a lie. She really loved it.

"It was Penny's bachelorette party, and we took a car service, so drinking was a requirement. Of course, it didn't help that Amanda made Penny wear a veil. So many free shots just because of a damn slip of lace," she groaned. "Wait. What are you doing here?"

He shifted around, grabbing his cell and swiping the screen on. She glanced at the string of texts that included:

Hi. You up?

I totally drank too much and I'm going to be hungover in the morning. I need the hangover cure in your pants.

I want your cake.

She dropped her head to his chest. "Shit. That's not embarrassing at all."

"And then you called a few times until I picked up."

"Oh God. I'm never drinking again." Her words were muffled against his shaking chest. She tweaked his nipple, smiling against him as he grunted. "It's not funny."

"Come on. It's pretty funny."

"You should've just ignored me. I would've passed out quickly."

"I couldn't have you passing out naked and waiting for me. What kind of guy do you think I am?"

"Sorry for the booty call. Did you get any booty?" she asked, lifting her pounding head.

"Seriously? We need to reevaluate what kind of guy you think I am. You know I prefer you sober." He tilted her head up, giving her his best panty-melting smile, which totally would've worked had she been wearing panties, or anything for that matter. What the hell had she done last night? Her memory was fuzzy—stupid veil.

"So why are we naked then?"

"Because I like naked spooning. Don't worry. I didn't take advantage of you in your drunken state." He ran his hand along her bare arm.

Every trip across her skin shot bolts of desire through her, making her forget about her headache.

"I'm so sorry I made an ass out of myself," she grumbled, feeling his damn chuckles underneath her again.

"You didn't make an ass out of yourself. As soon as I got here, you mentioned something about dessert finally showing up, which apparently translated to making out against the front door. Then as soon as you got your hands in my pants, you passed out against me. Not sure how to take that, actually."

259

Oh hell. She was burning Penny's veil. That thing was a menace. "Oh God," she muttered, dropping her head back down to his chest. "I'm so sorry. There was a veil and free shots and, and, I'm going to kill Amanda."

"It's fine. Not that I would've let it go much further. I prefer you sober, remember?" He ran his hand down her spine, and she looked back up at him, giving him a small smile.

"Yeah. I don't know what got into me last night. And you didn't need to be so forthcoming in your description of my behavior last night. A little mystery never killed anyone," she said.

"Just being honest. And since you are now awake and sober…wait. You are sober, right?"

"I think so," she said, slowly.

"I do know the best way to cure a hangover." He rocked his body against hers, his hard erection pressing into her lower belly.

She shuddered against him. "It's always about sex with you," she laughed, looking up and catching his gaze.

His eyes held complete sincerity. "It's never just sex with you."

She stopped breathing, her heart in her throat. Dammit. Why did he have to say shit like that to her? She fused her lips to his to stop him from saying anything else that might damage her heart more.

"I could do this forever," Grant said with a groan an hour later as he rolled off her and pulled her shuddering body into his side.

She tried to ignore his words, and the meaning—that she refused to acknowledge—behind them. They were said in a moment of post-orgasmic bliss and meant nothing. They had to mean nothing. But even she knew that it wasn't just sex anymore. He'd made love to her. It felt different. When had it become more than just mind-blowing sex?

She burrowed her head into his chest, inhaling his spicy, warm scent, wishing she could stay there forever. But she couldn't, and with each day, the strings tightened. He was going to break her heart, and she was powerless to stop it.

"Hey, what's going on?" he asked, shifting her to face him, clear concern and question in his gaze, while his hand roved up and down her spine.

She shoved away the heat spiraling through her belly at his gentle touch. "Nothing. I should probably get up."

"I thought we could have breakfast. I know Abby is with your parents until later."

He brushed a kiss across her brow and she relished the affection. Just one more minute of...no. This had become way more than just scratching an itch, but she'd ignored her brain's warnings because he was so good at itch scratching.

"Umm. It's getting late, and I should probably get Abby." *You know, before I confess how much I would love to stay right here. In bed. Forever.*

"Are you sure everything is okay?" He tipped his head to the side, focusing on her face.

"Yep. Never better, thanks to your headache cure." She ran her hand down his firm belly. *Focus on the physical.*

She couldn't describe the look that passed over his eyes. One part desire, as she reached her target, and the other…

The other—she couldn't focus on the other.

"You know you can talk to me about anything, right?" he asked, clearly not believing her flippant remark.

Her phone dinged across the room and she jumped out of bed to grab it, welcoming any distraction.

"Hey, Amanda. How's Penny this morning?" she asked. She had a vague recollection of Penny falling last night, but the bachelorette had brushed it off and said she was fine.

"You busy?"

Lexi looked over at Grant, the sheet pooled at his waist, his ridiculously toned chest begging her to crawl back into bed with him.

"Nope," she said.

"So, Penny apparently dislocated her kneecap last night," Amanda blurted out.

"I'm sorry. What?"

"Guess that spill was worse than she thought. We're finishing up at the emergency room, and heading back to my place."

"Holy crap. She said she was fine."

"I'm still trying to get everything out of her, but she's not fine. Something happened with Michael. Can you come over? I know you probably have Abby, but Penny needs both of us."

"That doesn't sound good. And Abby's still with my parents, so I'll be right over. Do you need me to grab anything?" Lexi asked. Amanda's voice lacked her normal humor. Lexi walked into her closet, grabbing her clothes. She'd wanted an out this morning, but not this way.

"I think she's good on booze for now, but chocolate never hurt anyone." Amanda's bark of laughter held pain, and Lexi could only imagine what Michael had done. She'd string him up by his balls if necessary.

"I'm on my way," Lexi said, before hanging up and yanking on a pair of yoga pants. It sounded like a comfy clothes day.

"Is everything okay?" Grant asked, rising from the bed, the sheet dipping further down his body. Now was not the time to thank gravity. *Focus.* Hell, Penny was in pain and Lexi was thinking about bedsheets hitting the floor. She was a shitty friend.

"I have to go. Penny apparently dislocated her kneecap when she fell last night," she said, walking into her bathroom to brush her teeth.

"Ouch. Is she okay?" His voice sounded closer. *Please be wearing pants. Please be wearing pants.*

"Hopefully. Sorry, but no brunch today," she said, ignoring the heat spiraling through her as he wrapped his arms around her waist, and pressed a kiss to her nape.

"Don't worry about it. We can have brunch another time. During the next sleepover."

"You planning a lot of sleepovers?"

"As many as I can get before I leave," he said.

It was like dumping a bucket of ice water over her heated skin. She pulled free from his arms. "I really have to go."

"I know," he said, spinning her in his arms, pressing a kiss to her lips. At least he was clothed.

"Sorry again about last night."

"Don't worry about it. Text me to let me know if Penny needs anything. Or if you need anything." Why did he have to be so damn considerate?

She rushed around, grabbing a few items, while ignoring the sounds of Grant getting dressed.

"Tell Penny I hope she's okay," he said, slipping on his jacket, his disheveled hair begging for her fingers. She ignored that flutter in her belly. That flutter was a pain in her ass.

"Thanks," she muttered, shutting the front door behind them and walking to her car.

He pulled her against his body, the cold car at her back, his heat seeping in through her front. He pressed a hard kiss to her lips, and she melted against him. The shiver had nothing to do with the cold morning air and everything to do with him.

She pulled free. Dammit. She needed some control around him.

"Next time, I promise breakfast in bed," he murmured against her lips. "Call if you need anything."

She just nodded as he pressed one last kiss to the tip of her nose and then got in his car. She slipped into her car, warming it up, and watched him drive away. As she drove to Penny's, her only thoughts were of Grant and how it had gotten to this point. Her heart was doomed, and she was powerless to stop it.

* * *

"I will string him up by his balls," Lexi bit out.

"I'm running him over first," Amanda said with pure rage, that probably mirrored Lexi's, in her eyes.

Lexi had arrived at Amanda's less than an hour ago, and after chocolate was distributed and Ben and Jerry had made an appearance, Lexi finally heard the story that Amanda had dragged out of Penny this morning. That rat bastard, scum-sucking fiancé had cheated on her. With his boss. What a fucking cliché. Lexi knew something hadn't been right with Michael.

"What am I going to do? I can't marry him," Penny cried, absentmindedly rubbing her knee that was currently incased in a large brace.

"Of course you're not, especially since he won't be around after I murder him. No, first I'm going to cut off his balls and shove them down his throat. Then I'm going to murder him," Amanda said. The gleam in her eyes said she'd enjoy it, too. Lexi was a little nervous about her friend's clear bloodlust. Not that the bastard didn't deserve it.

"How did this happen? I mean, were there signs I missed? Seven years. I gave that man seven years, and now this. How long has he been cheating? How did I miss it? We freaking live together. I mean, I know I'm busy with work, trying to land that promotion, and planning the wedding. Maybe we haven't spent enough time together, but—"

Lexi grabbed Penny's hand, halting the stream of pain she was all too familiar with. "Now, you listen to me. This is not your fault. Yes, you may have been preoccupied recently, but that never excuses cheating. In fact, nothing excuses cheating. That heartless dick doesn't deserve you. You could do so much better."

Penny gave her a weak smile. "Thanks. It's just that the wedding is next weekend. Oh God, my mother is going to *freak*. All those guests. And all the money my parents spent. And the gifts I now have to return. And—"

"Okay, stop," Amanda said, wrapping her arm around Penny. "Take a deep breath. Or five."

Lexi hated herself for not saying anything whenever Penny talked about Michael always working late and not showing any interest in the wedding, but she'd wanted to believe that Penny could have the happily ever after. One of them had to.

"We're going to sit here and enjoy some ice cream, and then you can call your parents. If they get too overbearing, I'll take the phone," Lexi said, pushing the bowl of Fudge Brownie Batter toward Penny.

"Thanks. You guys are the best. And I guess I can eat all the ice cream in the world since I won't be squeezing into a wedding gown next weekend," Penny said through the tears that had started to gush. "This fucking sucks," she cried.

"Yes it does," Lexi echoed, hating the pain in her friend's eyes and knowing that whatever happened, it wasn't going to be easy.

* * *

A few hours later, full of cookie dough and brownie ice cream, Penny phoned her parents and called off her wedding. Lexi was pissed that Penny's parents had balked, telling her that these things happen and not to be hasty. Unfucking-believable.

Lexi was also almost positive that she and Amanda had convinced Penny to go on her honeymoon to Italy in ten days just to get away from everything. The trip was nonrefundable and Lexi would've gone with her if she didn't have Abby.

"How do you get through this?" Penny asked, looking directly at Lexi. "I mean, how did you pick yourself back up after Joe?"

"It took a while, and I'm not going to lie, it totally sucked, but I had you guys and Abby. Just take it one day at a time and eventually the pain will diminish, and you'll get to the point where you can move on, and trust someone," she said, honestly.

"Like you're doing now? With Grant?" Penny asked.

"It's true. I haven't seen you happier," Amanda said.

"Grant's great. But he's not forever. Just fun until he leaves."

"Is that what you tell yourself?" Amanda asked.

"Hey, it's not about me today. We're here for Penny." And she really didn't want to talk about Grant.

"I don't want to talk about me anymore. I want to talk about you," Penny said, sitting up, focusing her attention on Lexi.

Damn. This was so not the topic she wanted to talk about. She was having enough fun internally dwelling on it on her own.

"Fine. It sucks. Not nearly as badly as what you're going through, but I don't know what to do. He's leaving soon, and as much as I know I have to end it, I just can't." Lexi let out a soft snort. "Guess Amanda will have to put up with both of us being depressed for the foreseeable future."

"You don't have to end it, you know," Amanda said.

"Yes I do. He's moving to Florida next month, and I'm not going with him, not that he's asked."

"But what if he did ask?" Penny asked.

"I'm not moving. You guys know how I feel about this. I'm not uprooting Abby. My parents did that to me so many times. It sucks making new friends every few years. And Grant said he might not retire in four years. Then where would we be? Moving again? I'm not doing that," she said, plopping back against the couch and wishing her ice cream bowl wasn't empty.

"I thought you said he had four years left and then he was coming back here?" Penny asked.

"That's what I thought, but he loves his job, and he said he wasn't sure if he would actually retire in four years or not. I can't take that gamble."

"Have you talked to him about it?" Amanda asked.

"No."

"Why not?" Penny asked.

"Because I'm clearly a glutton for punishment," she mumbled. "I should just cut ties now. I can't ask him to stay, and I'm not leaving. And I don't want him to leave a job he loves just because of me. That's not fair," she said, hating the sadness in their eyes.

"You should try long distance," Amanda said.

"Yeah right. Long distance isn't easy for anyone, and I have Abby to think about, too," she said, wishing for once that she didn't have to be the voice of reason. Wishing she could just follow her reckless heart.

"Talk to him. I saw how he was with you at the bar. It's not just sex for either of you," Penny said, squeezing her hand.

"Ugh. Enough of this. Can we just say that today sucks and watch a movie before I have to get Abby?" she asked.

Amanda plopped down between Lexi and Penny, wrapping her arms around their shoulders and pulling them in. "Men suck, but at least we have each other," she said, a small smile on her face.

"Weight room in ten?" Matt called out to Grant.

Grant nodded, finishing up some final repairs to his gear. He was the back-up swimmer tonight so he wanted to make sure everything was patched and ready just in case. He didn't mind the sewing they were required to do. Not that he'd tell Lily that, or she'd probably sign him up to help make costumes or something at the kids' school.

He finished up and made his way to the gym. He was on a practice flight in less than two hours so he'd have to rush through his workout.

"Come on, man. You can do more than that." Matt was ribbing Tyler across the room, trying to add another fifty pounds to what Tyler was already lifting.

"Like you could lift this, old man," Tyler said with a pained grin as he dropped the bar back into place.

269

"Who you calling old? I'm in my prime," Matt boasted, adding more weight to his own bar. The idiot was going to regret that, but Grant kept his mouth shut and grabbed a few free weights of his own, settling on the bench next to Matt.

"Need me to spot you?" Grant asked after Matt let out a few labored grunts.

Matt grinned—it was a pained grin—and kept lifting. He huffed. "Nah. I've got this."

"Sure you do."

"Bet I could out-lift you."

Grant shook his head. "Not even going there. We have a flight in less than two hours, so try not to kill yourself."

Matt dropped the bar back into place and sat up. "You know you're going to miss us when you leave."

"Maybe."

That was the one part that sucked, but it was the nature of the job. You learned to trust and rely on each other, and when it was good, you became a family, but people were always moving in and out of that family and then four years went by, and you were moving on again. He'd done it so many times, and he was used to it, but this time was different. He'd been home for four years and it sucked to leave. For many reasons.

Lexi. He wasn't ready to give her up, but he had no clue how to keep her. She'd been off last weekend, and he'd felt the difference, almost as if she'd been pushing him away before Amanda had called.

"Damn. I'll have to find a new wingman. Tyler's not ready yet," Matt said.

Grant laughed. "He needs a little help with his game, but he shouldn't get his tips from you, or he'll always strike out. Maybe I should've taken him under my wing."

Matt let out a bark of laughter. "Right. You're not even trying. You've got a steady lay. And I've got great game."

"Going to match meet-ups just looking to score is probably not what eMatch intended."

"Say what you will, but I've had no complaints."

"Why? Because you're out the door before they wake up?"

Matt smirked. "That's harsh, man. Sometimes I stay in the hopes that they'll make me breakfast in the morning."

"Not helping your cause."

"And you should be thanking me. Without my meet-ups, you never would've met Lexi, and I believe you are still enjoying those benefits." Matt wiggled his eyebrows. Grant couldn't stop the anger that rolled through him.

"Don't talk about her like that," he bit out.

"Whoa. Sorry, man. You are totally hung up on her. You know you're leaving in three weeks, right? How did you think this was going to play out?"

"I don't know," Grant said, focusing on the weight in his hands.

"She still calling you every time she has a bad date?"

"Yeah." Wait. She hadn't had a date in a while. "Actually, I haven't had to rescue her in weeks."

271

"Maybe she's figured out this dating thing on her own."

"No. I don't think she's had any dates." He tried to remember his last rescue. It'd been more than a month ago when he'd punched her date. She'd been so shaken by his behavior. Had she stopped calling him to rescue her because of that? No. He was almost positive she'd mentioned not having any dates the last time they'd talked. And it hadn't come up again this past weekend.

"Hey, where'd you go?" Matt asked, pulling Grant from his runaway thoughts.

"I don't think she's dated anyone in over a month," he said.

"Well shit, bet she's as hung up on you as you are on her," Matt said, grinning.

"It doesn't matter since I'm leaving."

"I can't believe I'm going to say this, but maybe you should talk to her about your feelings."

Grant chuckled. "Wait. Are you talking about feelings? Who are you, and what did you do with Manwhore Matt?"

"Hey, I resent that." Matt tried to sound offended, but his laughter gave him away.

"What part?"

"Both. Not that I can believe those words just came out of my mouth, but have you tried to talk to her? You like her more than just a hook-up. Even I noticed that."

"I don't know. She's got Abby, and I know she wouldn't move. I've got at least four years left, on the other side of the country, starting next month."

"It's a shit situation, but would it hurt to ask? Yeah, you've only known her for a few months, but you should know what's going on between the two of you before you leave. How'd you see this thing ending, anyway?"

"Honestly, I've avoided thinking about it," he said. That was a total lie, and judging by Matt's expression, his friend didn't believe him for a second. Grant had spent a lot of time thinking about what happened when his time with Lexi was up.

"Just talk to her. You'll regret it if you don't," he said, sounding like he spoke from experience.

"Thanks, man," he said.

"Now don't get all emotional on me. We've got a workout to finish and a training flight," Matt said, then grabbed another set of weights.

Grant chuckled and moved onto another machine. It was sad when love-em-or-leave-em Matt was giving out relationship advice that made sense. He should just ask Lexi out and clear everything up now.

Chapter 17

Grant eyed the tiramisu on the counter and swiped his phone on knowing he should probably wait for her to contact him.

Grant: What are you up to tonight?

Lexi: Nothing much.

Grant: So a little bird told me that you might be lonely tonight.

He could've worked up to that, but dove right in instead. Patience wasn't his strong suit.

Lexi: Oh really?

Grant: Are you up for some cake?

Lexi: Literal or figurative cake?

Grant: Both. Well, tiramisu. My mom dropped off another one yesterday.

Lexi: I could definitely go for dessert.

Lexi: My place or yours?

Grant: Nice to know that the way into your pants is paved with my mom's dessert.

Grant: Okay. That sounded way creepier than I intended.

Lexi: LOL. Slightly creepy, but I'll forgive you.

Grant: How generous of you, even if I know you're just in it for the dessert.

Lexi: I'll be there in twenty.

Grant: See you soon.

Grant ignored how fast he'd jumped up from the couch and inspected his house. He hadn't planned on

274

company, but he pushed a few boxes into the corner and set out a couple wine glasses next to the dessert. He refused to feel pathetic for texting that he missed her earlier today and then texting again tonight. Every time he looked at the dessert his mom had dropped off yesterday, his only thought was to see if Lexi wanted to come over. She might've ruined him for future dessert. Would he ever eat another lava cake without tasting her in each bite? That was a damn crime in itself.

Twenty minutes later he heard her knock, and he wrenched open the door.

"Hi," she said, her grin wide as she walked into his house. A wavy strand of auburn hair rested on her cheek. She was beautiful.

"Hi."

"So a little bird told you I was home alone?" she asked, her eyes sparkling.

"Yes. It's Keira's first sleepover. Abby's too?" he asked.

"Yep."

"How are you holding up?" he asked.

"Aside from secretly hoping that she calls me to pick her up early and hoping that she doesn't? I'm totally fine. And an awful mother," she said, her shoulders shaking with laughter.

"She'll be fine. I bet my mother is over there getting in on all the fun and filling them with dessert."

"Speaking of," she started, peeking around his body and looking into the kitchen. "There it is."

He chuckled. "I swear, you're only here for my dessert." He pulled her close, pressing a hard kiss to her lips that left both of them panting when he finally let her go.

"Totally not true," she said, her voice breathless. "I'm here for more than just dessert."

He pressed her against the front door that he'd just shut behind them. "I missed you," he said, wrapping his arms around her waist and pulling her tight against him, nipping kisses along her jaw, feeling her pulse race beneath his mouth.

"Missed you, too," she said, cupping his face and fusing her lips with his.

Her tongue darted out, tracing his lips, and he opened, tangling his tongue with hers, swallowing her moan, and rocking his hard body against her soft curves.

She clutched his shirt, and he cupped her jaw, holding her, consuming her mouth.

Her hands trailed down his shirt snaking underneath, and scraped her nails along his chest. He hardened more, if that was possible, at her touch, his stomach muscles clenching under her fingers.

He hadn't kissed her in what felt like ages, even if it had only been a week. He sucked on her lower lip, her hot breath coming in pants as she cupped him, scraping her nail over his fly. His cock hardened to the point of pain, and he needed to get them both naked now.

She broke free of the kiss and dropped to her knees. He stared down at her, his chest heaving as she smiled at him, slowly lowering his zipper, inch by torturous inch, her hand slipping inside his boxers, cupping his cock.

"I thought you wanted dessert," he bit out while she stroked him.

"I do," she said, shoving his jeans and boxers off of his hips, and licking the tip.

He fisted his hands at his sides, trying to resist the urge to sink his fingers into her hair and guide her exactly how he wanted her.

His entire body clenched as she drew his cock into her mouth, her warm heat enveloping him. She pulled back until just the tip was in her mouth, applying the lightest suction before she took him into the back of her throat, swallowing around his cock. His entire body shuddered.

"Holy shit. Yes," he groaned, his head tilted back against the door, his eyes drifting shut.

She bobbed up and down, making a soft humming noise that vibrated right through him.

Hell. He was close. It was almost embarrassing how fast she could get him to his breaking point. He squeezed her shoulder, letting her know that he was almost there. She pulled back, sucking on the tip, before taking him fully into her mouth again. He came with a groan, his body shaking as she finished up her torment.

She sat back on her heels, her cheeks flushed, a grin on her lips.

He slid down the door, ignoring the cold tile under his ass, his body not wanting to move or hold him upright.

"Now I'm ready for that tiramisu," she said, her eyes twinkling.

He let out a soft laugh. "You might be the death of me," he said, reaching up and twisting an auburn wave around his finger, pulling her close. "But what a way to go."

She laughed. "I aim to please."

"Your aim is perfect," he whispered against her cheek.

He tucked himself back into his jeans and stood up, pulling her along with him. She fell against his chest with a soft laugh, and he pulled her tighter into his body, tilting her head up and pressing a hard kiss to her lips.

Her fingers tangled in his hair, holding him locked to her, their lips sealed.

They were both panting when she finally pulled away.

"Stop distracting me. I want that dessert," she demanded, her cheeks and neck flushed pink.

"You're the distraction," he groaned, pressing his forehead to hers.

"Maybe we could bring it to bed."

"As much as I'd love to dot the creamy filling all over your body and lick you clean, I don't think I'd be able to look my mother in the face again," he said, chuckling.

She sucked in a hard breath. "Well, that wasn't what I intended, but now that you mention it, that would be both hot and weird. We'll eat fast," she said, pulling him into the kitchen and slicing up the dessert.

"Oh my God. Why is it so amazing?" she moaned, taking her first bite. He refused to think that her flush of excitement was due to the dessert and not the fact that she was currently perched on his lap.

"I'm jealous of a dessert," he said, grinning and taking the forkful she offered. "Always the best."

"Aren't you going to miss this when you leave?" she asked, taking another bite.

She stiffened in his lap, the silence awkward.

"Guess I'll have to visit as much as possible," he said, shoving another bite in his mouth before he could beg her to come with him. He'd mulled it over for the last week, wondering how insane it would be to ask her to think about moving with him. The school year was ending in a few weeks. No. It was crazy. They'd known each other less than six months, but he wanted to ask.

They finished their dessert without much conversation, kissing in between bites. Thoughts of Florida and Lexi in a bikini top left his mind as he focused on the here and now. As much as he hated it, this might be all the time they had left, and he was going to enjoy every second of it. His heart be damned.

She was such an idiot. Why did she have to bring up his leaving and make it awkward? She'd spotted the half-packed boxes when they'd entered his living room but she'd pushed those cardboard squares of doom from her mind and focused on attacking him against his door, like she was a starved animal. His groans had filled her head, blocking out all thoughts of him leaving.

But she'd brought it up again. Seriously. Enjoy the moment. Now was not the time to be sad. There was plenty of time for that next month.

"You okay?" he asked, pressing a kiss to her nose.

"Never better," she said, placing her empty plate on the kitchen island and wrapping her arms around his neck. "I think I'm ready for my second dessert," she whispered, rocking her hips against him.

"Me too," he said, scooting the barstool back. He wrapped one arm around her waist and the other under her knees and stood, holding her close to his chest.

Her hand immediately went to his chest, and his heart raced under her palm.

The fact that he carried her down the hallway, in his arms, without a hitch in his breath, was still hot as hell. Okay, maybe just one hitch, but that was probably because she'd scraped her nails against his chest.

He dropped her to the bed, and she scooted back, reaching for the bedside lamp. She wanted to see every touch, gaze on every part of his body, and push away the thought that this could be the last time.

She took in a shuddering breath. She would not think like that. She would relish the moment and focus on his glittering eyes as they raked over her body, causing desire to pool low in her belly. She'd never wanted anyone as much as she wanted him. *Needed* him.

Their clothes were yanked off in a hurry, and she bit back her giggle as he hopped on one foot, removing a sock. Her giggle died in her throat when he stood up and shoved his pants and boxers off. Even though she'd just had him in her mouth, and it's not like she'd never seen him naked before, he was still glorious sans clothes. And in clothes, for that matter, but without...holy hell, yes please.

"Why do you still have clothes on?" he asked, his eyes skating over her bra and panties.

"Just admiring the view," she admitted, knowing her cheeks were a brilliant shade of red at her honesty.

"Me too, but at least I can multi-task." He stalked toward the bed with a predatory gleam in his eye that sent a shiver to her toes. He leaned over her, yanking her panties down her legs as she rushed to unclasp her bra, leaving her as naked as he was.

He ran a finger down her chest to her belly, and she took in a shuddering breath.

"Lexi," he whispered, his head descended and his tongue darted out, tracing around her nipple but never touching the exact center.

So it was torture he planned tonight. She shifted her hips against his belly, rubbing her core against the soft dusting of hair on his stomach.

He groaned against her breast before drawing the tip in his mouth.

She fisted her hands in his hair, holding him to her as he ravaged her body, a moan slipping from her lips, with a soft "yes."

He released her with a pop, paying homage to her other breast before spreading kisses down her chest and over her belly.

Her back arched off the bed, her eyes drifting shut as he worshiped her. No inch of skin left untouched, until she was gasping his name and begging him to get inside her. His tongue traced her lower lips before zeroing in on her clit, all attention focused on that little nub of desire. And then she was crashing around him, her orgasm singing through her body.

He kissed back up her body, then sealed his lips with hers.

Her fingers sunk into his hair, holding him close to her as their tongues tangled, inhaling each other's moans.

He pulled back, nibbling on her lower lip, and she opened her eyes. Only the thinnest ring of chocolate remained, his pupils dilated with desire. One that matched her own, even if she was still recovering from her last orgasm.

"So beautiful," he whispered against her mouth, his hands cupping her face like she was a treasure.

"You're not so bad yourself," she said with a husky chuckle.

He grinned at her before dropping a kiss on her nose, then with lightning fast reflexes, he flipped them over so she was on top.

She gasped. "You trying to give me whiplash?"

"Nope. Just prefer the view of you over me," he said, his tone serious.

Her heart stalled in her throat, watching him stare at her. His pure need evident in his gaze and pressing against her core. She wanted him inside of her. She reached down, stroking his hard length, feeling the power she had over him as he shuddered.

His hands skimmed up her belly, her core clenching, and he cupped her breasts, his thumbnails scraping across her nipples, the pebbled points begging for his touch, his mouth, anything he would give her.

She leaned over him, pressing her lips to his, tangling her tongue with his, her hair shielding them from everything, including the boxes in the corner. *No.* She focused on him, on his lips, his warm and spicy smell as his hands cupped her face again, ravaging her mouth. She rocked against him, his cock slipping through her wet fold, her moan swallowed by his kiss.

She pulled back. "I need you," she whispered. More than she cared to admit out loud.

His eyes glittered under the lamp light, his cheeks flush, his lips wet from her kiss. She paused a minute, taking him in, committing him to memory. Who was she kidding? He was burned in her brain and, unfortunately, in her heart. Shit. She couldn't love him. It was too soon. Too messy.

"Are you okay?" he asked, running a finger down her arm, linking his hand with hers and tugging her down until she was pressed to his chest, his lips barely an inch from hers. His erection pulsed between them, and she needed him inside her. Maybe he could screw away her fears. The thoughts she didn't want to think about. There was plenty of time later for those thoughts.

"I will be once you're inside me," she said, focusing purely on the physical. The sex she could handle. The rest...

"Are you sure?" he asked, clear question, with a touch of concern, in his eyes.

"Of course," she said, pulling back and grabbing the condom next to the pillow. She stroked his cock twice before rolling the latex down his hard length.

He groaned as she lightly squeezed him.

Lifting her hips, she slowly sank down on his cock until he was seated to the hilt, their groans intermingling when her body was flush with his. Her hands skated up his body, gripping his chest. She raised her hips before sinking down on him, her core squeezing with each downward motion, his hard cock filling her.

He linked his hands with hers, bringing her down for a kiss, before pushing her back up, his muscles flexing as he moved her. Holy hell, his strength amazed her and turned her on more than she thought was possible.

She rocked against him, her clit rubbing against his pelvis, the friction causing every nerve in her body to center on her core. She gasped, moving against him, searching for her release as he continued to hold her upright and lift his hips.

"You feel amazing," he groaned, pulling her down to his chest, his chest hair scraping against her over-sensitized nipples.

"Oh yes," she moaned. "Don't stop."

"Wasn't planning to," he gritted out, grabbing her ass and plunging in and out of her body, her core clenching around his cock, wanting him to stay put right where she desperately needed him.

She leaned back, her hands on his thighs, her eyes focused on their connection. He released his hold on her ass, his hand snaking around, his thumb narrowing in on her clit, pressing tight circles on the nub and driving her breath from her body as she moaned.

"Oh, God, yes." She squeezed her inner muscles, her walls clamping around his cock.

"Yes," he echoed, the words harsh with need.

Her eyes locked with his, her belly shaking with her impending release.

"Touch yourself," he growled.

Her breath in her throat, her hands skated up her belly, cupping her breasts, tweaking her nipples as he continued tormenting her clit and rocking in and out of her body. She was so blissfully close to falling over the edge, but she wanted him right there with her.

"Are you close?" she asked, her gaze never leaving his, the depth of his need shaking her.

"Yes," he grunted, the circles he was making on her clit speeding up with every thrust of his cock inside her.

"Oh yes," she shouted as her orgasm took over, heat spiraling from her core to every point in her body.

He followed with a loud groan, moments later, and she crashed to his chest, her body a boneless quivering mass. He pressed kisses in her hair, and ran his hand down her spine while they both tried catching their breath. She would never get enough of him.

"I can't get enough of you," he echoed, his whisper skimming over her ear.

She snuggled into his body, unable to move a muscle, his soothing touch lulling her to a blissful sleep.

Chapter 18

His stomach clenched as she let out a soft moan and snuggled deeper against him. The sunlight was streaming in through the window. He hated to wake her, but he had no idea what time she had to pick up Abby today. Not that he was ready to let her go. If she could stay in his bed, in his arms forever, he wouldn't say no. He was definitely in far deeper than he'd intended. This thought should send his heart racing with panic, but it no longer did. He just wasn't sure what to do at this point. Asking her to move to Florida in three weeks was drastic, but he also knew that he wasn't ready to let her go.

"Lexi," he said, running his hand down her side.

She shifted against him, squirming away from his touch. "You're so mean. I was sleeping and you tickle me?" she grumbled, twisting around and glaring at him.

"Sorry." She was adorable when she was sleep-angry, with her hair mussed, and her cheeks flushed.

"How would you like it if I did that to you?" she asked, clear annoyance in her tone.

"I'm not ticklish," he said.

"I don't believe you." She reached down, her nails scraping along his skin, trying to find a ticklish spot on his body, and when he started to harden against her, he repeated the mantra that he wasn't ticklish. Worked every time Keira or Nathan had tried to get him to squirm.

He tightened his arms around her, halting her attempt at torment. "Told you."

She huffed. "Fine. I'd ask why you woke me, but I think I can feel the why against me."

He rolled her over, settling on top of her. "You *think* you can feel that," he growled.

She giggled. "Men are so easy."

He ducked his head into the curve where her shoulder and neck met, nibbling behind her ear, and she shuddered against him.

"You're insatiable," she said.

"It's just you. I wish we could stay here forever," he said.

She stiffened against him. "Me too." He couldn't ignore the wishful tone in her voice, and it gave him hope.

"What time do you have to pick up Abby?" he asked.

She glanced at his alarm clock and sighed. "In a few hours."

"Great. Are you busy Sunday?" he asked.

"I have Abby."

"Family-friendly fun," he started.

"Grant, I don't know if that's a good idea. She's getting too used to you, and you're leaving soon," she said.

Hello, elephant. Nice to see you. He figured saying "Come to Florida, I think I love you," was a bad idea. He paused at that thought. *Love.* Was that what this was? He was pretty sure he already knew the answer to that, but she wasn't ready to hear it.

"It's the last playoff game and, win or lose, we are going to Lanzi's to celebrate or commiserate. Keira and Nathan will be there. You'd keep Abby from her BFF?" he asked, trying to bring in some levity.

287

She chuckled. "Nice guilt trip. That's so not fair."

"Damn straight." He grinned at her. "So you'll come, right? Don't you want to see me play hockey? I've heard from multiple sources that women find it hot." He wiggled his eyebrows at her, and she pinched him. "Hey. Now who's not nice."

She glared. "I can't believe you just laid a guilt trip on me involving my kid and then followed it up by talking about your previous puck bunny conquests."

He let out a bark of laughter. "Not puck bunnies. This is a rec league. I don't think we even have puck bunnies. The other guys on the team mentioned it."

"Sure they did," she eyed him.

"And I've heard Lily go on and on about her favorite players. Just come. Have some fun. Maybe some tiramisu after."

"Now you're bribing me with dessert."

"I know what you really want," he said.

"Fine. But only so Abby can spend more time with her BFF."

She'd caved so easily. He laughed. "Sure. For Abby." She swatted his shoulder and he continued to chuckle, pulling her head back into the crook of his arm. He had some work to do on her, but definitely didn't have time for that today. He couldn't rush this, even if his days were numbered.

"Mom, that was so much fun," Abby said, her eyes shining and her cheeks red from the cold air as she bounced on the metal bleachers.

The game was over and Grant's team had won. She wasn't a hockey fan, or even a sports fan, but she'd listened to him talk about hockey, and he'd been unstoppable in his determination to win his final season with his friends. She refused to think of it as wrapping up loose ends, hating to think that maybe she was one of those loose ends, too.

Stupid over-analyzing train of thought. *Stop.*

Grant on the ice was something she couldn't describe. He'd held his own, showing complete ownership of the ice. And his skill...she'd already known he was good with his hands. Desire flooded her belly. Yes, it was that hot. She'd cringed every time he took a hit, even though the hits in a rec league were nothing compared to the NHL, or so he'd told her.

"Celebratory dessert and drinks at Lanzi's," Grant's step-father called out as everyone made their way out of the arena.

"Mom, we can go, right?" Abby asked, her eyes pleading.

"We should probably get home."

"Nonsense, dear," Rose said, sidling up next to Lexi. "It's still early, and you haven't had my tiramisu, have you?"

Lexi's mouth watered. She loved that freaking dessert and what usually happened after that. She felt the heat stain her cheeks. Having those thoughts around the woman who gave birth to him was so wrong.

"I've had it, and it's amazing," she said.

"You have?" Rose asked.

"Yes, I stopped by Lanzi's for dessert once."

"Right. With Grant." Lexi didn't miss the smile on Rose's face, and it wasn't so much of an, "I'm proud of my son" smile, but more of a knowing smile. Oh hell.

"Please, Mom," Abby pleaded again.

"Okay. But not for very long. Tomorrow is a school day," Lexi said. Luckily, Grant's team had played the game early, so it wasn't even seven yet.

"Yes," Abby exclaimed with a fist pump, and Lexi couldn't help but giggle.

"Great. Grant is meeting us there in a bit," Rose said, an unmistakable twinkle in her eyes.

Fantastic. Let the scrutiny begin.

* * *

A short while later, Lexi was settled into a booth next to Lily. Their kids had scampered off with Rose. Something about helping her with ravioli prep.

Lexi focused on the menu, even though she knew she would split the lasagna with Abby, and tried not to stare at the door waiting for Grant to walk in.

"You've been spending a lot of time with my brother," Lily said. Wow. Getting straight to the point.

Lexi slowly swallowed the bite of bread she'd just taken. "Ahh. Yes, but we're just friends." Her statement came out quickly.

Lily raised an eyebrow. Lexi should've just bundled Abby up into her car and gone home. Being surrounded by Grant's family was not a good idea, especially since she'd been grilled the last time she'd come in here by his cousin, and she had no idea what Grant had told them about their weird relationship.

Okay, "grilled" was the wrong word, but they'd definitely had their eye on her.

"Really? You know he's leaving soon, right?" Lily asked. There was no malice behind Lily's tone, just a friendly, yet stern, reminder.

Right. Like that knowledge didn't sit in her belly like a super-rich dessert, taunting her for enjoying something she knew she'd regret later. Not that she regretted any moment with Grant so far, but he was leaving in three short weeks. She should've ended it by now. Shouldn't have gotten in as deep as she was. But stopping it, cutting herself off from him was about as easy as giving up chocolate.

"Yes. I know, and we're just friends," Lexi repeated, schooling her emotions and wishing the kids would pop back up and lighten the mood.

"Just don't hurt him," Lily said, concern in her gaze.

"Grant," voices burst out before Lexi could reply.

Her eyes swung to the door as Grant stepped into the restaurant. His hair slicked back, still wet from his shower. A grin spread across his lips as he stalked toward her, his attention not on the well-wishers and back-slappers, but on her, a predator on a mission. She took in a deep breath, partly hoping he wasn't going to out them, but secretly craving his touch. He wouldn't. Oh shit, would he?

"I can't believe we finally won. That last goal. Man, it was beautiful," he said, stopping in front of her. His words coming out in a rush of pure happiness.

She didn't stop him when he gripped her hand, pulling her from the booth and wrapping his arms around her. His lips crashed on hers, and all the sounds in the room disappeared. An "oh shit" moment rocked through her before his entire being consumed her, and she could only focus on this unbelievably happy man kissing her, making her forget about the questions she'd have to answer once the kiss ended. Her hands clutched his shirt, holding him to her, an unconscious move that she'd regret.

After a few endless moments that were probably only a few seconds, he pulled away, a sheepish smile on his lips. "Shit," he said.

"Shit is right," she murmured back, trying not to smile or freak out. Who knew it was possible to hear a pin drop in a restaurant? She dreaded looking around.

"Mom, why is Mr. Parker kissing you again?" Abby asked, her voice clear and painstakingly loud.

Again. Crap. Crap. Crap. She ran through her mind every time Abby could've seen them kissing. She drew a blank. Shit. Had he kissed her during their hike with the kids? Or at the museum? Or…shit. How had they gotten to the point where that many options were available?

Grant squeezed her hands. "Stop panicking," he whispered.

"I'm not panicking," she bit out.

He had the audacity to chuckle. "I can see the wheels spinning. I got this."

Grant crouched down to Abby's level, and Lexi tried to ignore the squeeze on her heart.

"Your mom and I are just friends, Abby. I got a little excited about our win tonight and kissed her," he said.

"Yep. Just friends," Lexi echoed.

"Gross. Why would you kiss her? She yells at you," Nathan piped in.

Hell. One time. One freaking time. Her cheeks were probably a brilliant shade of red. She attempted to ignore the few awkward chuckles around the room, along with the curious expressions on everyone's faces, including her daughter. This is exactly what wasn't supposed to happen. No strings. It was supposed to be no damn strings, and now she was tied up like a freaking marionette.

"Nathan, really," Rose admonished her grandson, drawing more attention to their little circle.

"What? Kissing is gross, and Uncle Grant shouldn't kiss Abby's mom. She probably has cooties." Nathan crossed his arms over his chest and harrumphed, like he'd just stated a scientific fact.

"Nathan, I need your help in here," Grant's step-father called out from the kitchen. Lexi wanted to kiss that man, too, but it would probably outrage Nathan more.

"So. Just friends, huh?" Lily asked, her gaze darting between the both of them.

"Lily, be nice. I'm sure they both know what they are doing," Rose said.

"Thanks, Mom," Grant said.

"And we love Lexi and Abby, so you don't have to hide your relationship from us," Rose continued, her smile brilliant.

Lexi's heart plummeted, her stomach clenched into a ball. She wanted to take Abby and escape the endless looks and questions that she didn't have the answers to.

"So what are you going to do when he leaves? Long distance relationships work. Or maybe you're going to move?" Rose asked.

Black hole. Please, any time you want to open up.

"Ahh," Lexi stuttered, her gaze locked on Grant's, willing him to respond.

"I want to go to Florida. That's where Rapunzel is," Abby piped in. She'd plopped herself on the bench seat in the booth, next to Keira, and both girls were staring at her.

This was blowing up in her face. In front of her daughter. Her exact nightmare come to life.

She crouched down to her daughter's level. "Abby, honey. We can't go to Florida. We live here."

"I'd miss Grandma and Pop-Pop," Abby said.

"I know, honey. I just need to talk to Mr. Parker for a minute. Can you stay here with Keira?"

Abby nodded.

"Grant, can I speak with you privately?" she said, trying to remain calm as Rose and Lily looked at them, concern in their eyes.

"Sure." He squeezed her hand and pulled her down a hallway and into a small office.

She dropped his hand and whirled on him. "What the hell was that?"

"Look, I know that was bad," he started.

"Bad? You kissed me. In front of your family." She paced in front of him. This couldn't be happening.

294

He let out a small chuckle. "I know. I was there."

She swatted his shoulder. "Don't be cute about it. This is a nightmare, and Abby's seen you kiss me before, and your mom's questions about where this is going. It's going nowhere. It can't go anywhere, and we knew that from the beginning." *Oh hello, verbal diarrhea, thanks for making an appearance.*

He gripped both of her hands in his. "Lexi, calm down. We can figure this out."

"No. We can't. This went too far. You're leaving. I'm not. I have my daughter to think about…her feelings to worry about. God, I should've stopped this weeks ago." The hysteria was starting, and she bit the inside of her cheek to stop the emotions swirling through her. Hell. If she cried…nope, not happening.

"What if you came with me?"

His words were met with silence, as if all the air and sound had been sucked from the room.

"What? Are you kidding? We've known each other for a few months, and I'm supposed to pick myself, and Abby up, and move across the country with you? With no job, no friends, and no family?"

"Why not?"

He hadn't planned to ask her to come with him, but it felt right.

"Why not? We aren't even a real couple."

He couldn't stop his flinch. Wow. That hurt more than he wanted to admit, even though she was right.

"This doesn't feel real to you?" he bit out, grabbing her and slamming his lips on hers, swallowing her outraged gasp and drinking her in.

She didn't fight it, sinking into his body, her lush curves molding to him. He snaked an arm around her waist, keeping her close, giving into the raw desire they had for each other and relishing every second she didn't pull away. This. He wanted this.

He broke the kiss and stepped back, catching her when she weaved in front of him, trying not to smirk at her reaction to the kiss. How could she fight this? Ignore this?

"That's not real?" he asked, his frustration and anger clear in his voice.

"It's just sex." Even as the words came out of her mouth, he knew she was lying. They were more than just sex.

"Wow. Just sex? You can't tell me that you don't feel that this is more than just friends who eat cake and screw," he growled.

"It doesn't matter, because that's all it can ever be, and I should've stopped it weeks ago," she said, staring at her feet. "You're leaving, and I'm staying. I can't uproot my child and move out of state with no job. And you can't stay. You literally have orders to leave," she continued, finally looking up at him. The pain in her eyes killed him, but also gave him hope.

"And why couldn't we try long distance for now?" he asked, knowing he was grasping, but refusing to give up.

"Because it wouldn't work. And now Abby's seen us together as more than just friends. I don't want her to get her hopes up that you'll be around for her future. You're leaving

296

for four years. Maybe more. You said you hadn't decided if you were going to retire at the end of this term. So it would be another move, another change. I just can't," she said, dropping her head, shielding her eyes from him.

"So that's it? You won't even try? Won't even admit you have feelings for me?" He hated the pleading tone in his voice.

"What about you? It's not like you're offering to quit your job and stay here," she said.

"I'm only four years away from my complete pension. I would be an idiot to give that up now. It's not the same," he said, instantly wishing he'd reworded that statement, if the anger in her eyes was anything to go by.

"So I should rearrange my life. Leave my job, my home, my family, and just come with you. Rely on you until I get a job. Watch my daughter try to make friends that she'll probably have to say good-bye to in four years. How can you ask that of me?"

"Look. I understand where you're coming from. Really, I do. But...you would give up us? Give up the chance to be happy?" He grabbed her hands, pulling her close. "You can't tell me you aren't happy with what this is. With what we have."

"You don't know what it's like. Moving to different schools. Trying to make new friends with kids that have had their group of friends since kindergarten and aren't welcoming to newcomers. Kids can be so mean to outsiders," she said, staring at her hands again.

He put his finger under her chin, tilting her head up. "Abby is only going into the second grade. I moved to a new school when I was twelve, and I survived."

"I don't want her to be lonely," she whispered. He hated seeing the pain in her gaze.

"You can't push your fears on Abby. She's only six. Kids are resilient," he said.

She shook her head. "I just can't."

"So that's it? We're just ending this now because you are too afraid of change? Of finally finding a guy who loves you and your daughter? Did it ever occur to you that I meet every stupid check on that damn list of yours? Yes, the sex is amazing, which I believe was one of your requirements, but it's not just that. We just work together. I could list all the reasons, but I'm pretty sure you know them."

"Love? You love me?" Her eyes shone with tears, and he couldn't believe he'd just thrown that declaration out there, but it was true. His heart hammered, not with the fear of saying something he didn't mean, but with the joy of finally admitting it to her, to himself.

"Yes. I love you. Believe me, this wasn't my intention. I tried to avoid this because my leaving is a huge issue, but you wormed your way into my heart. I want you to be the first thing I see in the morning and the last thing I see at night," he said, squeezing her hands. "Lexi, you can't tell me you don't feel the same," he said, brushing her tears away with his thumb.

"It doesn't matter. It won't work. I have to be realistic."

298

"Realistic? How is this not working? I know you love me, too. We can figure this out," he said, feeling her slipping away from him, his desperation grasping at any solution.

"But every suggestion involves me changing my entire life, and you aren't changing anything. I'm not going to rely on a man to take care of me while I'm looking for a job, or settling my daughter into a life where everything she's ever known is a plane trip away. It's unfair of you to ask this of me."

"So you expect me to give up my job, step away from sixteen years of service, four years away from my pension, because you're afraid of change? Of relying on me? Of trusting that we can find a way to make this work? Your happiness. Abby's happiness. It's important to me, and I know we can figure this out," he said. He'd beg if he had to. How did she not understand that?

"I'm sorry, Grant. I can't do this." She pulled free from his grasp and took a step back, not looking up at him. "It won't work. I have to go. Thank you for..." she trailed off. Was she really thanking him? For what?

"So that's it. Thanks for the cake and screwing my brains out, but it's over?" The anger and hurt vibrated off of him.

"I'm sorry I let it go this far," she said.

"Go, Lexi. Just go. Be afraid of change. Of finding happiness, because it's right in front of you, and you won't take it," he bit out.

She looked at him one last time, through watery eyes, and he glared back. She flinched, and he hated this. She was slipping away, and he couldn't figure out how to fix it. He

299

also hadn't missed the fact that she never admitted that she loved him. He refused to believe that her emotions weren't as heavily involved in this as his were.

"I'm sorry," she said one last time before escaping through the door. He slammed his hand down on the desk, the force vibrating through his arm.

What the fuck just happened? Grant sunk into the office chair, his head in his hands, trying to ignore the sounds of the party going on without him. The party that was for him. And while he wished he could escape without anyone noticing, that wasn't an option.

Fuck. Tonight hadn't gone as planned. Not that he'd set out to tell Lexi he loved her or that she should drop everything and move to Florida with him. It was selfish to want that, but he'd never told another woman who he wasn't related to that he loved her. And what had he received in reply? A fucking, "Thanks for a good time...it's over."

He couldn't wallow in the office. His family would have questions. Questions he didn't want to answer. He stood up, rolled his shoulders, and headed back into the party, grabbing a beer off the bar. He knocked it back in a few lengthy pulls, then grabbed another.

"Hey man, everything okay? Lexi was acting weird when she bailed," Adam said, stopping next to him.

No, he wasn't okay, but he sure as shit wasn't going to start sobbing on his friend's shoulder.

"Fine. Lexi had to go." He didn't even sound like himself.

"Okay. She looked like she'd been crying. She just mumbled goodbye to your mom and Lily and rushed out."

Shut up, Adam. He didn't want to hear about her crying since she'd broken his heart. He sounded melodramatic. The timing sucked and that's all there was to it. Not that he had been flexible on his part. They could've tried long distance, but that never worked.

He spent the rest of the night knocking back beers and ignoring questions about Lexi. He didn't miss his mother and sisters' concerned expressions, but there was nothing he could do about it. He was grateful that he had tomorrow off because the hangover he was sure to have would make his job miserable for him and dangerous for others.

After Adam drove him home, Grant plopped down on his couch, staring at the partially packed boxes mocking him. His finger hovered over her name on his phone. He wouldn't look at their last text chain, before everything had blown up in his face. He threw his phone on the coffee table, watching as it bounced to the floor, wondering how his life had been turned upside down without him knowing, and fearing that he'd never speak to the one woman he'd ever loved, again.

Chapter 19

"All packed and ready?" Grant's mom asked him as he sat down for one last meal with his family before he flew out tomorrow.

"You know I just threw stuff in boxes, mom," he said, grinning at her glare.

"You should've asked. I would've come over and helped. I should've just come over," she grumbled.

"Mom, it's not like I've never done this before. I am capable of packing my stuff," he said, taking a bite of meatball. Man, he was going to miss his mom's cooking. Maybe he could convince her to come with him, as a vacation, and load up his freezer. Not that he'd had much luck convincing the women in his life to move with him.

Lexi. He didn't want to think about her, or the fact that he hadn't heard from her in two weeks since she'd walked out of the family restaurant. No texts, no calls, not a peep. Not that he'd reached out to her, even though he thought about calling her at least ten times a day, probably more.

He wasn't going to plead with her to come with him if she refused. She clearly didn't care for him as much as he cared for her, and that made him feel like shit. He was such an idiot for telling her he loved her. Especially since she hadn't said it back.

He'd been so sure she was in the same place as him, blindly ignoring every hint she ever gave at not wanting to move. And now he hated that their last interaction with each other was a fight. That he wouldn't hear her voice again, her laugh. Or kiss that spot behind her ear that drove him insane.

Jesus. He needed to stop. She'd made her feelings known loud and clear, and he would never beg. He wasn't that pathetic.

"Have you talked to Lexi?" his mom asked, her concern obvious. Had his pain been so obvious?

"Nope. We ended things." He hoped his tone was nonchalant, but her raised eyebrow gave him doubts.

"I really liked her," Rose said. "And Abby is such a dear girl."

"Yes, she is, but the timing was wrong, and we were really just friends, nothing more," he said.

Lily let out a soft snort. "Friends, my ass."

"Liliana Jane," Rose admonished. "There are children here," she whispered.

Lily had good thought to look sheepish at their mother's scolding, even though Grant was pretty sure Keira and Nathan hadn't been paying attention.

Grant couldn't decide whether to smirk at his sister for getting in trouble or glare at her for her remark. He chose to ignore her. That tended to piss her off even more.

"I just worry about you, Grant. I thought you really liked her," his mother said.

Hell. He did. And he didn't want to think about it, let alone admit it to his mother. Nothing would change. Lexi had made her decision.

"I'll be fine, Mom. I am going to miss your meatballs. You could come with me. Stock my freezer. Have a vacation?" He shot her a smile, trying to get her to stop thinking about his love life.

"I wish it'd worked out. Could you find a way to stay here?" she asked, her gaze hopeful.

"Other than getting a guy to switch places with me or taking a desk job, there aren't a lot of options. I'll be home in four years, so there's not much else I can do."

"Four years is a long time to wait for someone," his mom said.

"And no one is waiting for anyone," he replied. As much as he wished otherwise, they hadn't talked about it. After so many conversations about everything under the sun, how had they not talked about what would happen?

Right. Because he was a chicken shit and hadn't wanted to ask questions to which he already knew the answer.

"I just want you to be happy," Rose said, reaching over to squeeze her husband's hand. Grant's step-father shared a look with Rose. That's what he wanted. It'd just come too early, and he wasn't ready. Well, if he'd been up for retirement or he'd stayed in San Francisco, he'd be ready for it now, but the what-ifs game would kill him. Lexi wouldn't bend, and it made no sense for him to try.

"I'm happy. I'm finishing up my service in the sunshine." He ignored those knowing looks again.

"We can visit, right?" Nathan asked, breaking the tension. Man, he loved that kid.

"Of course," Grant said. "Whenever you want."

Grant focused on his family for the rest of the night, pushing Lexi to the back of his brain where he knew she'd linger, making him want things that he couldn't have.

* * *

The following morning, Grant sprawled out in a chair at the airport, his carry-on gear beside him. His flight left in less than an hour. He gripped his phone in his hand, willing Lexi to call. Say she was on her way to see him. But it remained silent in his hand.

He'd thought about her all night, about what options they had, and he'd wanted to reach out to her. See if they could find a way to make it work. But he held back, remembering that she still hadn't said she loved him, even with his multiple confessions. He'd been so sure of her feelings when he'd declared his. Apparently he'd been wrong.

"How was Italy?" Lexi asked, their first round of drinks in front of them. Lexi had desperately needed a girls' night. It'd been a week since Penny had returned from her fake honeymoon. Ten days since Grant had left. God. Why couldn't she stop thinking about him? She shook her head, focusing on her friends.

"It was nice," Penny said, her cheeks pink, her eyes bright, and Amanda immediately jumped on her.

"Something happened. Oh, and I bet it was good. What happened?"

"Nothing. Italy was just really nice. Lots of museums and carbs. I didn't want to leave," Penny said, her cheeks still glowing.

"It's something else. You're really happy," Lexi said, jealous of Penny's joy when the only thing she got joyful about these days was Abby. Desserts had lost their appeal, well, most of their appeal. She hadn't become a completely different person, and a cookie had its place.

"It was relaxing and refreshing," Penny said, clearly evading.

"Spill it. Please tell me you hooked up with a local and he rocked your world," Amanda said, grinning.

"Okay, so there was this guy..." Penny started, twirling her martini stem between her fingers, focusing on the swirling liquid, her cheeks a flaming red at this point.

"I knew it," Amanda shouted.

Lexi laughed, watching a few heads turn to look in their direction.

"But it doesn't matter. It was a fling that I needed and nothing more. I'm never going to see him again."

Lexi didn't miss Penny's frown, and her first thought was Grant. Never seeing him again. She was a mess.

"Was he a local?" Amanda asked.

"No, from New York. But we didn't exchange numbers or last names."

"I'm impressed," Amanda said, clinking her glass with Penny's.

"How did you leave it?" Lexi asked.

"I left him a note saying thanks," Penny muttered.

"Wow. Now I'm really proud of you," Amanda said with a chuckle.

"Yep. Just an itch to be scratched," Penny said, staring back at her now empty glass.

Lexi gave a soft snort. *Just an itch.* Hell, she hated the term now.

"Speaking of itch…" Amanda trailed off, looking directly at Lexi, her head tilted to the side like an inquisitive puppy.

"What?"

"Yes. What happened after I left? With Grant?" Penny asked.

"Nope. You can't change the subject. We want to hear more about mystery man," Lexi said, hoping to keep the focus off herself.

"There's really nothing more to say. I had a great time. Some great sex. And now I'm back, and ready to move on with my life," Penny said with a confidence that she'd been lacking even before she'd caught Michael cheating. Mystery man must've been amazing.

"Oh, don't worry. We'll keep grilling her until we get all the juicy details, but we want her to hear about what happened with Grant since you've been avoiding us, and I know he was supposed to leave for Florida over a week ago. I gave you your space until Penny got back, but you can't avoid us now," Amanda said, sheer determination in her eyes.

"Oh no. What happened?" Penny asked.

"It's over with me and Grant," she said, hating how her heart clenched at those words.

307

"Do I need to hurt him?" Amanda asked, her eyes narrowed.

"No. I ended it," she mumbled.

"And you're obviously not happy about that, so what did he do?" Penny asked.

"Told me he loved me." She stared at her glass, not wanting to meet her friends' eyes.

"That bastard. How dare he confess his love for you. Something I saw coming a mile away," Amanda said.

"Shut up," Lexi grumbled.

"So he tells you he loves you and then what?" Penny asked.

She shrugged. "Umm. I said thanks for everything and that it was over."

Penny's eyes widened. "Wow. Seriously?"

"Kinda harsh," Amanda said.

Lexi shook her head. "It doesn't matter. Nothing changes the fact that he's on the other side of the country for four years or longer, and I can't go."

"Because he didn't ask you?" Penny asked.

"No. He did. But I can't just up and move. I wouldn't have a job. I don't want to move Abby away from everything she's ever known, from her family, her friends. Hell, we've never even been on a date," she said, repeating the same words she'd said to him.

"But you always *end* your dates with him," Amanda said, her brow arched.

She huffed. "It's so not the same."

Penny's eyes softened. "And you've done things with him and the kids, outside of your train wreck online dates, right?"

"Those weren't dates. The kids are friends and they wanted to get together, and Lily was busy."

"Okay, it's not a typical relationship."

"It's not a relationship," Lexi said, cutting Amanda off.

"Yes, it's not traditional, but have you ever had more fun with a guy? Great sex. You're always talking about how you never run out of stuff to talk about. You like doing things together. Sounds like a great relationship to me. You just make it weird by throwing in a few random dates with other guys that were never going to go anywhere. Wait. Did you pick shitty guys to date just so you could spend more time with Grant? How were your dates always on nights when he was free?"

Lexi hated the gleam in Amanda's eyes almost as much as she hated the complete sense that her friend was making. "I did not plan that."

"I don't believe you. So what is the problem?" Amanda asked.

She glared at her friend. "Hello. He moved across the country."

"It's not freaking Guam. It's Florida," Amanda said.

"I'm not moving." She wrapped her arms around her waist. She probably looked like a pouting toddler.

"Because you're afraid it won't work out? That you'll be stranded and homeless in Florida when he disappoints you?" Penny asked.

309

"I'm not moving for a man. I moved so many times growing up. One place to the next. Each one was supposed to be better than the last. You know what that's left me with? Not having a childhood home to go back to. Not running into friends I've known all my life. Not *having* friends I've known all my life. I don't want that for Abby. I don't want her to walk into a new school with no friends. It's lonely, and it sucks," Lexi said, her voice rising, emotion heavy in her tone. She glanced around the bar, hoping no one had heard her pathetic outburst.

"Look, I get it. Your parents moved you right before your final years at each school, fifth grade, seventh grade, and right before your senior year. It sucks. Especially that last one." Amanda reached out, squeezing Lexi's hand. "And just so you know, running into people you grew up with, especially ex-boyfriends, is not something you're missing out on."

"I guess," she muttered.

"Abby will be fine. She's only six, and you know that Grant wants to move back to be close to his family once he's out. That's only four more years and then you could stay put here forever," Amanda continued.

"And what if he doesn't retire in four years? That's a giant possibility because he loves his job so much," she said.

"Yes it is. But he could retire, and you know he wants to move back here. There are no guarantees in life, so panicking about what could happen down the road will just drive you crazy."

"And what if I can't find a job? I can't rely on him to support me and Abby. Or what if he decides I'm not giving him enough attention. What if we get married and have a kid, and he leaves..." she trailed off. She was getting so far ahead of herself, letting her old insecurities get the better of her.

"Like Joe?" Penny asked.

She nodded, sipping her wine, focusing on the glass stem.

"First of all, he's nothing like Joe. Joe was a selfish asshole who never wanted to think about others," Amanda said.

"Couldn't that be said about Grant? He won't leave his job. He wanted me to drop everything and change my life, and Abby's life, drastically, and he wasn't going to change anything on his end with his job so he could stay."

"Okay, now you're grasping. Let's be reasonable here. Joe was a spoiled brat who didn't want to share your attention with his own freaking kid. Grant can retire in four short years, with a full pension, and do whatever he wants. He would be an idiot to give that up. They are not remotely the same. And you've seen him with Abby, with his niece and nephew. Don't think we haven't heard that wistful sigh when you talk about how great he is with kids," Amanda said.

Lexi didn't miss Amanda's triumphant grin.

"But it's too risky. I can't do what my mom did. Pick up and move every time her husband commanded, losing a bit of herself every time she gave in to what he wanted." She bit back the emotion that threatened to spill out of her.

"Do you love him?" Penny asked.

"Yes," she said, her tone both hopeful and sad. It was the first time she'd admitted it out loud. "But it doesn't matter."

"So there's no other option aside from you moving or him giving up his job?" Penny asked.

"She wouldn't know since she hasn't spoken to him since she told him thanks for a good time," Amanda stated.

Lexi took in a fortifying breath and glared at her friend. "What was I supposed to do?"

"I don't know. You love him. Maybe talk it out instead of running away," Amanda said.

Lexi didn't enjoy her friends' version of tough love.

"I agree with Amanda. Just talk to him," Penny said. "You guys had something, and it's been so long since we've seen you happy in a relationship."

She couldn't believe Penny's response. The woman's relationship had just imploded last month. She should be fully entrenched in man-hating, but she was encouraging Lexi not to give up. There was definitely more to her Italian fling.

"He probably doesn't even want to talk to me. He didn't call or text me," she said.

"Do you blame him? He tells you he loves you, and you tell him it's over and you would never move with him. What guy is going to go back for more after he bares his heart and you shoot him down?" Amanda asked.

"It's weird that she's become the voice of reason," Penny said, grinning as she eyed Amanda.

"Very funny. You know I choose to date a lot, not because I can't get guys to stick around. I actually know what I'm talking about," Amanda said.

"I know. I just don't know what I'm supposed to do. It's been a few weeks. What if he's moved on? Found some hot bikini-clad chick to ease his heartache?" Lexi mumbled.

"I highly doubt that. Just call him," Penny said.

Lexi hated the matching concern in their eyes. Tonight was supposed to be a fun night out. Hear about Penny's amazing trip over yummy cocktails, and not dwell on Lexi's love life falling apart. A love life that was never supposed to happen. Stupid damn itch.

"What am I supposed to say? Sorry for not completely changing my life so we could be together when you never offered to do the same?" she bit out, annoyed that everyone thought she should change everything for him. She would never change everything for a man. She'd seen and experienced how destructive that could be for one's well-being.

"That's not what I meant, and you know it," Penny said. "You never even asked him to think about options. Sounds like you ran out before a real discussion could happen."

She dropped her head down, staring at her still empty martini glass. "It was just too much," she said.

"I know, but you're miserable without him, right?" Penny asked.

"I'm doing okay," she muttered.

"You're a shit liar, you know that?" Amanda said.

313

"I say you call him. Or just send him a text to see how he's doing," Penny said, nudging Lexi's shoulder.

"And say what? How's Florida? Do you miss me?" Lexi replied with exasperation.

"He loves you. He's not going to care what you say, just that you bothered to contact him at all. He left the ball in your court," Amanda said, her voice of reason shining through again.

"And what if he doesn't respond?" Lexi asked.

"Then you move on, knowing you tried your best," Penny said, grabbing Lexi's hand and giving it a squeeze. "But he'll respond. I saw the way he looked at you. You don't get over that in just a few weeks."

Lexi grimaced and pulled out her phone. "Fine, but if this doesn't work, you guys owe me a huge dessert."

"Like an actual dessert or sex? I never know what that means to you these days, and you know I don't swing that way," Amanda said, grinning.

Penny snorted. "Seriously, Amanda?"

"You guys are the best for offering, but I definitely meant actual dessert," Lexi said, letting a small smile slip through. Then she stared at her phone as if it would jump up and attack her. "What should I say?"

"Ask him about the dessert in Florida," Amanda said.

"No. Then he'll think she's asking if he's had sex since he moved," Penny said.

"True. But they connected with dessert and sex. So I think it should be something funny or cute about dessert," Amanda said.

Lexi half-listened to them bicker back and forth while she thought of the perfect line. This was ridiculous. She was so tempted to just type "hi" and leave it at that, but she knew she needed something more.

She grabbed her phone, her fingers hovering over the screen, waiting for an amazing and perfect line to magically appear in her head. A line that made her sound witty and happy. Hell. This sucked. Why was this so freaking difficult? Not that she could text him and tell him she missed him. Loved him. She wanted to bang her head on the table.

"For the love of..." Amanda said, grabbing Lexi's phone.

"What are you doing?" Lexi screeched.

Amanda shielded her body away from them, her fingers moving, before sliding it back across the table to Lexi. "There. Done."

Lexi stared at her phone like it was diseased, scared to pick it up. "Oh God. Did you send something to Grant?"

"You were taking too long and overthinking it," Amanda said, clearly proud of herself.

"Oh God," Penny muttered, her gaze darting between Lexi and the phone.

Lexi peered down at her message:

Lexi: Dessert isn't the same without you.

"Seriously? That's what you sent? Now he's going to think I'm having sex with myself," she bit out.

"It's been a few weeks, so aren't you? And, it's just a conversation starter. I bet he answers in the next hour," Amanda said, looking a bit too smug.

315

Lexi stared at her silent phone, both willing it to ding with a new message and hoping the text hadn't actually gone through.

And the following morning when it still remained silent, she was glad it was the weekend so she could curl up into a ball and not see anyone. Abby was at her parents' house so Lexi truly was alone. She wished she could show her face at Lanzi's because she could really go for some tiramisu.

Chapter 20

Dessert isn't the same without you.

Grant stared at his phone that morning, hoping he wasn't reading too much into it, and holding back a smile at her timing. He'd stared at that text since he received it last night.

It'd been almost four weeks since she'd walked out on him, and he'd thought about her every day, wishing he'd tried to talk to her before he left, but knowing nothing would've changed her decision. But she'd reached out to him, and he had to respond. That had to count for something. Not that he expected her to tell him that she changed her mind about relocating and was on a plane to see him. The irony in that would've been amazing.

He wasn't sure how to take her message, but he couldn't stop the rush of heat in his belly at the thought of her enjoying their version of dessert on her own. They hadn't done that in all their time together. Shit. He wasn't supposed to get turned on by a short text message.

He was pathetic.

He wanted to be angry with her, but that had faded soon after his arrival in Florida. Now he was just sad. He missed her. And not just her dessert.

He opened his messages.

Grant: That's because you don't have my mom's tiramisu.

Easy, friendly. Keep it simple.

And then he stared at his phone like it was a bomb waiting to go off in his hand. But nothing happened.

Twenty minutes later, he heard the elusive ding.

Lexi: Hi. Her tiramisu is the best.

Grant: How are you?

He was diving right in, and he didn't care. Watching those damn speech bubbles move endlessly made him crazy. Especially when they disappeared for a moment and then popped up again.

Lexi: I'm good. You?

Hell. Who knew it was possible to be awkward over text? People texted solely to avoid this shit.

Grant: Good. Missing the family.

And you.

Lexi: I'm sure.

Her responses were short. Odd. She'd started this conversation with her text last night. Had it been a drunk text that she later regretted? This was ridiculous. He hit the phone icon next to her name. It rang three times before she picked up, like she'd hesitated, and again, he wasn't sure how to take that, and his nerves ate at him.

"Hi," she said.

He even missed her voice. This conversation was going to go one of two ways. He could only hope for the one in his favor.

"Hi. I figured I might as well call."

"Umm. How are you?" she asked, her voice soft.

"Good. You?"

"Good," she paused.

"Well this is awkward," he said with a short laugh.

318

"Sorry." She paused, and he wished he were there to see her expression.

"You texted last night, so I assumed you wanted to talk. I can hang up if this isn't want you wanted," he said, feeling like every type of fool for calling. Clearly last night had been a drunk text.

"Sorry. No. I want to talk. I just don't know what to say. And it was Amanda who actually sent the text."

"Why? You really didn't want to talk to me again?" he asked, trying to mask his irritation at his misguided hopes.

"No. No. It's not that." She let out a small laugh. "I just couldn't figure out what to say and she grabbed the phone. I wasn't sure how you'd take that text. I was ready to kill her."

He grinned. "It's an icebreaker."

Lexi groaned. "I could really kill her. That's not the only thing we were about."

"I know that. I miss dessert with you, too. And not just the bedroom kind."

Her laugh rolled over him. He missed her more than he'd thought possible.

"I miss you, and I hate how everything ended," she rushed out. He could only imagine how pink her cheeks were at her admission.

"Me too," he said.

"So everything is good?" she asked, steering to an easier topic.

"Yes. For the most part. Getting used to new co-workers and a new station is always a learning curve."

"I bet," she said.

He heard the sadness in her voice and hated it, but it gave him hope.

"I want to hear all about it," she continued.

He told her about his flight down to the Bahamas earlier that week, only pausing his story when he had to pay the driver and grab his bag.

"The weather must be awesome. It's decently warm here, but I can only imagine the sunscreen I'd go through down there." Had he detected wistfulness in her voice?

He laughed. "You'd need it by the gallon."

She sighed. "God, this sucks. You're over there, and I'm here and…it sucks."

His heart thrilled at her pain…and then he felt like an ass.

"I just wish you were here," she whispered.

"Open your door," he said.

"What?"

"Open your door, Lexi."

His heart sped up as footsteps approached the other side of the door. She flung it open, her cheeks flushed, and her eyes bright with hopefully happy tears.

"Hi," he grunted as she barreled into him, his bag falling to the ground, her arms locking around his neck.

He buried his face into her hair, breathing her in, before she pulled back.

"How are you? Why are you…? What are you doing here? I only sent that text last night. How is this possible?" she rushed out.

"I had the weekend off, so I'd already planned to fly in this morning. I was tired of missing you. Of being an idiot that night. For expecting you to change your life for me, when I wasn't going to do the same."

"Wow," she said in shock. She couldn't believe he was actually here.

He linked his hand with hers. "So can I come in?"

She let out a soft laugh. "Sorry. Of course." She squeezed his fingers and pulled him inside, shutting the door behind her. "How are you? You look good. Tan."

He chuckled. "Florida will do that for you."

"Not me," she grumbled. "I'd end up looking like an over-cooked lobster."

"Is Abby here?" he asked.

"No. She's at my parents' for the weekend. Grant, what are you doing here?" She hated to cut to the chase, but her sanity required it.

"I'm here to see you. To have the conversation we should've had last month," he said, tugging her away from the door and into the living room.

"So did you go A.W.O.L.? Are you home for good?" She pushed back the hope that fluttered in her chest.

He pulled her down on the couch, shifting to face her, squeezing her hands. "Not exactly. I'm expected back Monday morning."

Her heart sank.

"Oh. So, why are you back?" She still couldn't believe he was in her living room. Had he really just flown in to see her? Just to torture them both if he wasn't staying? She stared at their linked fingers, willing her heart to slow, waiting for him to explain why he was here before she got way ahead of herself imagining both the worst and the best options.

"Just to see you," he said, drawing his thumb across her knuckles, and she sucked in a breath.

"Really? Your parents don't know you're here?" she asked.

"No."

"Oh, man. Your mother better not find out," she said, smiling at his sheepish expression. His mom would be pissed for not knowing he was back.

"So," he started.

"So," she said at the same time. They both laughed. She hated how awkward it was trying to dive into a conversation she feared would crush her.

"I saw your sister last week when I was picking up Abby. She glared at me."

He shook his head. "Yeah. She's a little over-protective."

"What did you say to them about us?"

"They knew how I felt about you, and after you left that night, I avoided talking about you at all," he said, squeezing her hand.

"I'm sorry about that. I was scared, so I ran." She looked up at him through lowered lashes. "I should've stayed."

"No. I never should've sprung that request for you to pick up and move. I knew it wasn't something you wanted to do, and I shouldn't have assumed I could convince you to change. And I could've chased after you. Called you before I left. But I didn't do that either. We can't change what

322

happened that night. It's in the past, and I think we can find a way to make this work. I mean, if you want this to work," he said, the vulnerability in his eyes threatening to cut her at the knees. She'd done that. Had that strong of an effect on a man. A good man. She hadn't believed that was possible.

"I want more than anything to make this work." She raised her other hand to his cheek. "I love you, Grant. It wasn't supposed to happen, but it did, and I felt awful for saying thank you instead of telling you how I really felt." Her heart galloped in her chest at her admission, but she'd needed him to know. She'd always regret her words when he'd confessed his love that night.

"Oh Lexi. I love you, too. I never stopped." His tone was reverent, and when he tugged her into his lap, she melted against him.

"I hated being apart from you. The number of texts I almost sent...but didn't." He shook his head, a soft chuckle escaping his lips. He brushed a kiss across her cheek, then pressed his brow to hers. "We are going to make this work. I refuse to give this up."

"But how? You live three thousand miles away. It's unreasonable for me to ask you to give up your pension, and I can't move," she reiterated, hating the pain in her voice. They'd just confessed their love for each other, but she couldn't bask in that. She had to be practical.

His eyes locked on her, sheer determination in his gaze. "We'll figure it out."

She'd never wanted to believe anything more in her life. "Promise?"

"Yes. I just had to talk to a few people. Do some thinking," he said, straightening away from her.

"I know you don't want to be a recruiter. Isn't that the only option?" she asked.

"No, it's not. It's just the easiest option. Although I don't know many guys that would willingly give up swimming for a desk job."

"And I can't ask you to do that. Your job means so much to you. And you help so many people. I know it's unfair for me to ask you to chain yourself to a desk," she said, dropping her head down. She'd hated that part of their fight. And if he'd taken that position and regretted it, she'd blame herself.

"So another option is to switch with another swimmer. It rarely happens because the Coast Guard won't pay your moving fees to transfer again," he said.

"Can you find someone to switch with you, then? Would you do that? Give up your fun in the sun?" she asked, her hopes rising.

He chuckled. "It's sunny here."

"Yeah, but it's not like Florida and the Bahamas."

He pulled her closer, pure love in his gaze, and heat fluttered in her belly. "No, it's not. But it has other perks."

"Like your mom's tiramisu?"

"I do miss that."

"I can't believe you didn't bring any," she pouted.

"She doesn't know I'm here, remember? How did we get off topic?"

Her cheeks heated. "Sorry. Distracted by dessert."

He grinned. "Not surprised at all."

She swatted his arm. "Continue."

"So I just had to find someone to switch with me at the station here and hope that they are willing to move to Florida. And pay for the move," he said.

"Will that take a long time? Is there someone you could ask? Will they get mad at you for switching?"

"No. They won't get mad. And, as it turns out, a buddy of mine just transferred to San Francisco last month. We were stationed together in Alaska."

"So you could ask him?" She could feel the weight on her heart lifting.

"I actually talked to him last week. He has family in Florida. It's where he's originally from, actually, and he's willing to move."

"So you can move home? When can you move back? And then you could retire in four years and never have to move?"

He wrapped his arms around her, keeping her anchored in his lap. She didn't understand the hesitation in his gaze.

"In theory, yes. We should be able to move in the next month or two. And yes, I will stay here until I'm up for retirement in four years."

"And you'll really retire then?" she asked.

"I've debated this for a while now," he started, and she pulled back at his expression. He kept a firm grip on her.

"What does that mean?" she asked.

"I do plan to retire eventually, but I love my job. You know I love my job."

Oh God. The weight was returning.

"Yes, you do," she stuttered.

"I just don't want to shut that door right now. Most likely I will retire, but if for some reason I'm not ready to, I need to know that you won't run again." He kept his eyes locked with hers, hope clear in his gaze.

"I don't want to move, Grant," she said, her voice barely above a whisper.

"I know you don't. But four years is a long way away, and I just don't want to say that this part of my career will be over and not be able to discuss the option down the road."

"So we're in limbo again?" she asked, panic setting in. She almost had everything she ever wanted, and she was afraid it was slipping through her fingers again.

"No. When we get to that point, we are going to sit down and talk about it. About where we are and what we want to do with our lives. You and me. This is forever, and we are going to make decisions together. I'm just keeping the conversation open. I know you moved around a lot, and you hated it. You moved at terrible times in your teenage years, and I get that you don't want that for Abby. I just don't want you to completely forbid the conversation. Just be open to what's best for us as a family. Because that's what I want. I want you and Abby and whoever else down the road. I want this for the long haul, and your opinions, hopes, fears...they all matter to me, because I love you. I wasn't supposed to find you yet. It wasn't in the plans, but you snuck your way in, and I'm not letting you go. Now or ever. I will do everything in my power to make you happy, and I'm just asking for that in return."

She felt the moisture on her cheeks before she realized she was crying.

"I don't want to upset you. I'm just being honest," he said, brushing away her tears.

"They're happy ones. I promise," she whispered.

"So, you'll keep our future plans open?" he asked.

It meant so much to her that he'd asked. And she knew, without an inkling of doubt, that he would take her opinions to heart and do everything in his power to keep her happy. He wouldn't demand they move without talking to her. They would be equal, and that's all she ever wanted. To be valued. To be loved.

"Yes. I love you, Grant," she said, wrapping her arms around his neck and pressing against him.

"I love you, Lexi. More than I was supposed to. More than I thought possible," he said, before pulling her in and sealing his lips with hers.

She sunk into his embrace as he deepened the kiss, his tongue tangling with hers, her fingers sinking into his hair.

After an endless moment, she broke the kiss, skating her fingers down his chest, relishing in his indrawn breath.

"We should celebrate, but since somebody didn't bring any actual dessert, I guess we have to go out," she said, fighting back her grin at his growl.

"Or we could stay here and have our own dessert. And I promise to take you out for lava cakes later," he said.

She chuckled. "I love you almost as much as I love the fact that you said cakes, as in multiple."

He sealed his lips with hers, and they proceeded to indulge in all the dessert they'd missed.

Epilogue – One month later

Hell, she was nervous—like going out on her very first date nervous. She'd spent the last four weeks talking and texting with Grant like teenagers, and tonight he was home—for good. She bit back a laugh. It was their actual first date. She'd traced every inch of his body with her tongue, but tonight was their first date. Normal relationships were overrated.

She pressed her palms down her hips, smoothing out the non-existent wrinkles in her dress, attempting to ignore the slight shake in her hands. Jesus. She needed to relax. She'd barely heard a word her mother had said when Lexi had dropped off Abby a few hours ago. In fact, her mind had been scattered since he'd gone back to Florida last month.

She looked back toward the kitchen, debating downing a glass of wine—or a shot—before he arrived, but she wanted all of her faculties to be in order, or as ordered as possible, tonight. But now everything was done. Chicken cacciatore simmered on the stove, and the table was set. She sat down on the couch, resting back in the cushions and crossed her legs, her foot bouncing. She stood back up, pacing around the room.

This is ridiculous.

She huffed out a breath and darted down the hall to check her makeup again. For the tenth time. Like her anxiety could sweat her makeup off. It *was* warm. Maybe more deodorant? She'd just reached her bathroom when the doorbell rang.

Oh God. He's here! Her heartbeat galloped in her chest, the sound pounding in her ears as she made her way to the front door. She took one last calming breath and slowly opened the door, trying to fight back her over-excited grin.

And there he was. She scanned his body, drinking him in. Had he gotten hotter in the last month? The deep green shirt stretched across his chest under his jacket, and brought out his new tan. The top two buttons were open at his throat. Her gaze travelled up, across his scruffy jaw that she'd missed so much, to his chocolate eyes that made her think of lava cake and late night promises. She saw the humor in his eyes as he kept his mouth shut while she looked him over like a prized piece of cake.

"Can I come in?" he asked, grinning. Damn. She'd missed that dimple.

"Only if you come bearing gifts," she said.

"My presence isn't good enough?"

She grinned. "Your mom knows you're home now, so I was hoping…"

He pulled the dessert from behind his back. "You are too easy."

"I'm so not offended," she replied, taking the tiramisu in one hand and dragging him inside with the other.

"I missed you," he whispered against her hair, pressing a kiss to her brow.

"I missed you, too," she said.

He glanced down at her. "I'm not sure if you're saying that to me or the dessert."

She smiled and set the box down before wrapping her arms around his neck and pressing her lips to his. "Definitely you—well, mostly you."

His arms wrapped under her ass, and he lifted her, swallowing her squeak, and carried her into the living room.

Their heads tilted, finding that perfect angle, and his tongue traced the seam of her lips. She opened for him instantly, relishing in his touch, the taste of his mouth, the warm scent that was only him. This was what she wanted. What she needed. She kissed him with all the desire in her body. She wanted to sink into his embrace and never leave.

Her oven timer went off, the shrill beeping breaking their kiss. Stupid oven had the worst timing.

"Hold on," she said, pulling away from him and grabbing dinner from the stove.

"Wait? Are we actually going to have a meal together? From start to finish?" he asked.

She rolled her eyes at him. "Don't start, or I'll have to call Matt to come rescue me. I think my mom broke her hip again," she said, grinning.

"Wait? Did you call Matt for your dates after I left?" he asked.

She laughed. "Of course not. You ruined me for dating anyone. And I bet Matt isn't as good at rescues."

He pulled her close. "He's terrible," he mumbled against her neck, pressing a kiss to her throat that sent a shiver through her.

"I only want you to rescue me," she said.

"I'll gladly rescue you for as long as you'll let me," he said, drawing her down into his lap, their cooling dinner forgotten. Who needed dinner anyway? It was dessert that held her heart. And a snarky rescue swimmer who'd turned out to be her best match.

Adam and Lily's story is next.

Grab your copy of Last Call *today!*

Lily Pierson's life has been turned upside down. Now a single-mother raising her seven-year-old twins, and stuck in a long and painful divorce, she's ready to move forward, but fear holds her back. She should be focusing on getting her life back on track, of avoiding distractions, but she can't stop thinking about Adam. A boy she grew up with, a lifelong family friend who's been absent recently. But he won't leave her thoughts, nor will the kiss they shared when they were kids. A kiss he doesn't remember.

Adam Byrne's life is finally where it should be. After an injury took away his dream of playing professional hockey, and his father passed away, Adam found himself running the family bar. Happy in his new role, Adam is content with life and even decides to expand the business. He's been avoiding Lily, but she's the best realtor in town, so he enlists her help, knowing that the more time they spend together, the harder it will be to fight what's between them.

Can Lily truly let go and give love another chance? Can Adam find happiness with the woman who has been there all along? Could this be their Last Call for love?

Prologue

Tonight she was going to kiss Adam Byrne whether he wanted it or not. Not that she planned to tie him down, but if he knew what was good for him, he wouldn't fight it. Lily's cheeks heated at that thought, and she took another sip of liquid courage. Actually it was lukewarm light beer.

Liquid courage should taste better than this.

She could do this. Gird her loins and all that shit and walk over to the guy she'd loved since her older brother had brought him home with him when she was eight. For ten years she'd watched him.

Hell, that sounded creepy.

She'd been the annoying little sister tagging along after her brother and his best friend for years. Adam would ruffle her hair, and she'd look at him with sad, pathetic eyes, but he'd never noticed—until this summer. She refused to believe that she hadn't caught a new look in his gaze a few times since he'd been home. And now it was the last night. Her last chance. He was leaving to start his professional hockey career tomorrow, and she was headed off to college in two weeks. If she didn't gather the courage to tell him how she felt. To feel his lips against hers just once, she'd regret it.

That's what the light beer was for. She overanalyzed at a slightly lower level with some booze in her belly.

"God, he's so freaking hot," her friend Emily said, nudging Lily's shoulder, making her step out of her daydreams and look up.

"Yes he is," she whispered, spotting Adam immediately, looking all hot and dreamy standing next to the keg and laughing with his friends. His head back, his strong shoulders shaking, his hair danced in the firelight, longer than he usually kept it.

Danced in the firelight? She snorted. At least the booze had started working.

What would it feel like to sink her hands into it, the soft strands clenched between her fingers? She ignored the voice in her head that told her he should be off limits. The voice that sounded annoyingly like her older brother Grant's. But since Grant was off in the Coast Guard, his opinions were no longer the boss of her. She'd stomp her feet in defiance to her brain telling her that this could go bad. So very bad.

"Wish he'd look at me like that," Emily continued. "You totally need to go for that tonight."

"What are you talking about?" Lily tucked a short strand of brown hair behind her ear and watched Adam from under lowered lashes. She refused to outright stare at him. Let him think she was mesmerized by her pink toenails and not by his green eyes that reminded her of new spring leaves and soft grass.

Shit. She was completely hopeless.

"Adam. Obviously. Honestly I don't know how you haven't made a move on him yet. And Grant isn't even here to be a pain in the ass. What do you have to lose?" Emily asked, her eyes darting between Lily and Adam.

Lily pinched her friend, ignoring Emily's squeak of outrage. "Everything. And stop staring at him. How do you know he even wants to kiss me?"

Yes. How do you know? And please let your reasoning make sense so I can believe I'm not imagining this craziness.

"Oh please. He can't stop looking at you. He's leaving tomorrow. You've wanted him all summer, and it's your last chance before he goes off to training camp and finds the puck bunny of his dreams," Emily said, grinning behind her cup.

"You just had to go there, didn't you?" Lily grumbled. She didn't want to think about when he left, or the puck bunnies of his future. This summer had been perfect. After running into each other a week after her graduation, a few months ago, they'd spent endless amounts of time together. Movie nights, days spent hanging out in the city, even a few hikes through Muir Woods. It'd been like dating, but without the fun stuff. The *fun stuff* she wanted more with each passing day, and that clearly wasn't happening since he was leaving tomorrow afternoon and hadn't so much as moved in for a kiss in all the times they'd hung out.

"I think I'll grab another beer," Emily whispered, squeezing Lily's arm. "Have fun."

"Where are…" she trailed off as she looked up to see him walking toward her, that stupid smile on his lips that did things to her belly she didn't want to talk about.

"Hey, Lil. Did you just get here?" Adam looped his arm around her neck and pulled her into his body.

336

She breathed him in, his warm, spicy scent surrounding her when he pressed her to his chest. If she could bottle it up, she'd make a fortune. She took in another shuddering breath before tilting her head back to look up at the giant that spent way too much time puttering about in her head than was healthy. Maybe if she finally kissed him tonight, she'd get him out of her system. She bit back her snort, knowing how unlikely that was—the kiss and exorcizing him from her every thought.

He shifted his head to the side, his eyes locked with hers. Oh right, he'd asked her a question. She wished she could blame the fuzziness on the booze, but it was just him.

"Just got here. With Emily," she said, gesturing toward where her traitorous friend had disappeared to. Not that she wanted Emily to stay by her side all night, but now Lily was nervous. Which was so ridiculous, because she'd been alone with Adam countless times in the last few months. But tonight felt different.

"Awesome," he said, pulling back and ruffling her hair.

"Stop. Don't mess up my hair," she screeched, moving away from him, but not completely pulling from his hold. She hated and loved when he did that, since even though it was annoying, he was touching her. And she'd take what she could get. Ugh. So pathetic.

"Calm down, it's fine." He steered her over to a bench, dragging her down next to him, and looking out at the fire pit. "I can't believe I leave tomorrow."

He turned to face her, excitement sparkling in his eyes, and she bit back the pain in her chest, pasting on a smile that wasn't totally genuine. And then she felt like an ass. She was happy for him. This was his dream—all he ever wanted—and she was leaving, too. But a part of her wished she could stay right here, with him. Change freaked her out, and what if it was never better than it had been this summer?

"You're going to be a hockey superstar," she said, pushing her fears aside.

Vibrations from his laughter rolled over her as she pressed into his side, his warmth setting her ablaze more than the fire ever could.

"It's just the minors, Lil. I know I'm not a top player, but hopefully I'll get called up to the big show at some point."

"Of course you will. You're going to be a superstar and forget all about us little people at home," she said, biting back the sadness in her tone. He didn't deserve that.

He pulled her closer. "Stop making fun of your munchkin stature." He chuckled and she pinched his side. Not that there was much to pinch. Stupid, rock hard body.

"Ouch. And don't worry. I'd never forget you," he said, and she sucked in a breath, hearing something in his voice that she couldn't, or shouldn't, name.

"See that you don't," she huffed, trying to bring some levity back.

"And you're off soon, too. Any idea what you're going to major in?" he asked.

She laughed. "Not a clue."

"You'll figure it out," he said, leaning back, his arm resting along the top of the bench, his fingers periodically brushing the short hairs on her nape and sending bolts of awareness down to her toes.

She was definitely kissing him tonight.

Adam glanced over at Lily a few hours later as she laughed with her friends. Light from the fire warmed her cheeks and made her glasses sparkle. Fuck, he was in trouble. He should've stayed home tonight. Booze and Lily in close proximity could lead to disaster, mainly him giving in to what he'd wanted all summer.

He'd wandered off to grab more beers, just to stop himself from pressing her petite body into his again. She fit perfectly against him and those were thoughts he couldn't—shouldn't—have. He'd spent the night by her side, alternating between staring at her and telling himself that he needed to walk away. Grant would rip him a new one if he knew how Adam was lusting after Grant's little sister. He'd tried to fight it all summer. Hell, probably even longer than that, but no matter how many times he told himself this could go nowhere, he couldn't stop himself from dropping by her house to spend all of his free time with her.

And now he had a healthy buzz, so his will power to resist her was dropping with each gulp of beer. But it wasn't just that he found her unbelievably attractive, with her short pixie haircut that matched her perfectly pixie body. Just enough curves for him to mold his hands around. He wanted nothing more than to pick her up and carry her away. He groaned. Those thoughts couldn't happen. This couldn't happen.

Shit. When had she stopped being his best friend's annoying little sister? He'd spent half his time ruffling her hair, trying to remind himself that she was just a kid, but he really did it just so he could touch her. Fucking pathetic.

"Those beers are getting warmer by the second," Lily called out, her grin infectious, pulling him toward her, and taking a cup from his outstretched hand.

"Hey man, aren't you off to Wisconsin tomorrow?" a guy standing next to Lily asked.

"Yep. Training camp starts next week," he said, the conversation turning to hockey, a subject he felt safe talking about. He glanced at Lily, her eyes bright, her smile just peeking past the edge of the cup he'd handed her. She was not safe.

* * *

He should've listened to himself hours ago and taken Lily home before she'd had too much to drink. Before their inhibitions softened with the buzzy beer flowing through them. They'd wandered away from the crowd an hour ago and sat on a bench overlooking the beach. His hands played with the wisps of hair at her nape, the strands soft between his fingers, and he couldn't stop touching her. She'd snuggled into his side, one hand tucked against his hip, while an empty red cup dangled from her other hand.

The last hour had been perfect. The conversation never waned. Dammit. Why did she have to be so amazing? When everything screamed at him to walk away, he still couldn't fight her. Fight this draw he'd always had toward her.

She dropped the cup, her hand moving to trace along his belly, and his stomach muscles clenched, need spiraling through his body.

"Rock hard," she muttered. "So unfair. I've seen what you eat."

He choked out a laugh. "Have to stay in top shape for camp, and my metabolism is awesome."

"Still annoying," she grumbled, before looking up at him, her warm brown eyes locking with his.

He refused to think about how kissable her full lips were, even pursed in irritation, but he couldn't resist tightening his hold on her. He didn't miss the hitch in her breath when he did, and he was asking for trouble.

He dipped his head down, not missing her widening eyes. "You're so going to miss me when I'm gone."

"Of course I am." Her voice was breathy, and he swallowed hard.

"No you won't. You're going off to college. The whole world is available to you."

"Not all of it," she whispered. "There's one thing I can't get in college."

"What?" he asked, his head lowering, not heeding the screaming warnings in his brain.

Her hand stopped tracing along his belly and moved to cup his cheek. "Your kiss."

His heart stopped, air stilled in his throat.

She ducked her head. "Sorry. That was super cheesy. I don't know what I'm thinking."

He reached out, taking her face in his hands, and banishing every voice that told him to stop, he lowered his head those last few inches. "Stop thinking," he murmured before sealing his lips with hers.

He tilted his head, groaning as she sunk her hands into his hair and tugged him closer. He kept his lips closed, letting her lead, calling himself every kind of fool, but refusing to pull away like he should.

The tip of her tongue darted out, tracing along the seam of his lips, and that was all he needed to deepen the kiss, his tongue surging into her mouth, tangling with hers, swallowing her moan as he kissed her with everything in him.

After an endless moment, she pulled away, her cheeks flushed, her chest rising and falling as fast as his. "Wow," she whispered.

His chuckle was strained, and he bit back a groan, when she dove in for more, locking her lips with his and kissing him again. Her breasts rubbed against his arm, and he ached to hold them in his hands, to trace her pebbled nipples with his thumb and hear her shuddering breaths as he tormented her as much as she was currently tormenting him. Fuck. He shouldn't do this. But it would kill him to stop.

He needed her closer. Needed no air or space between them. He lifted her up, swallowing her squeak of alarm, and settled her in his lap, her firm legs gripping his hips as she pressed against his erection. She rocked against him, and he bit back his groan, continuing to ravage her mouth, inhaling everything she gave him.

Her hands sunk into his hair, gripping his scalp. He felt the tug of her fingers down to his toes. She pressed closer, and he deepened the kiss, swallowing her every moan, tangling his tongue with hers. How had he fought this for so long? He'd never wanted anything as much as he wanted this moment to never end, but they had to stop.

He broke the kiss, leaning back. Lily's eyes glittered in the firelight. Even in the low light, he didn't miss her flushed cheeks and her shallow breaths that matched his own. He dropped his forehead to hers, their pants intermingling.

"We have to stop," he said. "This can't happen." She stiffened in his arms, but there was no other way.

"Why?" she whispered. She shifted off his lap, and he couldn't bring himself to look at her.

"For so many reasons, one of which is your brother. He would kill me," he said, finally lifting his head and catching her gaze. A mixture of hurt and anger in her eyes.

"Leave Grant out of this. He's gone, and I don't care what he thinks," she gritted out.

"And I'm off to Wisconsin tomorrow, and you're leaving in two weeks. We're friends, Lily. That's all it can ever be. We had too much to drink and weren't thinking," he said, cursing himself as an idiot with every word.

"That's total bullshit," she bit out, and he hated himself even more.

"Don't hate me, Lil. I can't take that," he said, gripping her hand and squeezing. He needed her in his life, just not like this. Not when he knew how much her life could change once she was in college. Her friendship meant everything to him this summer, and this was not how he'd planned to end it.

"Just go," she whispered, breaking his gaze and staring into the fire.

Fuck. He never should've kissed her.

He wrapped his arm around her shoulder, tugging her into his side. "This is for the best," he whispered against her temple. She didn't budge an inch, and he wanted to punch something, like himself.

"Just go," she repeated. "I think I'll see if Emily is ready to head home," she said, still not looking at him.

"Text me when you get home," he said.

She nodded and he stood up, looking at her one last time before walking into the crowd. His buzz was gone, and he needed to build it back up again to attempt to forget what had just happened.

He grabbed a shot and knocked it back, following it up quickly with another one. It burned down his throat, hitting him hard. He knew the saying about beer before liquor, and he'd probably curse himself in the morning, but he needed something to wipe away the memory of her sad eyes. He should've stayed away from her, but she'd drawn him in, just like she had for as long as he could remember.

The following morning Lily walked downtown with Emily to grab breakfast. Her head ached from last night, but not from the booze. Luckily, Emily had appeared at her side shortly after Adam had left her, and Lily had convinced Emily to take her home. She hadn't heard from Adam after she'd sent him the text saying she was home. Her belly churned remembering last night and wondering if she would see him today or if their horrible goodbye last night was it.

"Ugh, I need bacon...stat," Emily grumbled when they slid into a booth at their favorite diner. "If this place didn't have the best stuffed French toast, I would've killed you for waking me up."

Lily grinned. "You know you'd do anything for their French toast. And it's not early. It's noon. Quit bitching," Lily said over the top of her menu.

"We're still on summer break. Anything before two is early," Emily muttered.

Lily laughed. "Man, I hope you set your schedule for all afternoon classes first semester, or you're screwed."

"Shut up and spill your guts about last night. You refused to say anything on the way home," Emily said. "Was he a bad kisser? God, that would be a total crime."

Lily bit the inside of her cheek. She didn't want to think about last night ever again. She wished she could blame the booze on her idiotic attempt to make-out with Adam, but aside from a light buzz, she'd been in complete control of her faculties. Even if she hadn't been in control of her common sense.

"I really don't want to talk about it," she said, focusing on the menu she'd memorized years ago. The waitress chose that perfect moment to come over, drop off coffee, and grab their orders.

"Seriously. Spill your guts right now," Emily ordered as she dumped an obscene amount of sugar into her cup.

"Did you see Bethany last night?" a voice from the next booth asked.

"No. Who'd she hook up with now?" another voice asked.

"Freaking Adam Byrne. Totally all over him."

Lily's chest squeezed. *Adam. Freaking Bethany.*

"Wow. She's been after him every summer since he graduated," the first girl continued.

"Yep. He was bombed, but he totally seemed into it. Hell, Bethany was bombed, too. Wonder if she'll remember her triumph when she wakes up today," the other girl laughed.

"Ignore them," Emily said, her eyes filled with concern and rage. "Gossipy bitches probably don't know what they saw."

"You don't know that," Lily whispered, staring at the stuffed French toast that no longer held its appeal. "Fuck, I'm so stupid."

Emily gripped Lily's hand, squeezing it. "Stop. You don't know what happened."

"I do. He kissed me within an inch of my life. Made me feel like I was the only girl in the world that he wanted, and then he stopped, said we couldn't do this, and he walked away. Apparently into a bottle of liquor and the arms of skanky Bethany." She shook her head, trying to clear that image from her mind. Wishing she'd been drunk enough last night to forget kissing him to begin with.

"Oh Lily," Emily whispered, clearly unsure of what to say.

Lily blinked back her tears. She would not cry right now. She'd save that for the solitude of her bedroom. "I'm not hungry," she said, pushing her plate away. And then she

346

wanted to punch him, because he'd caused that amazing French toast to lose its appeal. Now that was criminal. "I think I'm going to go," she said.

"We'll get to-go boxes and go back to my place, okay? You're going to want to eat this later."

Lily offered Emily a pained smile. Emily really was a good friend.

In no time, they had to-go boxes in hand and were headed home. Lily tried to push what she'd heard about Adam from her mind, but it festered there like an open wound.

"Lil. Wait up," a voice that she both longed and dreaded to hear, came from behind her.

She halted and slowly turned around to see Adam loping toward her, an easy smile on his face, and her cheeks heated. He looked so happy to see her, and her heart raced. Maybe he had an explanation for last night. Maybe Bethany had thrown herself at him, and he hadn't kissed her at all.

She held back a snort at her delusions. Adam was a big flirt, and she didn't doubt that he'd made out with Bethany if he'd gotten bombed. She just didn't want to believe it. A part of her held on to the thought that he wouldn't make out with her and then immediately turn around and make out with another girl, but that part was shrinking, and she hated it.

"Hey Lil," he said when he caught up with them. "How's your hangover this morning?"

"I don't have one. I only had a few. Shouldn't I ask you the same?" She wasn't sure how to play this conversation.

"Fucking sucks. I didn't want to move when I woke up. Last night was pretty much a blur."

So this is what it was like to have your heart plummet to your toes. It hurt a hell of a lot more than she'd expected.

"It's a blur? You don't remember anything?" she asked, her voice tight and low.

"Did I make an ass out of myself?" He reached out, ruffling her hair, and she pulled free. "Sorry if I did."

She choked back a sob, and Emily's hand tightened on her arm. She had to get out of here before she lost it.

"You were fine," she whispered. "We should go. I'm pretty tired after last night."

"Can't interest you in breakfast again?" he asked.

"No. We should go. Glad I got to see you before you left." She gave him one last smile and started to turn away.

He pulled her against him, in a bruising hug. "I'm going to miss you, Lil. Have a blast in college, but make sure you get some of that work done," he whispered against her hair.

She hated how quickly her heart was beating. How could it race like that when she was sure there was a jagged slice going right through the middle?

"Good luck in Wisconsin," she choked out, refusing to take one last inhale of his spicy warm scent that she loved more than the cinnamon-sugar sprinkled on her French toast. Hell. Who was she kidding? She was pressed to his chest and breathing him in as subtly as possible. He shouldn't smell this amazing. He should smell like booze and regrets.

He pressed a kiss to her hair, and she locked her knees. She had to escape. *Now!*

She pulled away, locking eyes with his spring green gaze one last time, wishing she could see something to tell her he remembered the kiss, but there was nothing there to give her hope.

"Bye," she whispered, one last time, before she dropped his hand and let Emily lead her away. She kept it together until they got to her bedroom, and then she cried until she was dehydrated, wishing she'd kneed him in the gut or yelled at him for not remembering. It didn't matter. They were both just starting their lives and were headed in different directions. It was for the best. She'd tell herself that until she was blue in the face. It didn't make the fissure in her chest ache any less.

Chapter 1

13 years later

"Tomorrow's the big day. You nervous?" Emily asked, sliding into the chair across from Lily's desk, a gleam in Emily's eyes that Lily was all too familiar with. Lily slowly sat back, pressing her spine into her chair, and eyed her friend warily.

"And why would I be nervous?" she asked, removing her glasses to polish off an invisible speck before putting them back on.

"Come on. I saw who's on the schedule. You blocked out a huge chunk of time," Emily said, grinning.

"I don't know what you are implying, but Adam asked me to find him a few properties, and we are going to look at them tomorrow. We are friends, and this is business."

Emily nodded, grin still in place. "Uh huh."

"What is up with you? How much coffee did you have this morning?"

"Don't try to change the subject," she said, pointing a finger at Lily. "You know exactly what I'm talking about."

"It's just Adam. No need to make a big deal out of it." *Yes, please stop making a big deal out of it or I will.* Hell, she already had. When he'd randomly texted her last week, she'd hoped they were finally going to talk about what was going on between them, but he only wanted her real estate skills to help him find a new property.

"Really? Because I'm pretty sure you've scoured every listing at least twice before presenting it to him."

"I'm just thorough." She plucked her glasses off, setting them on her desk. "I'm great at my job because I take the time to find the perfect properties to show. I don't like wasting the client's time." Not that she sold a lot of commercial real estate, but this was for Adam, and she'd done her homework. That's all it was.

Lily had spent the last week looking up listings for him. He'd rejected the first few because the location wasn't perfect, but since his price point wasn't unlimited, the pickings had been slim. He clearly wanted to show that he was successful, but opening a new pub in the high-end areas he wanted was an extremely expensive risk. Yes, he was her client, but he was also her friend, regardless of how awkward they'd become, and she refused to set him up to fail. Bars and restaurants were always a risk, and the higher the price point, the higher that chance of failure.

"Laying it on a little thick, aren't you?" Emily said, her eyes narrowing as if she was trying to burrow her way into Lily's head. "And I'm happy for him too, but that's not the point, and you know it."

And this was the problem with hiring her lifelong friend as her assistant. But Emily had needed a job years ago, and she was extremely detail-oriented. Something that made her an amazing assistant. Unfortunately, it also meant she knew all of Lily's dirt—well, most of it. Lily hadn't been completely candid with Adam's recent avoidance. Emily didn't need to know how often Lily thought about it. Hell, she shouldn't be thinking about it as often as she did, but she couldn't stop herself. Just one more thing in her life she could no longer control. That list was getting extensive and more frustrating every day.

"Stop fishing. Everything is fine," she said.

Emily jumped on that before Lily could continue. "You know that fine never actually means fine, right?"

Lily pinched the bridge of her nose. "Shut up. It's going to be fi...great." She ignored Emily's grin. "We are friends, and I'm so happy that his business is doing this well."

"Friends? Don't think I haven't noticed that he hasn't been around lately. Wonder what that's about?" Emily mused.

Me freaking too.

"He's probably just busy."

"Or maybe he hasn't been around because he secretly has feelings for you and now that you're free, he's nervous about jumping your bones whenever he's around you."

And there it was. That ridiculous idea had taken up residence in her brain, even though she knew just how ridiculous that idea was.

Lily choked on her coffee, setting down her cup with a bang and grabbing a napkin to mop up the mess. "Jesus. Could you warn a girl before you bust out your insanity. No more soap operas for you."

Emily giggled, wiping the splattered coffee off her own arm. "Just calling it like I see it."

"Oh really. Not that I believe you for one second, but please enlighten me with your bat-shit crazy idea." She shouldn't encourage, but she couldn't stop herself from asking.

"I know that he broke your heart when we were kids, but that was so long ago and you guys have become great friends again since he came back all those years ago. Maybe the timing wasn't right, but could be now."

"First of all, you are definitely certifiable. We are friends. I tried for more, and it didn't work. And secondly, in case your delirium clouded your brain, I'm still married," she grumbled.

"Don't remind me. And you're almost out. You have your court date in a month, right? Hopefully the final court date. Billy is gone—good riddance—and you are free to go for Adam. Hell, just have a fling if that's what you want. Do something," Emily said, her eyes bright.

"You're insane. Adam and I are just friends. That's all we will ever be, and I came to terms with that ages ago," Lily said, popping her glasses back into place to read the appointment that had just popped up on her email. "Now are you going to grab us lunch? I have to be on a call in thirty minutes."

Emily huffed. "So grumpy. You know what would fix that? Sex. With Adam."

"You are not funny," Lily grumbled.

"Just calling it like I see it," Emily said, before exiting the office.

Dammit. She attempted to push Emily's comments out of her mind, but they lingered. How could they not?

Books by Stephanie Kay

Unmatched
Last Call

And look for the first in her
San Francisco Strikers series:

Breakout (coming in early Spring 2017)

About the Author

Stephanie Kay has always loved a good romance. Reading them, writing them, and watching them on TV. She got hooked on the dirty ones at the tender age of 14, when she told her mother that if the cover wasn't a bodice ripper, then there was no sex in the book. As an avid mystery reader, her mother never checked to see if Stephanie was lying. Twenty years later, Stephanie's most prized possession is her Kindle, and she may have a Hallmark movie obsession.

Stephanie loves strong, swoony heroes and independent heroines that go after their dreams. She married her own strong, swoony guy, and convinced him to get married over the anvil in Gretna Green, Scotland, so she could live out her historical romance dream. Since he agreed, she decided he's a keeper.

She has called California, Maryland, and Rhode Island her home, but now lives in New Hampshire with her husband where she asks him incessant questions until he escapes to go hiking in the mountains. That's the only time she can get him out of the house so she can get her writing in. Married couples shouldn't both work from home!

Stephanie loves to hear from her readers. Please sign up for her newsletter, on her website, http://www.stephkaybooks.com, for upcoming releases and exclusive excerpts.

Author's Note

Did you notice the local hockey team mentioned? The San Francisco Strikers? I have a total hockey obsession, so of course I had to make up my own team. They're a national hockey team that will be featured in a spin-off series starting next year. I couldn't leave you hanging with Penny's story, so look for her to find love on the ice in the first Strikers book, scheduled to come out in Spring of 2017.

I tried to be as accurate as possible with Grant's career, and any mistakes are my own or were used to further the story. There are three ways a Coast Guard Rescue Swimmer can stay at his current base after the required four years are up: become a recruiter, test to become a captain and magically have a captaincy opening at the base, or switch with another swimmer. That last option is very rare, but possible, and since Grant would never give up the job he loves to be a recruiter, and I didn't want to make him captain, I decided to have him switch with a fellow swimmer.

59939435R00198

Made in the USA
Lexington, KY
20 January 2017